I0825206

Ingram

Ingram

A Novel

LOUIS C.K.

BenBella Books, Inc.
Dallas, TX

BenBella Books, Inc.
8080 N. Central Expressway
Suite 1700
Dallas, TX 75206
benbellabooks.com
Send feedback to feedback@benbellabooks.com

BenBella is a federally registered trademark.

Printed in the United States of America
10 9 8 7 6 5 4 3

Library of Congress Control Number: 2025023435
ISBN 9781637747902 (hardcover)
ISBN 9781637747919 (electronic)

Copyediting by Joe Rhatigan
Proofreading by Jenny Bridges and Michael Fedison
Text design and composition by PerfecType, Nashville, TN
Cover design by Sarah Avinger
Cover illustration by Ralph Voltz
Printed by Versa Press

This book is dedicated to boys everywhere.
And to my mother, Mary Louise Szekely, a wonderful mother of one boy (and three girls).

Acknowledgments

I would like to acknowledge Nancy Shayne, Jenny Gersten, Theo Von, Chris Rock, my sister Cathryn Szekely, and some interesting strangers at a place called "Fiverr," all who read early versions of this novel and gave me some needed encouragement and help to make it better. I'd also like to thank my manager and friend John Sloss who has been a valuable support and encouraged me to share this book with the world. Special thanks to Lea Cohen, who was my personal assistant and has become my booking agent and trusted producer of all of my recent work. She keeps the world moving and steady for me, which helped me focus on this work. Lastly, I'd like to thank Tim Walker, who helped me find some inner peace and quiet for Ingram to come into.

The path to publication for *Ingram* was made possible by my optimistic, thoughtful, and talented literary agent, David Halpern; and by the kind, serious, and talented staff in every department of BenBella Books; and the insightful, creative, and intelligent editing of Rachelle Bergstein, whose questions and ideas opened crucial avenues that helped me round out the book and make it whole. Most of all I would like to thank Glenn Yeffeth for taking a chance on Ingram and on me.

Contents

Part One

Part Two

Part Three

Part Four

Part One

Chapter One

Leaving Home

When I was a small and new boy, I'd sit outside the house with the animals. The animals were all over. Dog here, pigs around, horse grazing right next to the house, chickens underfoot, and no one thought anything of it. It didn't bother my mother or father, the animals being all around, nor did they take any pleasure in it. Animals were part of the home and part of every day. Feed the dog. Slop the pigs. Lay seed on the ground for the fowl, and tend to the horse in all the ways a horse needs tending.

I liked watching the animals walk around, sniff the ground, and make their little movements with no reason except to do the next thing they'd set themselves to do. I'd watch the chickens fight, the hogs try to scratch where they couldn't reach. I'd watch the dog sleep for as long as he slept. Every day, I'd sit on the porch step or in the dirt, my mother in the kitchen or somewhere else inside the house. Only my father came and went. He'd come out of the door, his big legs striding by like two great silent, swinging trees. I'd be sitting in the dirt by a hog, my father paying me as much thought or attention as he would to one of the hens pecking the ground as he stepped by it. I wouldn't look up at his face. But I'd watch his back go, seeing how his hat sat on his head like it was part of him and how his hands and arms hung down heavy, swinging like iron tools in the shed when the wind got to them. I'd watch my giant father as he got smaller and smaller, walking down the middle of the dirty road that ended at our front yard, as he went to town to get provisions. The dog would go with him. There had been another dog who followed him in a running crazy kind of way, but one night my father came back and the dog was dead. "Hit by a car," he told my mother, and then we got the next dog, who could walk behind him straight.

I walked up that road only one time, with my father, when he took me into town to see about me going to school. I had never left the house before that day, except for playing in the fields and woods behind and around it. I must have taken six galloping steps behind his every one, to the end of our road, which made a T with another road that was like a monster, covered with a hard gray stiff dirt, hot to your feet, with cars rushing past in both directions fast and loud and big rattling roaring trucks. I'd only ever seen these things before as little hissing, whizzing things off in the distance, from the porch of our house, making all one sound like wind or rain. But walking on that road, behind my father, every car and truck had its own dark color and terrible growl and roar, so fast and loud. I thought I would go deaf and blind from too much hearing and seeing.

I scrambled along the side of that hard gray road forever and ever, the hard, gray dirt cuffing my feet, which had never felt hurt before, having only run around in grass and dirt and swimming in muddy water, running behind my father's simple stride, his tree legs swinging away, one after the other, his hat never moving—him never looking back at me or saying a word. Till we got into what could only have been *town*.

Town was a place with suddenly so many houses, one after the other, and square buildings made of all brick like our fruit cellar but so much bigger. The people were dressed so neat and strange, with straight trousers and shiny brown shoes. So many people walking past each other, not looking, not knowing each other, and I couldn't notice all of it for fear of losing sight of my father's heels, which suddenly turned toward a great big clean building of brick and windows, bigger than anything I'd ever seen in my life. I followed my father through the door, which felt like being eaten by a brick animal except we were opening its heavy metal mouth and walking in on purpose. My father pushed my shoulder down, making me sit in a wooden chair that set against a wall, and he left me, himself going inside a door made of wood and glass. The floor that was a perfect marvel of cold straightness, felt smooth and good to my bleeding bare foot bottoms. Through the wood and glass door I could hear a woman talking, and I could hear my father's voice talking back, him only saying one word at a time, like when I'd hear him with my mother in the kitchen. After a very short time, he came back out of that door and walked past me, back outside. I scrambled to my feet to follow him out of the door, out of town, down the gray hard shaking monster road, all the way home.

"They don't have a bus that come here," I heard my father say to my mother. And so I was not to go to school. I guess I was relieved because I'd been so shook-up and shocked by the walk to town and back, which took the whole day. I was head to toe with sweat and my face sunburnt, so I stripped down to naked and got in the pond. Things went back how they'd always been—me and the animals sitting in the dirt, eating when my mother had food and otherwise living without thought or expectation.

One day, as the sun got low behind our house, a car came driving down up the road, dragging a long shadow behind it. The car, which was dark blue like the coffee boiler and made almost no sound except the crunching and pocking of rocks spitting out from under its creeping black tires, stopped. Two men got out. They were both wearing full suits of gray clothes and black shoes, and they had ropes of cloth tied snug to their necks, something I'd never seen and looked to me like two Guernsey cows had yanked their ropes in half from where they'd been tied to a fence and had run off and got themselves a car. Except only one of those men was heavy, and he wore a black beard on his face, which was trimmed up even and neat as his gray suit-coat. The other man was thin and his chin was as naked as my mother's. These two men got out of their car and came over to the porch where I was sitting, asking if my parents were home. I pointed inside, where they went and talked for a short while, and came out a few minutes later, got in their car and drove away.

"From the bank," my father said those men were, and the next day he slaughtered every animal on the place except the horse and the dog. He told my mother to smoke the pork and cook the chickens and he saddled the horse, saying he would ride into the town and sell it.

"But we don't have any wood cut for the smokehouse," my mother said, but my father got on the horse and rode off like she'd said nothing. I watched from my seat in the dirt, wondering why I wasn't slaughtered or sold, as my father clopped on the horse up to the busy road, the dog following behind. He never came back.

After that there was no animals at all. Just me and my mother, who let me sleep in her bed that night and all the nights after. I hadn't slept in a real bed in something like years. It was my father who forced me to sleep in the shed, and my mother letting me come inside at night was what made me know he would never come back. She cried and cried in bed at night and most of the day. I'd look at her. Days and days went by. I could never know how many. We ate the chickens and what eggs they'd laid before dying. My mother tried to keep the pork going but most of it rotted. What little was good my mother fed to me and she quit eating. She never said a thing to me.

I knew it was all coming to some kind of end, and I didn't know and couldn't imagine how that would look. My mother got so hungry and tired that she stopped crying, and she got less well looking. The skin on her neck got red and rough and she'd scratch inside of her dress so I knew it was all over her. My mother's hair, which I'd known to be a simple dark color, or not a color at all, had always been tied up tight, up in a ball on the back of her head. But around the time she got that rash, she one day untied a string and let her hair come out. I was laying on her bed and she was sitting on it with her back to me as her fingers, which had got like bones, pulled at her hair, which kept coming longer and thicker out of that ball like it was pouring out from somewhere in the middle of her head.

Her hair was colored like long burnt grass that is brown when you're walking by it thinking of something else, but from up close, looking right at it, becomes many colors, some white and some gray and even some green. My mother let her thick heavy hair cover her whole back and her head and it was even over her face like a long lampshade, and out from under it I heard her make a sound I had never remembered hearing come out of anyone except myself. My mother was taking deep breaths and then letting them out in low, yelling, sobbing sounds that put a bad fear in me and made me jump out of that bed and run outside and into the shed, where I slept that night without being told.

The day after, that car came back down the road, with the same men from the bank in it, but instead of coming in the house, one of them just barked out the window to me, "Tell your mother two more days," and they drove away.

The next morning, the very beginning of it, when the sky is purple and the land is black, my mother put a hat on my head, which she said was my brother's. I didn't know what she meant, me not having a brother and not remembering ever having had one. I never had a hat either and it felt funny on my head. My mother walked me out of the house and onto the porch and gave me some pork she'd tied up in a rag, and she said, "You need to head off, Ingram. There's no home or family here now. Your luck and lot are worse here than anywhere in the world. And I don't have one thing to give you by way of food or protection. So you head out now before that road starts roaring and do what you can." This was more than I could recollect my mother, or anyone, having ever said to me directly, so I didn't have the words or even thoughts to put together by way of a response. My mother put her hands on my shoulders, squatting down right by my face, looking too tired to be sad anymore, and she said, "I can't tell you how to survive or even live, Ingram. All I can say is live and keep going as long as you can, any way you can."

The way my mother was looking right into my face made me feel better than I ever had in my life. Her eyes and mouth and the skin along the lumps of her features looked a certain shining way to me.

When she rose up from her squat I turned my back to my mother and walked away from her, because I knew she would do the same and there was a bad feeling in my chest that if I saw her do it I would never make it in the world. I just walked on, down the porch steps, past where I used to sit in the dirt, not looking back, down our dirty road, knowing if I was sitting in the dirt watching myself, I'd be getting smaller and smaller, but a whole lot quicker since I was little to begin with.

I reached the hard gray road, which was quiet in the early morning. Instead of walking toward town, which was the most fearful thing I'd ever seen, I turned the other way, to where I didn't know what to expect.

Chapter Two

Under the Great Road

I walked on that road as the sky paled out from white and then into blue and as the cars and trucks went from one passing every now and again to all of the trucks and cars in the world roaring past in both directions, the wind coming off of them shaking and rattling me. I was thankful that I could walk my own way, without my father's big legs striding away ahead of me to catch up to.

I ate my breakfast of pork from my mother's kitchen rag. But the work of walking and the heat of the beating down sun shrunk the feeling of that little bit of food down to nothing in my stomach. Soon I was hungrier than if I'd eaten nothing. I walked and walked till my knees felt like tree twigs you can snap with two fingers. Just when I thought the hot hard road, which had gone from gray to black, would come up through my feet and set my toe-bones on fire, I reached a long low square house off the side of the road. Cars were pulling up to it and stopping, with men and women of all sizes and loud voices getting out, slamming the doors of their cars and going in the long low building. Trucks pulled in too, one of them almost rolling right over me if I hadn't scampered to the side.

I didn't know what to do, but I knew that I was hungry, and the people walking out of the long low building looked the way my father did after a good fat meal, all pink and shiny and tired, and I could smell cooking from inside too, so I walked over there with no idea what to do except that my mother had told me to keep on going any way I could and that meant eating, so I waited for no one to be going in or out of that door and I went in.

Inside was loud and lively with voices coming from all around. The floor was all flat like in the school except in squares like checkers that my father played, with Uncle Bert, who stopped coming after they had a fistfight—"Over money," said my mother. There were tables all around the place in rows with long seats on each side, two or three people on each seat, eating off white plates piled with food of every color and smell.

Around one table, I saw a man and a woman and three children. One of the children was a boy, like me. The other was a girl child, which I knew because I'd met one. A woman I had never seen before, who my mother said was her sister, whose name I had forgot, came one day to our house bringing a girl child, a bit smaller than myself, whose name was Anna Lee. They came asking my mother for some kind of help, and my father made them leave the next day.

The other child at the table was so small, like a piglet, except a person. It shrieked and cried like a piglet too. I looked at that table with the man, the woman, and the three children and I knew what they were. They were a family. I wondered if this was their house, and all these people were their friends, except no one was talking from one table to the other.

It was then that a man with a big gut sticking out his front spoke to me from where he sat close by and said, "What's you doin', kid? Where's your maw?" I turned and looked at his face. His cheeks were all puffed out with food like his stomach was, and he had a piece of meat on his fork, holding it right near his mouth, waiting to stick it in there and chew it up before he was done chewing what he had in there already. I looked down at the plate on his table, right above his fat gut, and on that plate sat a cut of meat with some slop all over the top of it and something inside told my hand to reach for it so I did.

"Hey!" said the man as I jerked back my hand and put that meat in my mouth. The fat man reached out his fat hand and my body told me to duck away so I did. The man hollered, loud and angry, which made the place go quiet and I kept listening to my body and ran out of that door. The last sounds I heard coming from that building were lots of people laughing as that man continued to yell, but he never came after me, so after running down the road a bit, I slowed down to walking, as I finished the meat I had taken.

I remembered how a rickety, rattling truck had come down our road one night when we were all sleeping. I looked at the truck, the first one I'd ever seen, through the crack in the door of the shed where I slept. It had its lights off, but I could see by the moon that a man was getting out and unhooking the fence that pent up our pigs, who right off started bleating. My father, in his underclothes, came near flying out the front door and over the porch steps. I saw my father jump onto that man, who was trying to put our hog in his truck-back, and my father knocked him to the ground and began pounding his fists into that man's face.

I couldn't tell if the bleating I heard now was the man my father was beating or the pig he was trying to hold onto with his free hand as he covered his face with the other to stop my father's punching, which he couldn't. The man finally had to let the hog hoof go and my father got up and took the animal in his arms as the man scurried into his truck. My father and I watched that truck go back up the road, though my father didn't know I was watching with him. And I remembered how, the next morning at breakfast time, eating my biscuit on the porch steps, I heard my father tell about the man who tried to take the pig to my mother, who said, "Oh my."

And my father took a loud sip of coffee, saying, a bit louder, "Stealing can get you kilt." I knew what *kilt* meant because Uncle Bert said his "business partner" had *cut a man's throat till he was dead* and that he was in prison for it for the rest of his own life. I knew what dead meant too, though

I couldn't remember from what. I knew that dead was ugly and nothing comes after. And I knew that what I'd done that day, taking the meat from that man's plate, was stealing.

I walked until it got so dark I couldn't see my feet as they went one after the other at the edge of the road, away from where the cars had been going, though now it was quiet and I could hear crickets sing in the nature. Far ahead, I saw a tiny light growing toward me until it split in two and I could hear the car that was carrying the lights getting louder and louder. The horn of that car began to honk and the lights lit up the black hard dirt under my feet, making me see that I had wandered into the middle of the road and had to run quick to the side as the car swung past honking loud with a voice from inside the car hollering, "Watch it, Chucker-head!" and in my scrambling and running, I found myself tripping and falling over some brush or bush I couldn't see. I tumbled and fell to the ground. Laying there on my belly, in the dark, I only knew from the feel of damp, giving coolness that my face and hands were in some wet mud and I got overtaken by the need to sleep. Knowing that home was a day's walk back, I let my eyes go closed and the world slipped straight out of my mind.

WAKING UP TO THE KNOWING that bugs are crawling out of your mouth will make you promise to no one listening that it's better to die than to sleep outside. A bug going *into* your mouth may be one thing. You know it just got in there and you only have to spit it out. But to feel it coming *out* means it's been there for such a time that it did all it wanted. The thing about bugs is not what they can do to you, which isn't much, but the *idea* of them and the way they make you have that jittery juggery motion somewhere inside that makes you flap your hands around when you need something to stop that stopped already. I jumped up from laying out in the mud, stamping my feet, blowing raspberries out of my mouth, wiggling from head to toe, and slapping myself in the face and neck, trying to beat away that feeling of my whole body shaking with wanting to leap right out of living.

When my twitching was done, I stood there heaving my breath in and out, remembering all at once what had happened the day before and all the walking and hunger and confusion that had led to where I was, at the edge of a swamp, at the foot of a long slope of muddy grass, the tires zooming by like black streaks right above where I stood. I continued walking. Where I was walking *to* I didn't figure or even wonder. But being shy of the roadside, I stayed down at the swamp edge, the walking being stickier but kinder to my bare feet.

I was hungry. In fact, hungry is all I was. If you'd asked me what I was or what my name was, I would have said *hungry*. To distract me from the food I didn't have, I thought again of Anna Lee, holding the hand of her mother, who had a straw suitcase in her other hand. I had watched them walk all the way from the big road as I leaned against the porch step, with the dog laying in the dirt beside me, trying to cool his belly. About half way down our road, her mother bent down and picked up Anna Lee and carried her in her arms, something I never saw a person do to another. I'd seen my father pick up a pig in order to hang him up and slice him open. I wondered why my mother's sister did carry her child and my mother didn't carry me.

It might have been because Anna Lee was small, which she sure was. Anna Lee had legs like funny fingers dangling down from her puffy dress-bottom. Her arms were likewise thin and soft looking. Her eyes, that were so blue I could remember them better than the color of my mother's or father's eyes, were real close to each other and to her nose, that was barely a bump above her smooth face and mouth just below it. The whole look of her was what I thought of as tender, like a baby mouse. So I figured her mother wanted to carry her up above the dirt in the road.

Her mother too, was different from mine. When my mother and her sister sat beside each other at the kitchen table I could see through the screen of the door that my mother's eyes were like her sister's eyes but upside-down because her sister's eyes would open upward to the ceiling and my mother's eyes opened by the lower lids falling down to the floor. Her sister talked in a voice that started up high like a bird, and swooped down for sad moments but dipped back up again. Like when she said, "It has been a harder year than most, but we must remember that God watches over us all."

"I don't think he's much watching, here in this house," my mother had said back in her own voice, which was higher than my father's, but still low, like a bullfrog, but a girl, and never changing from one word to the next.

As I walked on my second day alone on the road, my feet got more and more stuck into the suck of the swamp, which was getting to be more water than mud, which made me have to go back up that bump of patchy grass, pulling on weeds to help me climb it, as it had become like the side of a steep hill. The road was roaring again with cars and trucks, only meaner and harder than before. I looked ahead and saw that the road was rising away off and upward, somehow off the ground, and it was broken into two great roads, each hugged on the sides by rippling metal rails, with car after car, only inches apart, side by side, one behind the other, driving fast as ferrets, up and down the swells and around the circles like they were thinking all together. My mind couldn't see it all straight at one time. It was a few seconds of looking before, under the hiss and roar of all this river of motor and metal, I heard the sound of my own breath, panting in and out fast like I'd been running from the mad dog that chased me home from the house behind, until my father shot it dead and drug it by its one foot, dangling it at his side till he threw it into the creek.

My head began to get light and dizzy, and I set myself on the rail of the metal fence, thinking that I'd found another world and hoping I would suddenly die so I wouldn't have to face anything more unknown and frightening. I let my head hang down to my chest so my hair flopped over my eyes and made a wall between me and everything around.

I DON'T KNOW HOW LONG I sat there but the edges of the railing were cutting into my hands and into my bottom through my coveralls. As the cars rushed by and by, my breathing was slowed down to not so quick and my legs got back to feeling ready to walk. So I got up, stamped my feet on the hard black ground of the road, and began walking the way the cars went, letting the tips of my fingers glide along the top of the metal rail, which felt warm to the touch and kept me knowing I couldn't wander into the road like I done the night before.

As I walked, I came to where the road was rising, like climbing a narrow hillside. I looked over the edge of it to see the ground, that had run along beside the road, was dropping fast away, further and further down. And worse was that the space beside the white line of paint, that was keeping me safe, aside from the cars, was getting thinner and thinner, with the rubber and steel getting closer to my body, tighter and tighter, till I had nowhere to walk at all. I was frozen in my tracks by lack of place to go and the cars and trucks were flying by so close it was whipping my hair around my head, and they honked long and loud at me, the sound of each horn getting from low to high and switching back to low as each car went away ahead. I knew I had to get off that road. I looked over the rail to see the ground beneath was so far below that trying to see it was like trying to see the bottom of a river, or the very top of a night sky. I was trapped by lines and corners and highs and lows, unfriendly sights and sounds. I had no way to go but back. But *back* was the one way I couldn't make my feet go. "Back to what?" my feet asked me. "Back to the swamp? Back to the man you took the meat from? Back to your mother who has nothing to offer you by way or food or protection? There has to be a way *ahead*, even if *ahead* is the way to dying. Because *back* is not a way at all."

I had to laugh at myself for listening to my feet as if they could talk. It was an inside kind of laughing. I never much laughed out loud at home, that being a loud noise, which was the kind I was better off not making around my father who could get mad at just about anything, or around my mother whose face would tighten with worry, which would quick bring my laughing to an end and make me feel remorseful for upsetting her. When I thought of something that ever struck me funny, I would keep my laughing on the inside which shook my chest a bit and put a warm tingle on the backs of my cheeks. It was that kind of *inside* laughing that came to me on the great rising road. The laughing didn't give me any better options, but it got me warm again. I told my feet that *ahead* would have to wait till I could go *back* at least far enough to climb off this road and walk down there, way below where I couldn't see from up there.

"If it's water down there," I told my feet, "I'll have to swim it. If it's mud, I'll have to crawl it. Because two more steps ahead the way I'm going, I'll be murdered by a truck, with no ways left to go."

I turned around and started back down the road. The cars and trucks that'd been coming from behind me were now barreling right toward me, toward right between my eyes, like I was walking into their path. I hugged as close as I could to the rail and my feet took off running, the white stripe now making a wider and wider path to run on. I ran and ran, pumping my hands, fingers pointed outstretched like my hands were stars of skin. I ran until the muddy side wasn't down below anymore but even with the road. Then I jumped over the rail sideways, landing in mud. This time, I made my hips squat down so I wouldn't slip and tumble, like I had the night before, and it sure helped that I could see.

I walked along the edge of the swamp, which had dried a bit from the sun, back in the direction I had called *ahead*, but now on the ground, the road rising up and up till it loomed above me, held up from underneath by trees of rusty steel. Soon I could look up and see where I must have been standing when I had stopped to look down to where I was now, and I nearly fell backward from looking up that high. I couldn't imagine a boy my size way, way up there at that railing. It's a strange thing to feel afraid of something you've done already and got away with, but looking up there from down at the bottom I got an awful fright of what might've been and for the first time since my father had last belted me, I cried a choke-full, quiet, mess of tears.

Crying won't fix anything. But it has a way of putting you back where you were before the trouble began. I wiped my nose on my arm and wiped my arm on my coveralls and kept on walking. Now my feet weren't being sucked down by mud, but they were fighting with the trash; cans, bottles, papers, old busted lampshades, and a bunch of rusty mattress springs sticking up in the air like daisies reaching for the sun. I knew what those springs were because my father had come home one time in another man's truck, hauling a mattress. He told my mother that the mattress had belonged to a man who was just dead, who had lived in the house owned by the man in the truck, and he had sold the mattress to my father for less than a dollar.

"He wanted five but I told him fifty cents," he told my mother. "Then he said three, and I said I'll give you a buck, but you haul it." My mother didn't like the idea of sleeping in a dead man's bed, which she said but once and quietly, knowing if she said *anything* twice or with insistence, my father would hit her. There had been an earlier time, hazy in my remembering, when my mother would argue against my father with more gust, and her face would be swollen black or she'd have red in the white of her eye from my father's angry hands. There was another time, even hazier, where the voices in our house were all different, back before I was made to sleep in the shed—when I slept inside, which I'd forgotten ever happened until I saw my father and that man dragging that mattress into the kitchen door and then they came out soon later with the one that was in there before. My father tried to get the man to haul the old mattress away but the man got angry and my father called him cursing names and let him go. Instead, my father tumbled that old mattress, end over end, just far away enough from the house to stop caring about it, and there it stayed, till all the cloth on it withered away with rain and baking sun, till the springs pushing from inside tore through the fabric and mixed in with grass coming up through the cloth. Those springs looked like wild daisies.

The road, getting taller and wider and wider above me, shook and trembled from the cars and trucks whooshing on it, making a sound like distant thunder that never got closer or further as all around me went to night. I might have felt afraid if I wasn't so hungry. But I had no room inside of me to feel anything except the biting and scratching of the hunger dog in my stomach, which would come, now and again, when my mother would say at dinnertime, "We ain't got none," and that old dog would start tumbling inside of me. I used to sit in the dirt holding my belly and whisper to it, "Come on, you dog. Quit scratching. It won't make the food come quicker. Don't you think I'd eat it if I had it?" But this wasn't home, and I knew it to be foolish to sit on the ground and hold my belly in such a dark and scary place, so I let the hunger dog holler to itself and kept on walking.

The only light I could see was strange cold bars of blue, coming from the edges of the road. It cast down to the ground under my feet, which was so covered in broken things that it was a peril to be walking anymore, and yet there was no place to stop unless I wanted to cut my face by sleeping on it.

Right ahead of me was one rusting metal tree, wider than all the others, reaching way up high, holding up the road on its rusting metal shoulders. I felt a certain safety at the sight of it, and walked over to see if maybe I could sleep against it. I walked until I reached the feet of the great rusted tree, where I found something that was like a tiny house made from plastic tarps like the brown one that covered the roof over our kitchen, where a tree had caved it in before my father got up and fixed it with new wood.

That had been a long time before, when my father was different. He was more moving around fixing things and planting in our field and having new ideas like when he had started bringing home animals to raise. That was before he stopped doing much at all and started saying things like, "Bad luck is all around."

I got up close to the tarp house that was lashed to the rusted tree with many kinds of rope to poles and wooden boards that leaned together to create a tiny inside, which I was eager to occupy, eager to stop, eager to sleep. I pushed aside a flap of tarp that was green when the rest was black or brown and inside the little made house was darker than all the dark I had been walking through. I squatted down and felt the ground inside and it was just a little dryer. Just a little warmer. My hands disappeared into the dark in front of me, and I followed them in with my knees, further and further in, crawling on all fours. The flap closed behind me, shutting out the sights and sounds of the whole dark world. I laid on my side on something that felt like a quilt and began to fade down into myself.

Chapter Three

The Mountain

I woke up because a large hot hand was holding my neck down onto the ground, only letting the tiniest breaths come in and go out. I opened my eyes to see what looked like a pile of stones, or a mountain, that began on my chest, looking down at me except I couldn't see eyes, but I knew what was on my throat was a hand by the way it was warm and tightening and quivering like you could feel the thinking inside each finger, which were so long and thick that one of them pressed hard against the whole side of my face.

"What you doing in my tent?" said a voice coming from the top of this mountain. The tarp behind it was lit and glowing from morning sun outside, making this talking mountain just a dark shape in front of it, a rocky heapness that started at my chest, where it sat. "What you want in here?" the mountain said. "You fixing to die before you grow to a man?" I couldn't answer for my throat being closed, till the fingers let go just one bit, letting me speak.

"I come in here . . . I was looking to sleep is all," I said, knowing it was time to talk myself away from a beating, something I'd done a number of times at home. "I didn't mean no offense," I said. The mountain closed its fingers back down, having heard enough, and I figured it would keep on squeezing till I was dead, but it let me just breathe as it breathed too, deeply and slowly for I don't know how long, till suddenly the mountain stood up, swung its legs off of me, and left out the door flap of what I now understood was a "tent."

I sat up, rubbing my aching neck till my breath came back regular, and I crawled out the tent flap myself, finding the world around me lit up by the sun, which, just rising, was still low enough in the sky to throw its light down there under the great road, which was once again roaring and shaking above me. A few feet from the tent, sitting on a plastic bucket in front of a small fire, was a man who looked even more like a mountain in the daylight. His face and hands had a dark color in the shade, but where the sun hit his skin, he glowed almost like metal. His hair wasn't in strands and strings like mine. This mountain's hair was thick and moss-like but tougher and in a great pile on his head with chunks sticking out like gray-black colored pinecones or like a hair fruit of some kind. His clothes weren't so much a pair of pants and a top as it was different kinds of cloth and plastic lashed together across his body just like his tent. He had a stove pan in one hand and a cooking spoon in the other, scooping out some kind of steaming stew and feeding it into his mouth, which was bright red on the inside. I stood there looking at him and he sat there looking at me, the only difference being I wasn't eating and it hurt real bad inside my stomach to see him doing so. My hands touched my belly and I saw his big warm eyes look down and see it.

"Come here, boy," he said. His voice was like a low, calm hum that I could feel in my chest. I walked a few steps closer, which brought the smell of his food to my nose and made me have a painful wishing for something to eat. "Come over right here, boy." He waved his spoon at me. I came straight over to him, till his face was right in front of mine, like only my mother's had ever been, like it was when I'd last seen her.

The man's eyes looked up and down from my brow to my chin as he chewed some kind of meat. His big hand, which had been cutting off my air in that tent, was now touching and squeezing me here and there, on my shoulder, on my hip, chest, like he was testing a peach for ripeness. His face, dark from a few paces back, close up, had many shades of dark and lightness. Black like night around the edges and cheeks, then a sort of red-brown, like turned soil, on the edges of his nose and under his eyes. There were many other colors, even blues and greens. He looked that certain shining way to me, like my mother had. I wondered if every face is such a perfect pleasure to see up close, since the only two I'd seen this way were to me, at least as far as I could remember. It felt inside, though, somewhere before remembering, like there had been a face I looked at from close and then forgot. The slight knowing of that other face put a shiver in me, and I quickly thought my thinking away from it, which somehow made me dizzy in my head.

"What you doing way out here?" asked the mountain, sounding angry, and I could smell the meat on his breath, which was more smelling of food than my mind and body could take. I felt my knees buckle, and I began to fall backward and forget living all at once, though in a curious way I never felt my back hit the ground. There was a feeling like floating, but bouncing. I opened my eyes, which I didn't even know I had closed, and the face of that mountain man was even closer now, as my head was on his chest and the sky was moving behind him. I couldn't make out in my mind what was happening till I lifted my head and looked down and around to see that I was in his arms, being carried back into the tent.

It was strange to be carried like Anna Lee had been. I was seeing the world from a bit higher than my eyes could see when I walked by myself. I wondered if I'd ever see the world from up there on my own, if I'd ever grow to be a man. It hurt to hold my head up from looking, so I just dropped it back onto the mountain's chest. The feeling of being straight against his warm body with every part of me was like becoming two people at once. I could hear the mountain grunt and breathe, but from the inside of his chest, which my ear was set against by the laying weight of my own head. I wondered what Anna Lee could hear inside of her mother when she was carried toward our house and then away from it.

I wished that the mountain would keep on carrying me or would let me somehow live in his arms and share his life. But I felt him let me down onto the floor inside the tent, and my mind slipped away again to that forgetting place.

I woke up to the sight of the mountain once again, but this time he was set beside me in the tent, watching me with a look of concern. When my eyes opened, he leaned across me with something like a bottle in his hand except it seemed to glow like a light bulb. He put his hand under my chin, opening my mouth, and let water flow from the bottle into my mouth. It felt a cool relief to have that water hit my lips, but as it flowed down past my tongue, and the wet of the water, which was colder than any water I had ever had, flowed into the dry crackling in the back of my throat, my chest got shocked and began to cough so I had to get up on one elbow and let some out.

"What's the last time you had yourself some water?" the mountain asked me, sounding vexed. I told him I hadn't eaten in a day, and that my last meal was only a bite. "Food you can go without, if you can't get none," he scolded. "But without water, boy, you're dead. Don't ever try going another day without it."

I hadn't ever considered the importance of water. It was the one thing we never lacked back at home. Even when the shelf was bare of food, the well behind the house and the spigot in the sink always gave water and there was the stream just past the meadow where water flowed that I could drink with my hands. Water never struck me like something important, because it wasn't scarce. But now that the mountain had given me the lit-up bottle to hold, I turned its fanny up and its head at my lips and sucked every drop of water out of it while he watched and made a clicking sound with his tongue. When I had finished, the bottle ceased to glow with light. The mountain handed me the stove pan from behind him and the cooking spoon and let me finish his breakfast. I couldn't say what kind of food it was. I just knew that I needed it. Once I'd eaten, all I could do was put the pan down and sit there breathing.

"Come outside when you feel like you can," said the mountain and he left the tent. When I came out of the tent, I found him sitting on the bucket again, looking at me with one elbow resting on his thigh, which was thicker than the middle of my body. I could feel the food and water working through all my parts as he looked me up and down. "Now what's a little white boy like you doing out in the middle of all this?" he asked. "Are you lost?" he asked, a little softer than the last question.

"Lost?" I said.

"Where are your folks?"

"I don't know where my father is," I told him. "My mother was back at home, but the bank men told her she only had two more days, so I guess she might be somewhere else now."

"Why aren't you with your mother?"

"Because she told me to go on my own."

"Hmm," he said. "That's what my mama said to me. I didn't think that happened much to white folks though." The mountain looked at me for a long time. Then he looked down at his hands. "Now I give you some of my food and some water to drink. I can't have you here no more. I don't have enough to raise a strange child. I didn't have enough to have my own child, or even a wife. I'm just trying to hang on here on my own. So, you need to move on." He looked back up from his hands to my face and he, all of a moment, got angry. "You go on now, then. You'll do fine. You're white." I didn't know what that meant, and I guess he saw a quizzical look in me because he said, "You don't know what I'm talking about, do you?"

"No," I said.

"Were you raised in a town? Or a farm?"

"I guess a farm," I said.

"You ever seen a black man before?" he asked, with a kind of funny grin.

"You mean like you?" I asked.

"Like me?" he asked back, and then he picked up his big hand, slapped it down onto his big thigh, and threw back his head and laughed so that it shook his whole body the way crying shook my mother's. He even had tears in his eyes, which he wiped away as his laughter simmered down like a wind that shook a tree and then gently changed direction. "Oh, lord," he said. "Am I the first black man you ever saw?"

"I guess."

He had finished his laughing and it took him to a place of quiet and calm. He nodded and then he said, "Look here. You're headed into a world that is split up into white folks and black folks. And you're white, which is the luckier thing to be. But all the same, you're headed out into a hard world, boy. No matter what you are, the world is hard and it don't care. It's full of sharp edges and slithering snakes."

"I've seen snakes before," I said.

"That's not how I mean it. I mean people that are like snakes out there. They shift and slither and sneak up. And by the time they bite, you're too late. You watch out for those that come to you with a smile, you understand?"

"Why?" I asked, thinking till then that a smile was good.

"I ain't smiling at you now, am I, boy?"

"No," I said truthfully.

"Was I smiling when I gave you water? Or when I fed you my own supper?"

"No, sir."

"When I set out alone in the world, I was but ten years old, about like you now. My mama had given me two silver dollars. I met a man on the street and asked him where I could get some supper. And he smiled like the moon at me while he fished his hand in my pocket and took all I had. Just remember that. Don't trust a smiling man. Never. You understand?"

I did understand and I kept listening. "It's a hard and twisted world, boy. You're just a soft little child. You don't stand no kind of a chance. But I reckon neither did I when I left home. And here I am." He sat thinking for a while longer. "You go on now," he then said. "You keep walking under the road and it'll take you to a big city called Houston. You ever heard of Houston?"

"No," I said.

"You go there and try your luck. You'll either make it somehow, or you'll die. But I guess your mama told you that already."

"My mama?"

"Your mother, boy," he said in a very serious way. "Your natural mother who had you and raised you from a baby. Now you may have a bitter feeling that she sent you away because you don't remember what she did for you as a baby.

"Your mama suckled and carried and tended to you, and if she hadn't, you'd be dead. You may not know it as you stand here in this mud, but she sent you away from her because she knew you'd die otherwise. Like so many mothers now who are too poor and weak to care for their own children so they send them off. Greatest shame of all time. But it ain't her fault any more than it was my mother's fault that I'm here. If she'd held onto me I'd have died beside her. So you never forget your mama, you understand?"

I didn't say anything. He stood up and came over to me, looking down at me from the high mountain of his head, and put a hand on my shoulder, turned me away from him, and gave my back a push. "Go on now," he said from behind me. "Get going. Don't come here again. I got nothing for you."

I walked away from the mountain. I didn't hear any footsteps behind me so I guessed he stood there watching me for a while. I walked and walked under the road as the sun began to set behind me. The road above my head had become twisted and looping and louder, and I started to understand that I was getting closer to a place called "Houston."

Chapter Four
The River

It was early in the nighttime, when the sun is just a stripe on the edge of the sky, like lamplight coming through the bottom crack of a shut door. I had walked away from the great road and was walking down a smaller road, with houses along the sides. Some of the houses were like my own—small and simple with whitewash boards on the sides and a short porch, and close together, one after the other, on and on down the straight road. But then sometimes there'd be a space between with only one house that was taller, still white but smoother like metal or plastic, without windows but a door in the front. As I walked along, the sky got dimmer and darker, and tall, steel poles along the sides of the road with lamps on the tops began to shine down to light up where I walked. And the houses along the sides were lit up with their own lamps in the windows of those that had windows, so I could see more in the night than in the end of daylight.

In the front yards of these houses were people, together in groups. Most all of them had darker skin like the mountain had. These folks were set on chairs in their yards or on the porches and they talked low and I saw that they watched me as I walked by. Now and then a car would drive past but going slowly, and the driver would holler and the people on the porch would holler back, and they'd talk this way in a conversation of yelling back and forth.

"Where's Diller at?!" a man called out from a car.

"He done left a long time ago already. You missed him!" answered a woman who was set in a chair in her yard close to the fence as I walked by. She had a high and crackling but powerful voice. "He said, 'I'm not waiting for that fool one minute longer!' Picked up his kit and went off!" she yelled while waving away with her hand, showing the direction this man called Diller must've gone.

The man in the car laughed and said, "Well if he ain't waitin' on me, then I ain't waitin' on him! You tell him I came by!"

"I'll tell him what I tell him!" yelled the woman as the car roared off.

She was lit up good by the light above on the pole and I looked at her face and saw that it was thin and sunken in like a starved animal and had many deep lines and grooves along the skin on her cheeks and across her brow like I never seen before. Her whole skin was almost like a chicken's where it twists and wrinkles around the neck before the feathers start. Her eyes were shiny but the middles of them were cloudy, and her hair was a shock of pure white, pulled back tight in a ball like my mother's. I guess I was standing and staring at this woman's face because she turned and looked at me. Her mouth spread wide into a grin, showing that her teeth were but one or two on either side. There was something in her smile that said welcome and hello and it gave me a pleasant sort of feeling, but then I remembered what the mountain said about folks who smile and I tore off running. I heard some men on the porch behind her laughing, and one of them called out, "What'd you do to scare that boy, Grandma?" I kept running until the houses stopped lining the road and there were no more lights on poles and I was running in darkness.

As I slowed down to a walk, I felt the hunger dog tumbling and scratching again. This time he was reminding me of the kind of things my mother would cook when she had them. I began to remember and almost smell when my mother would make cereal mash with eggs. I would watch her pour the funny colored shapes out of the box my father would bring sometimes from town, and she'd crush it up in a bowl and drop an egg in, whipping it all up and cooking it in a pan till it was a sweet hot mash that I enjoyed for the way it filled my stomach quick, resting the dog in my belly, who now, on remembering that mash, began to howl. I rubbed my stomach with my hand and said, "Quiet now. You know it's not food we need, but water."

Where would I find water? I started thinking on this question in that way of talking to myself inside like I was two people, except this time I let one voice inside of me sound like the mountain. I guess because he had talked to me with some wisdom and advice which I'd never had anyone give me before, and felt like something I sorely needed now. "You need water every day, boy," he had said back there under the great road. So now I asked him in my mind, "How do I find me some water?"

"How do you find food?" the mountain asked inside of me.

"I don't know," I said.

"How do you know that there is food when you can't see it?" he asked, sounding impatient, which made me think sharper.

"I guess because I can smell it."

"That's right," said the mountain. "You find food with your nose. Now what part of you can find water?"

I stopped walking so I could think on this question with everything I had. "If your nose can find food," I had the mountain ask myself again, "what part of you finds water?" And in the stillness of my hard thinking, the answer to that question came out of the air around me. The sound of a running stream.

"My ears!" I said out loud. "I find water with my ears!" The mountain didn't need to answer yes. I followed the sound of water in the darkness and it took me off the road into damp grass. The sound of water got louder and louder, changing from that far-off water hissing sound to the closer water sound, like a mix of crinkling paper and wind through trees. The grassy ground began to tilt downward, and I walked it careful, placing each foot heel first, then flapping down the toes, small steps down and down in the dark till I felt my feet hit cool moving water. I squatted down on my haunches and reached with my hands till I felt them both go wet, made a cup of them, and brought them up to drink. The water was cool and fine, like water is everywhere.

I drank and drank from my hands. I stuffed my cap into the front bib of my overalls and put water on my head. Every part of my skin that the water touched felt right away new and better. I slurped and drank, like the hog we had, who I named Henry. He never looked hungry but when food got in front of him, he'd gorge it down like he'd been starving for weeks. I splashed the water onto my neck and on my face and all the pain of walking began to leave me, and I knew I had to get my whole self into that stream. I took off my clothes and laid them on the ground where I couldn't see them in the dark. I stepped myself down and down, till the grass under my feet bottoms became mud and the mud became murk as the cool water tickled the top of my feet, then my ankles, then my shins as I went more and more in and down and I could feel the pull of the water's movement stronger and stronger. I stepped down a bit harder with each foot, sticking my toes into the mud, which was cool-curing the sores and cuts all over them from walking and was also keeping me, tight down, from being carried away. Back when I crossed the stream in our woods to get to the apple trees on the other side, I'd use this same trick of sticking my feet hard down into the mud as the water got powerful strong in the middle but thicker mud beneath. But as I walked out into *this* water, which I couldn't see in the darkness and wasn't familiar to me, I didn't feel the muck at the bottom getting thicker. And the pull against my legs, like a school of fish trying to pull me to their way of swimming, was making me step littler and littler steps and gave me a nervous feeling in my chest. Soon I felt my naked bottom touch the water, and I knew there would be more of me under than over. And I had a sudden thought, which was that I was dead tired of walking and moving through this world at the speed of my feet, and that I wanted to feel all of me in that water, from head to toe. Before I could argue with that idea, with concerns or fears, I pulled my feet out of the mud and up to my chest, drew a deep breath and held it and let my body drop like a rock into the cool water. I bobbed down and then up, and took a hard breath and right away, bobbed back under. I knew I was floating fast, away from my clothes and my brother's cap, away from the chore of walking to I didn't know where anyway.

I knew there was something very foolish in letting myself go down this stream without clothes or caution but something powerful pushed my cares away, and I laid floating on my back, letting the water take me down and down in the dark. Now and again, I could feel a floating branch or twig or something under the water scratch or graze across my back and bottom, so I'd tumble round in circles, swimming some, and drifting some, in the darkness of the stream.

Carried by the water, I was moving quick. Things around me were beginning to change. Bright lights appeared on the shores, streaming through metal fences. Then I saw a powerful light ahead in the direction I was fast drifting. It was a light like dawn in the sky, casting up from the ground. I was passing by a great brick building, far bigger than the one I'd walked into, in town, with my father. This building had no windows and had a round chimney that reached up and split the sky in two with a cloud of smoke churning out of it. And out of the bottom end of this building was a great pipe, like a chimney, but laying on its side just above the water. Out of this pipe was flowing something like mud, or tree sap, and it made swirls of green and black colors in the water, lit up by lamps on the side of the building that shone down on me as bright as ten cold suns. As I drifted past, the green-black swirls snaked around me, and I could feel them on my skin like a quick sunburn. My feet were beginning to scrape against sharp things, and I knew the bottom was coming up shallow. I didn't like the feeling of the stuff coming from the pipe on my skin, so I floated on my belly and began to swim in faster strokes. Meanwhile all around me was getting brighter and brighter. When I floated on my back and saw the sky, it was still pitch-black night, but all around me was more and more and more bright lights. I could see the edges of the stream now. It wasn't green grass on the shores but a white sort of hard dirt like the great road was made of. And there was chain fence along the sides that reached high up. The white hard dirt was getting higher and higher too, and perfect straight like walls, along the stream which was getting narrow, and up ahead I could see the stream was leading to a great wall of white, and the water was flowing right into a black circle in the middle of that wall, and I could see it was a hole, perfect round, as big as a house. I realized that if I didn't get out of that stream, I was going into that black hole myself and my body told me for sure that swimming into it meant dying. I swam to the side and climbed up onto the shore of white hard dirt and stood there, naked, realizing that the walls were too smooth and high to climb up and there was nowhere else to go.

I knew I shouldn't have done what I had done. I shouldn't have left my clothes on the grass and let myself drift so far down. I knew I couldn't go back up the stream. The hard walls and the fence were too high and the going too narrow for me to walk back to where I had started. I was, again, in a place where I couldn't go ahead, but this time I had no way back. I had made a bad decision in picking up my feet and plunging in, giving myself to the water. It had felt, at the time, like a good idea and the feeling of doing it was pleasurable. And now, because of doing what I did and had such a desire to do, there I was in a bad mess.

"You got to think more careful," I said to myself. "If you do something stupid, you could die." I didn't have the mountain say it to me, because when I thought of him seeing me naked and scared in this corner of hard and white, I felt ashamed. I wished I had someone else to talk to—to tell me the best things to do or not to do. I could almost give a name or a face to who that would have been. I almost thought I could see someone like that in my memory. I knew it wasn't my father, who was never interested in what I did except when it bothered him. My mother never looked up from her lap much to tell me anything. But the feeling I had, of missing someone who could help me, felt like it must have come from someone having been there. How could I miss someone who never was?

Chapter Five

The Gray Creature

I woke up late the next morning blinking at the sun, which was high in the sky already and punching its heat down onto me. The skin on my belly and chest stung like a burn but I didn't see how the sun could have cooked me that quick. I slept in the sunshine many times at home, when I'd swim naked in the pond in the hottest part of summer and then doze in the grass and let myself be combed dry by the low willows and reeds that grew wild around the water. I didn't have much time to lay there and think of that because the hard white dirt I was laying on had taken up the heat like a skillet and was burning me from under. I hopped up off of it, but then it burnt my feet. I hopped from one foot to the other, while looking around me for a way out of this bad situation that had only got worse with the daylight. I couldn't get back in the water because it was only a trickle now, way down under me. I hopped up and down and looked up, down, and all around, till my eye caught something above my head that looked like a ladder, but stuck to the wall and made of thin metal bars. It was just barely so high that I couldn't grab it with my hand, so I began to hop up, reaching up with my fingertips—but I couldn't get it. I knew my jumps were too short, but my feet would burn harder if I hunkered down any longer for a bigger leap.

"You gonna have to take the burn to get out of here, boy," said the mountain in my mind. So I set myself flat-footed, squatted my legs into jack-rabbit springs, and jumped my very highest. My hands stretched out above me, and sure enough I caught the bottom rung of that metal ladder. It was hard to hold onto—I used my shoulders to boost myself up and up, grabbing more and more of that rung until my palms were wrapped around it, and my feet dangled with relief below me. The metal rung hurt my palms, but not as much as it had my fingers, my palms being fatter, which gave me time to work out how to climb up. I had climbed up plenty of tree trunks, but this smooth white wall was hard to get a grip on. I put one foot on the white wall as if it was a floor and took a sort of step up to the sky, and in the half a moment where my body didn't weigh so much, I reached up with one hand and grabbed the next rung up. "That's it, boy," said the mountain. "If you can do one, you can do the rest." I grabbed the next rung, and then another, and soon I could get a foot on the first rung and now it was easy. I climbed that metal ladder up and up, hands and feet, higher than any tree I ever climbed.

Down where I'd started, where I'd woken up, trapped and cooked, in the white corner by the stream and the black hole in the wall, it all looked smaller, like a mole's hole as you stand above it. Seeing something so far down made me dizzy, and looking straight up made me hopeless, so I just watched my hands keep grabbing the rungs, which had been black at the bottom but were now painted red. Then there came a white rung, then the rest were white. I kept climbing. Then the rungs and the wall I was climbing were in a narrow strip of shade, which was making the rungs cool enough to handle.

The higher I climbed, a sound I never heard before got louder and louder. It was a scramble of different noises all twisted together and colliding with each other in the air around my ears. I looked up again to see where I was. I could no longer look down. I was too afraid. Above me, I saw that the rungs were coming to an end and there was a sort of metal railing now on each side of the ladder that came away from the wall, went up, and made a sort of loop that went over the top of the white wall. I climbed up from the last rung to see that I was sitting on top of a wall as thick as a bed, which went straight down on the other side, not near as low as the side I'd just climbed up but pretty far down, and the ladder of metal rungs continued down this next side, white, then red, then black at the bottom, like the way I came up.

The white wall I sat on went away from me both ways, and around, making a massive box, bigger than our whole farm and the one next door. And inside this white box was the world I had been hearing. There were men everywhere. So many of them but looking small in the bigness of this box, like ants swarming and milling around, in and out of clumped-up groups of men working with tools. Some banging with hammers, some sawing. Some men sat in trucks that were bigger than any I'd seen on the road, with tires taller than two men if one sat on the other's shoulders. Some of these trucks, which mostly were the color yellow, had shovels on the front that were digging down deep into the dirt, hauling up boulders, and the shovels rose up above all their heads and then turned and dumped all of those boulders into the backs of big yellow trucks with a BOOM sound like lightning, except without the crackle, that shook everything all around—but none of the men noticed for all else that was going on.

There were trucks with great metal barrels in the back, turning in slow circles with a kind of empty tail coming out the end, and it was dumping gray mud out of it into long boxes as men stood and stirred the mud with sticks. Some of them took that mud and spread it out onto what looked like a great floor just like the wall I was sitting on, and suddenly I put it together that this wall and the great road and even the smaller road near my home had been poured out of barrel trucks and spread out and must've hardened in the heat of the sun. The men were making a floor of the gray mud and another floor above it and there were steel beams like the one that held up the great road except the beams were making boxes after boxes, way up into the sky, with wooden planks being laid across them and the hardened gray mud going up their sides. And crawling all over all of it was men. Men moving and working and struggling, like worms picking over a dead fox. They were all dressed the same, in overalls and yellow boots, with hats that looked like baking bowls that glowed an orange color, and if I stopped looking at any one thing from high up on that wall, I just saw orange dots milling all around the ground with yellow metal animals lumbering around and all making more noise than any creature could ever make on its own. In my mind they must have been every person in the world down there. Every person who drove past me on the road since I left home and then some more besides. I knew that as I sat up there, naked as a baby squirrel, that this world I was looking down on must be Houston.

I sat my bare bottom down on that white wall, with my feet dangling over the edge. It was hot to my skin to sit down but there was a cool breeze higher up there that made it just cooler so that I could sit without stinging. I watched the men work for what might have been a whole day of hours. I'd look at a group of them set at a task in one area, and when my interest in them drifted away, I'd just look at something else, like a yellow truck with black smoke spewing out of a pipe on its back and a metal bony arm on the front with a yellow hand at the end plunging into a hole in the ground and dragging out more dirt than I thought the world beneath could contain.

There was so much to see that it made just seeing into something to do. And as I sat there seeing and seeing, I felt I could ignore the hunger dog who was so desperate he could barely move himself. "What happens if you go so hungry that the hunger dog dies?" I wondered. It was just then that I noticed one man, not in coveralls but in a gray suit, like the men who came in the car and told my mother, "You got two more days." And that man was walking toward the wall I was watching from. He stopped at a tall metal pole, which reached up in the air, and right by where I was, at the top of this pole, was a funny sort of rusted metal thing that looked like a coffee kettle but was big enough to boil a bathtub of water. There was a chain hanging off of it, all the way down, with a handle at the bottom, which the man in the gray suit pulled on, with a jerk. When he did that, the top of the kettle came off and white steam shot up out of it and a shriek filled the sky. It was the loudest thing in my life up till that moment. That kettle shrieked like a diving hawk and a honking car horn and an angry man screaming all together from one throat and never stopping. I had to smash my palms against my ears to keep from screaming myself. The man finally let go the handle. The terrible scream, now gone, had washed away every other sound, because all the men had heard it and stopped working. Every machine was shut off, every hammer was put down, and the mud barrels quit tumbling. The men set down where they were and began to eat, talk, and smoke.

Watching those men eat brought my hunger to where I had to move. But it didn't fall, to my mind, as a smart or safe idea to climb down into that white box amongst those eating men, with my whole body being naked. I used to go naked sometimes at home. There was never anyone but me and the animals, and they were naked too.

It never struck me as wrong or strange to be naked till the one time I wandered back to the house like that, as my mother was coming out of the back kitchen door to dump out some hot, dirty water. She saw me, set the pot down on the porch step, walked up, reared her hand way back behind her, and swung it forward, slapping me hard in my face. "You don't go round with no clothes on," she said. "It's disgusting to show your naked spigot and fanny to a woman. Don't never do it again." I remember the feeling of my face burning from the slap. I hadn't flinched to take the heat off it, like I may have with my father, because my mother had never hit me before, and never did again that I remembered.

I had my hand on my face, remembering that slap, as I sat naked on that wall, when it occurred to me that, down below, I didn't see any woman.

"Hey!" I heard a man's voice rise above the others, and I looked down and saw a face looking at me. "What the hell? Lookit up there!" The man looking was holding a sandwich in one hand and pointing up at me with his other. Suddenly all the men were looking at me. I must have had every one of those eyes on my naked body.

"Some kid!" said another man. "Hey, kid! How'd you get up there?" he called up to me. The man in the gray suit, the one who had pulled the chain that made the kettle scream, walked toward the wall I was sitting on. "Hey. You don't belong up there. Get on down off there, boy," he said.

"Is he nekkid?" someone shouted. All those eyes on me were like burning suns. I couldn't sit there any longer. But where to go? There was only back to the water and concrete behind and below me, down amongst them, or the wall that went around them in a square.

"C'mon down from there," said the man in the gray suit in a scolding way as he came to the bottom of the ladder that led to where I was. He put his hand on one rung and his foot on another, and I knew for certain he was going to come up to beat me with his hands. I jumped up and began running along the wall. The second I did that, the whole world of men beneath me broke out in laughing and cheering and hollering. That man and another one behind him, the one who had first seen me and yelled up, came scrambling up the ladder as I ran to the far corner of the white box and then turned, going along the next side. There was room for me to run along the top of the wall but the men chasing me were struggling to keep their balance on account of their being much larger. This was making the men below laugh and cheer more as I ran along the wall, like a mouse running along the edge of a bathtub. The clumps of men twisted around in twisting spin-out circles, like the seeds in a sunflower head, as they all turned to follow my running, all pointing and laughing.

"Get him, boss!" said some men. "Leave him be, boss! He just naked!" said others. One man yelled out, "That goddamn kid is naked as Jesus!"

I saw that the man in the suit was still behind me but the other man had gone the other way around, meaning I'd be running straight into him if I kept going along. But I had nowhere else to go. Soon they were on either side of me, both coming toward me in a cautious way as I ran a little toward one, then toward the other, till I could see plainly that I had no escape. I sat on the wall in the middle of the two, which made the men yell and boo and whistle in disappointment at the game being over.

The two men were standing above me on each side. The man in the gray suit had a cold stare.

"You can't be up here," he said.

"Hey, boss," said the man on the other side, "he just a kid." I looked up at him. He was wearing coveralls like the other men below. He had a look on his face like worrying. I could see he was careful how he talked to the man in the suit.

"Well, get him off this damn wall," said the man in the suit. Then he waved his hand over his head, yelling at the men below. "Lunch is over! Get back to work!" The men booed and hollered and cursed and went back to their machines and tools. I felt the other man's hand on the crook of my arm, pulling me up as the engines started roaring and screaming again below.

"Okay, kid, come on," he said in a way that was gentle. His hand was big, with thick fingers. I looked up at him. His whole body was thick and all muscles. His hair was dark and kind of oily and it covered all his skin which was pale white. His face was shiny with sweat. His eyebrows were thick and bushy and dark. He pressed my shoulder, moving me back along the wall toward the ladder. "How'd you get up here?" he asked me. I felt my voice staying inside and not wanting to speak. I looked down the other side of the wall, and he followed my eyes, looking way below at the stream of water ending in the black hole. "You came from down there?" he asked in surprise. I nodded my head. He took off his plastic hat and scratched his head. "That's a hell of a thing."

"Ernie," yelled the man in the suit, who had climbed back down already, "get that kid down and get back to work!"

This man who I now knew was named Ernie got down the ladder a few rungs first and then waved me to come down after him. I followed him down till we reached the ground. A few of the working men wandered over to get a look at me. They formed a circle around me. I looked up at them and they were like trees all close together.

"He's buck naked," said one man. I had forgotten this, and I quickly balled up, crouching down and holding my arms around my knees. The men laughed and kept saying things like "What the hell?" "He hatch from a nest up there? Looks like a baby bird." "He's skinny as hell. Must be starving." They talked about me like they were looking at a dead animal that couldn't hear them.

"Back to work, damn it!" yelled the man in the suit. I felt heavy cloth slipping around my shoulders. I looked up and saw that the man called Ernie had come up behind me and put his own flannel shirt over my body. I checked his face for a smile, but there wasn't one. "Where's your mother and father?" he asked me, as he got down on one knee to be at my height with his eyes. I didn't answer him.

"Ernie," barked the man in the suit, "get back to work!"

"Just a minute, Mister Lawson," said Ernie. "This young boy here—"

"Never you mind him, now. You're a foreman. I can't spare you for such nonsense." The man in the suit called Mister Lawson was standing above both of us now. "That boy washed up here from someplace, he'll wash right back. He's not your concern."

"But where'd he come from?" asked Ernie. "There's nothing around here."

Mister Lawson walked away saying, "Just get back to work."

"Come on, kid." Ernie took my hand and started to lead me away. My feet were in a world of sharp and edgy things and I couldn't walk easy.

"Jesus, you got no shoes either," he said as he picked me up. It was the second time in two days I found myself in the arms of a man. He carried me to a small house that looked like the back of a long truck but with windows and a door in it. Inside he laid me on a sofa. "Here. Just set tight," said Ernie. "I gotta get back to work." He hustled over to the door and then stopped, looking at me. "You must be hungry."

I said, "I need some water." Ernie looked excited or happy or something. He pointed at me and ran out the door, leaving it open. I listened to the sounds of the work, the machines, the pounding, the yelling of the men. Then Ernie ran back in, holding a black sort of metal box, which he opened up and took out a sandwich wrapped in some kind of paper.

"My wife packs me two sandwiches. One for lunch, one for later. You can have my later one," he said, handing it to me. I quickly put the sandwich in my mouth. I didn't know what type of meat it was, but I knew it was meat, and I got it down my throat without even chewing.

"Hold on there. Easy." Ernie took my wrist in his big hand, holding the sandwich back from my mouth. "Go easy, kid. Eat slow. Chew your food." I slowed down to chew more and he let my wrist go. "Water," he then said. "Let me see . . ." He went into a little door at the end of the little house. I heard a sort of hissing sound and he came out with a cloudy glass filled with water. "Here. Now if you need more water, or you need to use the can, go in there, got it? You finish that sandwich, but eat it slow. I gotta get to work. Don't leave this room, you hear?" I nodded, drinking the water as he ran out the door, closing it behind him.

With that man called Ernie gone, all I had to think about was that sandwich and that glass of water. I took smaller bites and chewed for longer, like he'd told me to, which made the sandwich last, but not forever. When it was gone, it was easier than anything in the world to tumble over onto my side. I could feel a sleep coming on, a kind of sleep that almost felt like at home, except that there wasn't the quiet of the night. The noise from the work was loud and constant. But in my mind I got to thinking of it as like a thunderstorm. I'd slept plenty of times in the shed, to the sound of hard rain and hail pounding on the tin roof above me, thunder rolling in the sky, and the twigs from the tree outside slapping the little window. This was no different except it was daylight and I could fix that by closing my eyes, which I did.

The first time I remember having a dream that frightened me was when I was much smaller and I had a fever that lasted many days. I'd heard my mother tell my father, "He might get took in the night by that fever." To which my father replied, "One less mouth."

I was laying on the sofa in the room beside the kitchen. It was strange to be sleeping inside the house. My mother wrapped a cold, wet sheet around my body. I felt my head begin to boil. It was that night when I slipped into a dream where there was a man of cold gray flesh, like that of a snail, laying on the couch beside me pressed up against my side with his head nestled under my arm like he was trying to feed off of my teat like a baby animal would. His eyes were red, without lids, and he stared up at me never blinking with a sort of unfriendly, hungry grin of sharp teeth. He had no hair on his head or body, and the coldness of him was sucking the heat off of my side, so that I began to feel a relief of the fever dropping until I understood that I would keep getting colder until I was cold like him and then I'd be dead. I wanted to wiggle and run off the couch, away from that cold gray man, but I couldn't move and the feeling, which I knew was death, was spreading up from my chest to my head. I tried to holler and scream but I was frozen stiff and dying quick and the gray man, who was more a creature, said into my mind by looking into my eyes, that he was my *death to be* and no matter if I survived that night, and no matter how many days or years I pushed away and struggled to be a living soul, he would always and forever be up against my side, draining away the heat of my body—and that in the end, I'd be cold and gray and dead and I would join him and become the red-eyed death of someone else. The knowing of this filled me with a kind of fear that shot through me. I screamed so loud that it was *too* loud to be me. My eyes shot open as I realized the scream was coming from outside myself, outside of the room, and all at once I knew it was the work whistle blowing again outside and I found myself on the sofa of that little truck-like house, wrapped in Ernie's shirt, soaking wet and burning hot.

I must have gone from remembering the dream of the creature to having it again on that sofa. I looked out of a little window and saw that the men were stopping work once again but instead of eating, they were putting away their tools and changing their clothes. The man in the gray suit came into the little truck-house and looked at me with that angry face and said, "What he put you in here for?" And soon after, Ernie came in and when he saw my face, he looked scared.

"Hey, that kid looks awful sick," he said as he came over and put his hand on my head. "He's burning up. I got to get him to a hospital."

"That's your affair now that it's quit time," said the man in the gray suit. I looked up at Ernie, whose face was so close to mine that it was the whole world I could see.

I woke up to the feeling I was rushing along somehow real fast, being carried away, like when I floated on the river the night before. I opened my eyes to see I was on some small kind of sofa next to Ernie who had a plastic wheel in his hands and was looking out of a big bright window. I turned to see that outside of that window, the sky, road, and whole world were flipping by like a running rabbit.

I began to put together in my mind that I was inside of a truck, and Ernie was driving us down a road. I also became aware of a sound all around us in the truck. It was like a mix of thumps and taps and something like twittering birds and warbling frogs and a woman's voice who was talking and then crying and then screaming and talking again in a way that sounded like the twittering and warbling. But there was no woman inside the truck. "What's that sound?" I asked Ernie.

"Sound?" Ernie asked, as if he couldn't hear it.

"Where's that lady who's crying?" I asked.

Ernie laughed and pointed next to the wheel in his hand and said, "That's the radio, kid. Don't you know radio? That's Harley Bard singing." I didn't know what he meant, but I listened closer. The woman was crying the same words again and again: "My heart is broken by your lovin'. So don't love me no more, baaaaaby."

"She sounds sad," I said. I tried to sit up higher to see more of the flying world through the window but the burning dizzy feeling in my head pushed me back down.

I felt Ernie's hand on my shoulder and he said, "Settle down, kid." And I dropped back down into darkness.

Chapter Six

My First Hospital

I woke up in a bed. I'd slept deep without any kind of dreaming. I was under sheets and a blanket and I heard the sound of rain on a window. I rubbed my eyes, which felt like they'd been shut off a long time, and then opened them up to see that I was in a very long room, like the one my father had took me to in that building, but with beds all along the walls. It was nighttime and the lights were off, but I could see, because so much cold electric light was coming in through many windows and making funny moving shapes on the walls from the rainwater hitting and pooling up on the glass of the windows that were behind the beds. I had something like a rope stuck to my arm, right where it bends in the middle.

There was a bed beside mine, very close, with no one in it. And beside that was another, with a very small boy who was sleeping. His head was wrapped up in a white cloth. On the other side of me was another bed with a girl on it who was bigger than me, but still a child, and she was sitting up looking at me. She had her knees up to her chest with her arms around herself, and she was staring at me with no expression, like a raven sitting on a mailbox. Suddenly the room was filled with quick light, then dark again, and the thunder that followed cracked loud and shook all those big windows. And I put my hands over my head thinking the whole room would cave in and the girl laughed at me. The funny shapes on the walls from the rain on the glass started to move into the inside of my mind, and I felt the bad burning in my head again—pain so bad that I couldn't stand it and that girl kept laughing like a raven's cawing and I got hotter and hotter and I felt myself peeing inside of my sheets, which was hot and then cold. And from that cold wet pee, I felt a cold lump growing against my leg. I kept my eyes shut tight, afraid to see, but I reached my hand down under the wet sheet and touched cold flesh that I knew to be gray and snail-like, and I knew it was that red-eyed creature of my dreams that called himself my coming death and he laughed along with the raven girl and grew bigger and bigger beside me as the heat in my head was sapped away into his cold head and I got to shivering and chattering my teeth and knew it was the very moment I was to die.

"He is not our child," said a lady's voice, which woke me up after what seemed like a sleep that was longer than my whole life. I opened my eyes and saw the lady who was talking. Her face was big, like a man's face. But I could tell she was a lady because her skin was creamy and her hair was long.

"We aren't responsible for him," the lady was saying. She was looking right at me from the moment I opened my eyes, so she must've been looking at me before.

Sitting next to her was Ernie, who looked behind him and said, "Is he dyin'?"

"He's not dying," answered a man who stood behind Ernie, wearing a white coat to his knees with a suit on under it. "He needs more care and he needs time to recover. What we need to know is who is paying for his stay here at the hospital."

While he was talking, this man was pulling the rope that was in my arm out. It had been inside of my skin with a needle like the one on my mother's sewing machine, which broke and never got fixed. I didn't know why they'd stuck that under my skin, but my mind was working slow.

"I thought we might look after him," said Ernie, "until he gets well. That's why I brought him here."

"This isn't a charity hospital," said the other man. "If you're not prepared to pay his bill, you should have taken him to the Union County hospital. They take charity cases."

"We're not responsible for him," said the woman again. "He's a stranger to us. My husband found him and brought him here is all. We have no money or obligation to pay for his stay."

"What will you do with him if he's not paid for?" asked Ernie.

"It's neither our policy or habit to throw sick children out on the street. Now that he's here he'll be cared for to a point. But arrangements must be made for his placement once he's—"

"Not by us," said the lady. She took Ernie's elbow in her hand and began pulling him away. "Let's go!" She pulled Ernie toward the door at the end of the long room full of beds. Ernie looked at my eyes the whole way to the door till they both left. The other man put his hand on my forehead. I could feel his skin cold against my skin, which was still hot, but not burning. The man put his thumb on my eye and pulled it up and open, and he took a tiny bright torch in his other hand and shined it right into it. I didn't like that and I tried to pull my eye closed, but he pushed his hand hard against my head and said, "Hold still." So, I held still.

"What's your name?"

"Ingram," I said.

"Ingram what?" he asked. I didn't know what he meant.

"You don't know your last name?" The man put away his torch and sat down on my bed.

"I only got one name," I said.

"Where are your mother and father?"

"I don't know," I said. "My father left and my mother told me to leave."

"God help this country," he said. "You're on your own?"

"Yes," I said.

"Yes *sir* is better," he said. "When you speak to an adult, particularly someone of authority or respect, you should answer 'yes, sir' and 'no, sir.'"

"Yes, sir," I said.

"Why were you naked when they brought you here?"

"I went for a swim. I left my clothes by the river. The river carried me away, sir," I said.

"That was a damn fool thing to do," he said like he was angry.

"Yes, sir," I said. Because he was right.

"The rivers in this city are full of sewage and industrial waste. You're lucky to be alive, or maybe not so lucky. In any case you can't stay here. Once you are well enough, you'll be moved to a home for orphan boys, if one can be found with space."

"What's a home for orphan boys, sir?"

"A home for children who have no parents. You are one of many abandoned children in this country. So many, in fact, that we might not find a place for you, in which case you'll have to fend for yourself."

"Yes, sir," I said. He got up and left the room. I looked up at the ceiling, which was perfect white, like the man's coat. Then I turned over on my side and saw that the girl in the next bed was sitting up, like she was before, and looking at me again.

"You're an orphan," she said.

"Yes, sir," I said, because she looked older than me.

The girl's laugh was so loud it was slapping against the walls and falling on the floor. When she finished laughing, she pointed at the bed on the other side that used to have a boy in it with his head wrapped up. "The boy that was in that bed died this morning," she said. "They said you were going to die too but you didn't. So now you get to be an orphan."

There was something in the way she said it that reminded me of my dad when he had drunk liquor. "Are children in Houston allowed to drink whiskey?" I asked her.

Another voice laughed from across the room. An older boy was sitting up in his bed. He had a magazine in his hands and he was laughing at what I just said. The girl turned her head away from me, looking mad, and that older boy came over and sat on my bed.

"How you feeling, kid?" he asked.

"I still feel hot but better than before," I answered. I was thinking that boy was older than me. He was thin with dark hair and his nose stuck out a lot further than mine. When he wasn't talking, his teeth still showed, like his lips wouldn't close all the way over them.

"My name's Tab," he said. "I'm here cuz I had PO-LEE-OH." He said these last three sounds big with his hands cupped over his mouth.

"What's that?" I asked.

"It's an old disease that's makin' a comeback. It's a kid killer. My brother died of it. Not me. But my heart came out my skin. It's on the outside now, pumping away over my skin. You wanna see?"

I looked to where he was unbuttoning his shirt, feeling a little scared to see a heart on the outside of a body. When my father slaughtered all our animals, he put their hearts in a pile and I saw them. Tab opened his shirt all the way down and then suddenly pulled it open. There was nothing there except a normal chest of skin with two small teats like any boy would have.

"Ha!" he suddenly yelled. "Just kiddin', kid. Boy, you'll believe anything."

Then a boy from another bed said, "Hey, Tab. Leave that kid alone, why don't you?"

Tab yelled at that kid, saying, "Shut up!" in an angry, vicious way. Then he turned back to me and looked calm again. "You better get some rest, buddy. We'll talk again tomorrow, okay?" I nodded yes and Tab went back to his bed. It was good he left me alone because I could feel the heat coming back in my head and I felt all my limbs in the spots they meet and join starting to ache something awful. I turned on my side and tried to fall back asleep.

I liked the way that Tab talked to me—like he was interested in me without being mad at me. The only other person ever talked to me with interest before was Anna Lee, when she came with her mother. I was sitting with the animals. She came right over and sat next to me and we both watched the chickens walk and peck and cluck. "What's their names?" she asked me.

"They don't have names. Just chickens," I told her. She looked down at the dirt. I knew she was sad because I didn't tell her any names, so I pointed out the hogs. "I call them Henry and Helen," I said. "I call the dog Rufus."

"You got to name the animals yourself?" she asked in an excited, wanting way.

"Well, my mother and father don't call them nothing. I give them names. Doesn't harm anyone."

"But you didn't name the chickens?"

"Nope," I said and looked at her face, which was sad again. "You want to name the chickens?" I asked.

Her face snapped wide into a smile like a sheet on the line suddenly caught by a gust of wind. "Can I?" she asked.

"Sure. You go ahead."

She looked at all the chickens real careful, like naming them right was the most important thing in the world. There were three of them at the time. She pointed at the one with red feathers and said, "His name is Red John." Then she pointed at the black and brown one. "His name is . . . Sammy." And then she pointed at the chicken that was mostly white and said, "And that one is . . . Jesus."

I didn't feel it important to tell her that these chickens was girls if she couldn't tell for herself, so I set my mind to remember those names, and that's the names those chickens had till the day they were killed for slaughter.

The next morning, I was woken up by the window above my bed being opened with a squeaking sound, and all the sound of birds and car horns and commotion got carried in by a cool breeze. I looked up and saw a lady all dressed in white. She had big, thick legs and a big backside and fat breasts, and she was putting some kind of latch on the window that held it open.

She saw me looking at her and frowned, and then she sniffed the air and said, "Did you wet your bed again?" And she grabbed the edge of the sheet and blanket I was under and pulled them down, and then she got even madder. "Why a boy your age is wetting the bed is well beyond me," she said.

My legs and my backside were wet. I thought it was from sweating like I'd been doing since I got there, but my head wasn't hot anymore so I guess I'd wet myself in my sleep.

All the other children in the other beds began waking up, and now they were all looking at me and laughing. Then Tab's voice cut them down as he said, "Shut up!" So the children turned away from me, and I was suddenly feeling private in a crowded room, and Tab, who was also not looking at me, was protecting me. I had once been walking by the fence in our back woods, and I saw a rotting wooden box. I took a stick and flipped it over and there was a cat with a slew of tiny baby kittens nestled against its belly. When I'd let the sunshine into their hiding place, those kittens mewed with their eyes shut. The mother cat stood up and arched her back, hissing at me real angry. I ran off. I told my mother what happened and she said, "She was protecting her young," as she peeled a carrot into the sink.

The lady in the white dress pulled the thin white pants I was wearing off of me and threw them into a bin at the foot of my bed as she said, "Disgusting. Disgusting." Then she took a clean white rag out of a little dish of hot water and soap and handed it to me and said, "Get out of that bed. Stand over here and clean your privates while I change your bed." I did like she said, running the warm soapy rag over my crotch, spigot, and backside and down my legs. She was flapping new sheets up and down and covering my bed back up as she kept muttering like she was speaking to the air in front of her face. "Children from the countryside are just wild animals," she said. Then she looked at me with her big pale pudgy hands on her white hips and said, "Okay, get back in bed. I'll bring you some new pajamas."

I got back in bed as she walked away, carrying my wet clothes with her fingertips, her white shoes making a *clock, clock, clock* sound out of the room, and she once more said, "Disgusting."

Tab came over to my bed again and said to me, "Hey, kid, you know, you don't have to do everything they tell you to do."

"What do you mean?" I asked.

"Grown-ups will always tell you what to do, right?"

"Yes, sir," I said.

He laughed, which made me remember the raven girl. I looked over to her bed to see that it was empty.

"You don't have to call me sir, kid. Gee, wow, you need to get some backbone. Especially seeing that you have no parents. A kid like you has to get tough and be his own boss. You may as well start practicing now. You gotta be in charge. You think that fat nurse cares about you?"

"Nurse?"

"Yeah, she's a nurse. That fat cow in the white dress just now."

He was calling that lady a cow. We never had cows but the neighbors did, and they had high-up rear ends, and so did she, and the idea of calling her a cow hit me so sudden as funny that I broke out laughing. Seeing me laugh made Tab laugh too. It was a new, sweet sort of feeling, like honey or sugar or something, to be laughing along with someone else.

"What's your name, kid?" asked Tab.

"Ingram," I said.

"Hey, Peach, Wilson, come meet Ingram." He waved to two kids in other beds. "Most of the kids in this ward are rats," he said, "but these two are okay."

The two other boys got out of their beds and came over to mine. One of them, Peach, was about my size. He hopped with one leg gathered up like a lame dog. The other boy, Wilson, was real small and skinny, looking almost like just bones. His skin looked paler than skin, especially with his eyes having such a dark color around the edges of them. They came over and sat on my bed on each side of me.

"Ingram," said Tab, "this here is Peach. He's lame, but spirited. And Wilson here's got cancer. But he's tough, alright. Boys? This is Ingram."

"Hiya, Ingram," said Peach, and he put his hand out in front of me. I had a real natural feeling that it was a good idea to put mine out the same way, and he grabbed my hand and sort of pumped it up and down like drawing water from a well. Then he let go.

"Hiya, Ingram," said Wilson, and then me and him did the very same thing.

I said, "Hiya, Peach and Wilson," and somehow that made all three of them laugh and I laughed too.

"Where you come from, Ingram?" asked Peach.

"I come from . . . our house," I answered.

"How'd you get here?" asked Tab.

"Walked part way," I said. "Swam some too. Then a man brought me here from where the end of the river was."

Peach looked at me funny and said, "You get less clear the more you tell."

"I'll say," said Wilson, his voice cracking a little like a baby bird that can't cheep too loud yet.

"You better begin at the beginning, kid," said Tab, putting a hand on my shoulder.

I liked how that felt. I liked the feeling of these three boys looking right at me and asking me about what happened to me. That happy feeling, the *liking* of all of this, was rushing over me in such a new way, that it was frightening. Why would I be frightened of something I liked? It was happening too fast for me to understand it. And at the same time, I was working in my mind to recall where I'd been so I could tell them what they wanted to know, and it put pictures in my head of the road where I walked, and the hunger I felt and the fear of the darkness beneath the great road and all of that gave me a sort of sudden sadness—a bad, bad feeling that I didn't even feel when those things occurred. And that bad feeling of remembering ran across me and collided with the good feeling of *liking* the kindness and attention of these boys—boys just like me—and the two opposite feelings knocked against me and shook me so hard that it put a hard rock in my throat that kept me from talking. The boys all looked at me with confusion, and then I burst out all at once crying, tears and sobbing and making gulping sounds and I had no control over anything I was doing. I looked up at the three boys but I couldn't see their faces for all the crying.

"Why's he crying?" said Peach.

"Aw, he's okay," said Tab. "He's had a rough go of it is all."

"I cried like that when they told me about the cancer," said Wilson.

"Shut up about your cancer, Wilson," said Peach. Their three faces were just blurry colors in a heap as they talked to each other about me.

My crying was winding down now. The storm of good and bad, fearful and happy, that set off the rain on my face was passing. I could remember sudden and powerful storms, on deep summer days, that had hit our place, tore tall trees in half and then kept on moving, leaving the sky clear above us but menacing some place further off and I'd think, "Well, someone else is hanging on and waiting for that same storm to pass now." And I wondered, sitting on that bed, whether someone else far off was crying from the feelings that had just passed through me.

Then that nurse with the big behind came in. "All of you get back to your beds," she said. And the boys went off, leaving me alone. I rubbed my eyes off on the sheet and looked up, seeing her holding some white clothes like the ones I'd gotten wet with pee. "Get out of bed and put these on now."

I remembered what Tab had said about saying no to adults.

"I said get out of that bed."

I knew her tone was the kind that comes before a punishment. I didn't want to get hit. But I didn't want to do what she said. I had never said no to any person who told me what to do. I figured I had to get used to doing something I hadn't been doing till then. So I looked at the woman and said, "I don't want to put those on."

She took a step closer to me. "Put them on, I say."

As I looked at the face of that woman in white, a feeling grew in me. I hadn't felt it before, but it reminded me of something I had seen—my father's face when he changed from plain to angry. I thought maybe I was feeling inside what he did. The feeling was hot and bitter, like I could taste my own blood with the inside of my stomach, and I felt ready to do something against this woman.

"I said get out of that bed," said the nurse. I wondered if she was fixing to hit me. And I wondered if a lady could hit like a man could, not slapping that stings, but a punch that can make you fall over and feel pain for days. This woman was big. She was angry. But she wasn't my mother or my father. And somehow that made me think that if she hit me, I could hit her too.

I saw her angry eyes look down at my hands, and I saw for myself that they were both tight, red fists. She changed her expression, taking a step back, away from my bed.

"A juvenile delinquent," she said. "Just what I thought. Well, that makes it easy. There's no room for you at the orphanage. We had been speculating that you probably escaped from a reform school somewhere, which is why you came naked. And you sound like a liar to me. Well, no worry. There is plenty of room for you in the one here in Houston. Clearly, that's where you belong." She dropped the white clothes at the foot of my bed and walked out of the room.

"Hey, Ingram," said Tab, "you better get on out of here."

"No kidding," said Peach. "Don't let them take you to reform school."

"What's reform school?" I asked.

"It's a place only for kids who are criminal and violent. You'll get flattened in a place like that. You gotta go. Now. Peach—he's your size. Give him your clothes."

"Give him my clothes?" said Peach, in an unsure way.

"Where do I go?" I asked Tab.

"Go out that door," said Tab, pointing at the only door at the end of the room. "You know how to read?"

"No," I said.

"Look at that sign," he said. "It says EXIT. Exit means out. Exit signs are always red with big letters like this, and if you go where they point, you'll get out of wherever you are. You got that?"

I looked at the sign he was pointing at. I didn't want to leave this place of boys who I could talk to and feel a part of. And a safe bed to sleep in and food. But the woman in white could take me somewhere real bad and then I'd be away from these boys anyhow.

"Ingram," said Tab, and he got close up to me, putting his hand tight around my elbow. "Did you escape from a reform school? You can tell me if you're lying. I won't care." He was asking in a low voice like he wanted only me to hear it.

"No," I said, "I'm not lying. I don't know what a reform school is."

"It's no good. Believe me," he said, even quieter. "Kids die in there. And nobody knows about it."

Tab looked afraid when he said this. Then he got back to looking tough like he'd been looking before.

"Peach, I said give him your clothes," said Tab.

"I can't, Tab. My parents will have a fit," said Peach.

"Pay attention, Peach," said Tab, coming over to his bed and turning hot and angry. "This kid ain't got any parents. You're lucky yours are around to give you clothes and to get mad when you lose 'em."

Tab started rummaging through a drawer in the little table next to Peach's bed. Peach was trying not to let him, though he was too small to stop it. "I don't know, Tab. Those are my clothes. I'm not exactly keen on giving away my clothes."

Tab turned on Peach in a quick and violent way and put his hand around his throat. "Shut up, Peach. Shut the hell up!" Peach's eyes were bugging out from not getting air, just like I was on the floor of the mountain's tent. Then Tab started coughing. His cough was from down deep and it made his knees bend. When he coughed, blood came out of his mouth and dribbled on his chin. He let go of Peach. Peach took Tab's elbow and helped him back to his bed. Then Peach came over to me with a pair of dungarees and a shirt and put them on my bed.

"Here," he said, "you better go before she comes back." And he went back to his bed. I looked over to Tab, who was lying on his side, trying to breathe better.

I put on the dungarees and the shirt, which went easily onto my body, and walked over to the door and turned to look back in the long room. Every child was watching me from their beds. Like they wondered what happens to a kid who goes out of the room on his own. When my mother had told me to go, I had done what she said. Because I always did what she or my father said to do. Now I had said no to that nurse and I was having to go again.

"Shoes," said Tab, his voice still soggy with blood. "Somebody gotta give him shoes."

"Why doesn't Peach?" asked Wilson.

"Peach gave enough," said Tab. "Someone give him your shoes." But no one said anything more. I went to the door and put my hand on it to leave. Then I turned around and looked at all of them looking at me and said goodbye and walked out of the room.

I was in another long room, with another door at the other end of it. Right away, over another door to the side, I saw a sign with the red letters Tab had told me said *EXIT*. I went out through that door. Then I was in a room of stairs. I ran down those stairs, which felt cool to my bare feet. Down I went, until the stairs ended in two big doors that had big metal bars on them, which I pushed with all I had in me and they flew open onto a world of cars, all arranged in rows with white painted lines around them. I didn't know where to go except away from this place and the people in white, so I just ran between the cars and away. I looked back one time at the place and saw a window up high with someone standing there who I felt was watching me go. I kept running.

Chapter Seven

A Hole in My Foot

There were buildings everywhere. Some were brick—not just red brick but other colors like bright yellow with windows all over their sides and narrow roads between them, crisscrossing each other, full of cars crawling around honking. The cars were bright colored and kind of shiny, making their own light like the mountain's water bottle had. I couldn't see where the driving road was and the walking road was but I hardly had to decide where to go because I was caught up walking with the river of walking people that went up and down the streets turning this way and that.

Every place where two roads crisscrossed each other, the folks would gather up like minnows in the elbow of a creek and wait until the cars stopped in one direction and then they'd burst across the road, colliding with the folks coming the other way and knotting up at the next side with the folks going against them in reverse. I found myself in a herd of legs and backsides, shoes and trousers and ladies' skirts. I was too occupied with not catching a strong knee to my jaw for me to look up at the faces of the folks who were striding past me faster than I could keep up, let alone have any clear thinking about where I ought to be headed myself.

I couldn't catch sight of the sun in the sky and I had a terrible feeling that I was going deeper and deeper into this place and that there was no way to trace my steps back, and yet the legs and knees kept rushing and I got pulled along—like all those folks were water but without the quiet that a river brings. Every person and every car was making their own separate holler or honk at the same time making such a chatter and bang inside my ears, I thought my head would pop away from my neck like a daisy-top picked off and chucked into a puddle. "You got to get out of this place, Ingram," I had the mountain say in my mind.

"How?" I asked his voice. But he had no answer. And in that moment, as me and a bunch of folks began to crisscross again, I brought my foot down off the walking part of the road and onto where the cars go, and my foot came down on something so sharp and cutting that I heard my own voice scream out in pain. I looked down at my foot and saw that I'd stepped directly on a green broken bottle and glass was sticking out of my naked sole. Blood poured out. My scream stopped a small circle of people who looked down at me while all the folks around them continued walking in all directions. "What happened, kid?" said a man. "He cut his foot on a bottle," said another. "Okay, get out of the street, kid."

I felt a hand take my elbow and begin leading me away. I hopped on one foot as the man who'd taken me said, "Sit down here against this building," which I did and just like that he was gone. I sat with my back to a window that went all the way to the ground. None of the people rushing by saw me. There was only a little narrow place to sit and I had to gather my knees up not to be stepped on. I looked at my foot and the glass was still sticking out the bottom. The hurt was so much that instead of being a boy with a hurting foot, I was a hurting foot who was barely a boy. I reached down and touched the green glass and it was like touching myself on the inside and it made me howl. I knew that glass had to come out. And seeing as it was me that stepped on it, it could only be me that took it out. I took a deep breath, held on to it, and pulled that piece of glass out of my foot. It was a relief, but the hole where the glass used to be made the blood come more and quicker.

I had been cut on my foot before. I stepped on a nail left in the dirt from when my father fixed the roof. I showed my mother the nail sticking out the bottom of my foot and told her it hurt real bad. She said pull it out and stop the bleeding with some damp soil and a rag. There was no soil around me there in Houston, and I had no rag, so I spit on my hand and rubbed off some of the blood, then I tore off a piece from the bottom of the shirt Peach had given to me and I tied it around my foot. The river of people kept on rushing by. "You can't sit here," said a man standing above me. He wore a dark blue suit that was closed up to his neck with shiny buttons, with one big shiny button on his chest, and he had a hat on that was sort of pointy on the sides and flat on top. That man held a black stick in his hand and pointing the end of it in my face. "Move on, kid," he said. That wooden stick was getting closer to my face. "Get up from there or you're gonna be in a world of it," said the man in the blue suit.

I stood up and said, "Yes, sir." Which made the man look calm and satisfied. He slid his stick into a sort of loop on his belt. I walked, limping on my rag-wrapped bleeding foot.

I walked along, turning this way and that. Each time I found a way that had in it less folks, I'd turn down it, and then turn again when the folks were even less. The rooftops of the buildings were coming down lower, letting the sky into view. Then the buildings became more like houses in rows, with a shop here and there, with now just a few people walking here and there, and those that walked did so at a pace closer to a heartbeat. The people in this quieter area were all dark-faced, where the more crowded area had folks mostly of pale color like mine. I remembered what the mountain had said—that the world was divided, white and black, and that being white, I was on the lucky side. But I sure felt more comfortable here, around the folks he called black, and could only feel sorry for the fast-walking white folks trapped like fish, with no choice in the matter at all.

I limped past a brick house where a group of boys, mostly a bit bigger than me, and some much bigger, sat on the high-up front steps. They had a loaf of bread and a plug of meat that smelled like pork, and they were passing it around, each taking a turn to rip off a chunk of each and eat it, and then pass it to the next boy.

"Boy, something you need to learn," said the mountain in my mind, "is to start looking for food before you're too hungry to find it." I stared at that pork and bread so hard that I didn't notice all those boys looking right at me.

"What the fuck do you want?" said one boy.

"Get on off of here, white boy," said the largest of them. He was sitting at the top of the steps and all the other boys looked at him when he talked, and then at me. All I could do was stand there and stare at the pork and bread as it passed from one boy to the other.

"I think he wants some of this pork meat," said a smaller boy.

The biggest boy climbed down the steps, grabbing the pork chunk from the boy who had it and holding it in front of my face. "This what you want?" he said. Having that meat so close to my face was more than I could take. I reached my hand out to grab it but it quickly became a blur as he yanked it away with one hand and swung his other around, bringing his palm to my face with a hard slap, which popped my ear and made every boy there laugh hard and loud. "Boy must be hungry," he said to his friends, and he held the meat again close to my face but carefully like teasing. "You want this meat, white boy?"

"Yes, sir," I said. Every boy laughed when I said that, except the biggest one in front of me. He looked at me in a curious way, like he was trying to remember my name. Another boy, maybe the next one down in size from him, climbed off the steps and stood in front of me with his chest up, making himself as tall as he could.

"What the fuck are you doing in these streets, white motherfucker?" he said, and he reared back, made a hard fist with his hand, and punched me straight in the mouth. I fell on my back. The boy climbed onto my chest.

The rest of them jumped off the steps and crowded around. I looked up at their faces which were laughing and hollering, covering up the sky, as the boy sitting on my chest punched me freely in my face over and over again. "White motherfucker," he kept on saying. I laid there and did nothing but let each new pain explode on my skin. The one thing I knew how to do in life, was take a beating. I had learned long ago that the less I did in resistance the quicker my father would figure he'd hurt me enough. Laying on my back and letting this boy hit my face over and over again, I had a quick-rising feeling that I didn't care what happened to me anymore. I didn't see much difference between being hit by this boy or not. I was hungry, tired, and had no way to make life better anyway.

The biggest boy pushed past the others, shoving them all away, one by one, letting the sky back into my vision, and finally he grabbed the boy on my chest from under his armpits and lifted him off me, throwing him backward like a spent tire, saying, "Get off him, Charlie."

I laid there with my mouth full of blood, which to my hungry stomach tasted at least like something. I wondered if a man who was starving to death could survive by eating pieces of himself.

"What are you doing here, kid?" asked the biggest boy, standing over me, with no anger in his voice. "Where you from?"

"I don't know," I said to his ankles, and then looked up at his face.

He looked down at me and shook his head. "Man, if you ain't one sorry white boy. Don't you know how to get home?" I didn't answer anything. "Don't you have no home?"

I didn't answer. He reached down, took my elbow in his hand, pulled me to my feet, and led me away from the group of boys. "Come on, then."

"Where you takin' him, Jerald?" one of the boys shouted at our backs.

"To Miss Maw's house," Jerald said loudly out in front of us, knowing that his strong voice would tail out behind us and reach those boys. He walked with me, saying nothing, and me saying nothing. I was happy to be pulled along the road by someone else's feet besides my own.

Chapter Eight

Family

Jerald took me through a hole in a low fence, to a little white house, kind of like my own, but painted better and looking more generally lively—the way a house can look dead or alive. My father used to say about our house, "This is a dead place." And my mother would look down at the floor. We walked up to the front door, which had a screen for an upper-half. Jerald knocked on the wooden frame of the door, which rattled around loose, and as we stood there waiting, a girl who looked exactly my age came up to the door and said, "Hello, Jerald."

"Hi, Sinema," said Jerald. Sinema had wide thick hair, like a black hedge growing even all around her head. She was wearing a bright yellow dress that stood out against her dark-skinned shoulders. Her eyes, big and bright, stood out, too, against her black face, like if the sun could shine in the midnight sky while leaving it black all around. Sinema turned her head from Jerald and looked at me directly in my eyes, and I looked directly into her eyes with my own, which got a strange moist kind of warmth in them—so much so that it said to me I would never have to blink again as long as I looked, with her, at *each other* in this way.

"Who is this?" asked Sinema, meaning me.

"Boy's lost," said Jerald. "Tell Miss Maw. I'll see you later." And Jerald walked away, leaving me there with this girl Sinema, who opened the screen door, which I forgot had been between us, and only made her colors and darkness more colorful and dark with the screen door gone. As the door closed with a *wap!* Sinema looked up and down at me, as before she was only looking at the balls of my eyes.

"What happened to your whole face?" she said with big surprise in her voice.

"Got beat up by a boy."

"One of Jerald's boys," she guessed right. She took my hand with her hand and pulled me into the house. The closest I'd ever come to having my hand held was when the mountain had put his hand around my throat. Sinema gripped my hand just as tightly, squeezing and tugging me along. But she could have squeezed harder and harder still without causing me the slightest pain or panic. After a few steps, though, she stopped to notice me again.

"How come you're limping?" she asked, looking down at my feet.

"I stepped my foot on some glass," I said, pointing at the bloody shirt-rag that was keeping my foot-bottom closed.

"Boy, oh howdy. You had a bad day, huh?" she said, looking concerned at my face. I didn't say anything. I just looked back at her and her mouth started to naturally spread out wide, in a grin of clean white teeth. Then she said, "You're all serious." And she started laughing a little, like she was trying not to. And then I started laughing. I couldn't help it. We both laughed. Standing there with this girl and laughing to each other's faces, like looking in the mirror, felt like something I must have at some point done every day in my life, because it felt just like living does. Like the thing you do without thinking.

Our laughing passed and Sinema took back my hand and said, "Come on." And she led me deeper into the house. It was cool inside in a soothing way to my skin, which had begun to burn from the sun outside. "What's your name?" Sinema asked as she led me to the back of the house to a kitchen. I told her Ingram as we came walking up behind a woman standing at a stove that sizzled with pans frying and bubbled with big boiling pots. The woman was about the size of the mountain but shaped as if the mountain was a woman. She had thick, tree-stump legs widening out to hips like a horse but then real narrow-like to her waist, and then wide again across her broad back covered by a thick, clean white dress with little blue flowers across it. And on her head was a bush of black hair just like Sinema's but twice the size.

As she did her cooking, the woman was crying and hollering in a voice like a small bird, too small for her body, and she was saying, "What a friend we have in Jeeeesuuss! All our sins and griefs to paaaay."

I asked Sinema, "Is she Harley Bard?"

"What?" Sinema said and she laughed. "No! This is Miss Maw." Hearing us talk, Miss Maw turned and faced us.

"Miss Maw," said Sinema, "this is Ingram."

Miss Maw looked down at us with a spatula in her hand. She used her sleeve to wipe sweat off her brow, which was as high as any brow I had ever seen and chestnut-brown in color rather than the midnight black of Sinema's face. When she saw my face, Miss Maw's head snapped back in surprise. "Well," she said, and then looked at me longer, as Sinema continued to squeeze my hand. "Ingram, huh? What notion in the Lord's mind brought a boy like you into my home?"

"Jerald brought him," said Sinema. "Said he's lost."

Miss Maw squatted down on her great legs, bringing her big brown face down to mine. "Who's done this to the boy's face?" Miss Maw asked.

"One of Jerald's wild boys," said Sinema. "And he stepped his foot on some glass." And then she started chuckling. Miss Maw looked at her kind of angry and I wondered if she was about to scream at her or hit her. But Sinema kept laughing and Miss Maw didn't get serious mad. She just clicked her tongue and looked at me again. I didn't laugh with Sinema this time. I was occupied looking at Miss Maw's face, which, from close to her, glowed like the honey that had burst from where I'd once thrown a rock at the beehive that had grown in the crook of a tree limb behind our house. That honey oozed down, glossy brown, swarming with the bees that fed on the field of wild buckwheat behind that tree. Miss Maw had skin looking just like that, from the edges of her eyes to her nose and down her neck.

"Sinema, you go on now and set the table for lunch with the others," Miss Maw said to Sinema, who let go my hand and walked away. Miss Maw reached up into her sink and got a wet cloth and dabbed at the hurting parts of my face. Then she put her hand on my arm and looked me up and down, testing my skin here and there just like the mountain had. "Well now, Ingram," she said, "how did you get yourself so lost and beaten up?" I wanted to answer her but I kept looking back at the stove behind her. "Your face looks like country, but those clothes look town to me. You from somewhere here in Houston? I know you don't live in Black Town."

"These clothes are not mine," I said.

She looked at the bloody shirt-piece around my foot and said, "Why don't you have shoes on?" There was some sort of sausages on that stove that were popping with hot grease and sending a smell to my nose that made me want to die rather than want something this bad. Miss Maw followed my eyes to the food. "Sounds like you've done some hard living, Ingram. Let's get you fed and you can tell me about it later."

Miss Maw led me to a separate room that had a long table with many chairs along each side of it and one chair on the end of it, in which she told me to sit, and she left me alone, returning to the kitchen. It felt good to sit in that chair. It was made of smooth wood that felt warm and held my bottom well. At first, I sat in that room all alone and quiet except for Miss Maw's voice crying from the kitchen, "What a friend we have in Jeeeesus!" Then I heard the screen door open with a *creak* sound and close with a *wap!*, then I heard it again, *creak, wap! Creak, wap!* as many voices, all sounding like girls, filled up the house, especially the kitchen, as Miss Maw called out many names. But the room with the table where

I sat stayed empty except for me and the smells of food coming from the kitchen, which were driving me so crazy I had to hug my arms around my belly and moan.

Then Sinema walked in, holding a big bowl, which was yellow like her dress, with steam rising up from a pile of what looked like mashed potatoes. She looked at me only for a second as she laid the bowl in the center of the table and then left the room. Then another girl, a little smaller than Sinema but looking like her and Miss Maw, walked in carrying a tray of fried chicken pieces, followed by more girls and more food. And suddenly the whole room was buzzing with talk as food was laid out and empty dishes placed in front of each chair with forks and knives and a dish put in front of me by a tall girl—taller than any girl I had ever seen, taller than my mother and maybe even my father. She had thin arms and legs and wore a thin red dress with blue birds pictured all over it and her hair was, instead of standing out in a great round bush, weaved into pretty rows along the sides of her head with tails sticking out the back. Her lips were red like cherries and shiny, different from any lips I had ever seen. When she put the plate down in front of me with her slender brown hand and long fingers, she looked at me with her eyes narrowed and suspicious and she said, "Miss Maw tell you to sit there?"

"That's no look-out of yours, Beth Anne," said Miss Maw as she laid a big bowl of green food on the table and then shouted, "Everyone make your plates and sit down now."

All the girls came in at once, all looking in their faces different but a bit the same, taking their plates and filling them up from the food in the bowls and sitting at their places, but not yet eating. Miss Maw took my plate from in front of me and handed it to Sinema, saying, "Sinema, make a plate for this boy." Sinema put some potatoes, greens, and carrots on my dish and then two pieces of fried chicken. She set it in front of me and I stared down at the biggest plate of food I ever had in front of me in my life. I couldn't believe this was to be for me—to eat by myself. Sinema let out a chuckle, and I looked up and saw that she was watching my amazement.

She went back to her own chair and soon we were all sitting with full plates before us. I had never seen so many people at a table together for eating. I had no memory of having sat at a table for eating myself. As far back as my thoughts could go, my mother put food on our kitchen table for my father, and I'd only see him begin to eat when she would take my plate to the back step for me to eat outside. I had no memory of seeing my mother eat at all. But sitting here at this table with this family, I knew I had done such a thing before. Even though I didn't know when.

Miss Maw stood near the door to the kitchen and told everyone to be quiet, and they were. "Beth Anne, lead us in prayer," she said. Everyone bowed their heads and closed their eyes.

I looked at Sinema who made a motion with her hand that I knew meant for me to bow my head, and I did, unable to close my eyes for looking at the food right under my nose, as I heard Beth Anne's voice say, "Lord, we thank you for the blessing of this food, for the roof above our heads and for another day of living. I pray to you, Lord, to look after Miss Maw and all my sisters here and—"

"And this boy, Ingram," interrupted Miss Maw, "who come to us for love and shelter."

"In Jesus's name we thank you, Lord. Amen," finished Beth Anne, and every hand grabbed a fork and every mouth started eating and talking as Miss Maw, who didn't make herself a plate, went back to the kitchen.

I took the fork next to my plate and buried it in the pile of hot yellow mash, and when I raised it, it came up covered with some stuff that was steaming and looked like potatoes but not quite and I didn't care. I put it into my mouth, closing my lips down over the fork, tasting salty, buttery, and I stayed just like that, holding that fork and food in my mouth, closing my eyes and breathing, unable and unwanting to move an inch of my body or to live past this moment in my life.

"Boy, ain't you never had some grits?" said a girl's voice. All the girls laughed, but kept on talking with each other, about what I could not tell you, because my world consisted only of me and that good hot yellow food, which I had yet to even swallow.

"Have some chicken, Ingram," Sinema said in a soft voice that I could hear under all the loud ones from where she sat. I opened my eyes and saw her looking at me and not eating herself. I took the fork out of my mouth, swallowed, and took a piece of chicken—a leg—in my hand and tore off the whole side of it away with my teeth. Now I had chicken flesh in my mouth, which I chewed but once before taking another bite, and another, and another fork-full of yellow mash and some salty sweet greens and more chicken and, as I ate faster and faster, I came to notice that no one was talking. They were all watching me eat.

"Why's he crying?" said the littlest girl. It was only then that I could feel the tears in my eyes and that I heard myself making a sobbing noise as I ate. I became ashamed at their looking and I put my hand, like a guard, over my face. I looked down at the table and tried to keep eating but it had all become too difficult. My mouth was full of food because I wasn't able to swallow for the jumping in my chest, from the crying, from the tears and snot coming out of my nose. I couldn't stop.

A glass of yellow water was put on the table in front of me, and I heard Miss Maw's voice, from directly above my head, say, "It's okay, Ingram. Slow down. Have some lemonade." I looked up at her and she nodded. I picked up the glass, which felt colder than anything I'd ever touched, and took a long drink of *lemonade*, which was something sweet, like drinking an apple, except it puckered my tongue and went down my throat just perfect. The lemonade cleaned out my mouth and sent all the backed-up food gently down my throat and the coolness of it cleared out my crying till my eyes were dry enough to see that all the girls were talking to each other now except Beth Anne, who stared at me with more anger and hate than even the boy who beat me up that afternoon.

Miss Maw went back to the kitchen. I continued to eat, but more carefully and slowly, telling myself inside not to forget a single bite of this food because I could never know when I'd eat again, let alone this much, and food tasting this good and I'd probably had my first and last glass of lemonade.

The girls' talk had slowed down to a quiet, until Beth Anne's angry voice cut through it as she said, "Sitting him at the head of the table. Waiting on him. Just 'cause he's white. In her own home. Dumb little white boy treated like a prince. It's shameful."

"It's not because he's white and you know it," said Sinema. "It's because she misses Martin, and this boy is just what size Martin was when he passed away."

"Shut up!" said the littlest girl. "Martin ain't dead."

"Martin IS dead," Beth Anne said to the little girl. "It's time for you to face it. He died just like we all will. Just like you will."

"I ain't gonna die!" yelled the little girl, who was crying loud and angry.

"Yes, you are, Charlotte," said Beth Anne. "You're going to die, just like Martin. Just like Miss Maw's gonna die and everyone here except maybe the white boy because white people never have to die—they just keep roaming around eating everything in sight and getting richer and whiter and—" As she went on, Miss Maw had walked back in from the kitchen. She came up behind Beth Anne and slapped her hard in the back of the head, stopping her short. Everyone was quiet now except for the little girl, Charlotte, who was crying with her lip quivering and her shoulders shaking.

Miss Maw came up behind Charlotte and put her big hands on the girl's arms and said, "You don't have to be afraid of dying, Charlotte. And do you know why?" Then she looked at me and said, "Are you afraid of dying, Ingram?"

"Yes, sir," I said.

"Yes, ma'am," said Sinema. "When it's a lady, you say ma'am, not sir."

"Yes, ma'am," I said.

"Do you know who Jesus Christ is, Ingram?" asked Miss Maw.

"I knew a chicken named Jesus," I told her.

"You were never taught the Word of God? And about the life of Jesus?"

"No," I said.

"Did you ever have any schooling?"

"No. The bus didn't come near enough our house."

"Did your mother teach you how to read and write?"

"No, ma'am."

"You mean you can't read nothing?" said Beth Anne.

"I can read an exit sign," I told her and everyone laughed, but in a way of friendliness—even Beth Anne was looking at me with something besides hate in her eyes now.

"Okay, let's clean up this table. Everyone get about your chores," ordered Miss Maw. Every chair scraped on the floor as every girl got up and began cleaning off the table. I got up too and began to pick up my plate but the food in my stomach made me suddenly tired and my eyes got foggy and I started to sway.

"Sinema," said Miss Maw, "take Ingram up to Martin's bed and make him lay down." I felt Sinema take my plate and put it down and she took my hand tightly in hers again and I guess I sort of floated, by the power of her palm, through the house and up some stairs, into a small room and onto a bed onto which I laid down and went directly to a deep and dreamless sleep.

I WAS WOKEN UP, IN the dark, by two sensations. A tickling on my cut-up foot and the warm rumbling sound of a man's voice, which shook the floor under Martin's bed where I laid. I could hear him talk, then Miss Maw's voice, then him again as the bottom of my foot was being stroked by something warm and wet. I opened my eyes and looked down and saw Sinema. She had a basin of warm, soapy water. She had taken the shirt-piece off my foot without waking me and she was wiping dried blood off of my sole with firm but easy strokes of a piece of white, wet cloth. Sinema looked up and saw me looking at her but she didn't say anything—just went back to washing my foot, except now that I was awake, she went about the work less careful, not needing anymore to let me sleep. She held my foot in the same firm way she'd held my hand, and she wiped harder, which stung and made me coil my leg back. But she gripped my foot firmly and said, "Don't move. I gotta clean this out good. It's starting to infect."

I kept my foot still as Sinema began to scrape hard at the place where it hurt, but the pain she was putting on my foot was anything but unpleasant because the pain came from her wanting to fix it. She was looking down at the hurt spot of my foot like it was the most important place in the world.

"When you got a hole in you," she said, "all kinds of bad stuff leaps to get inside."

I thought of saying something in return, but the man's voice downstairs rose up sharply in something that sounded like anger. Miss Maw's voice came up, just above his, in her strong calmness, to push the man's voice down gently. I looked down at the floor and Sinema said, "Pa has come home. He was working on the oil fields and Miss Maw didn't expect him for another week. But he's home now and knows you're up here." Sinema's voice was right in the middle of her family. It was calm and knowing-sounding, but also like a playing child.

"Who's Pa?" I said.

"My father." She smiled at my ignorance. "I gotta get you cleaned up so we can go down for supper."

"But we already had supper."

"No, that was lunch. Supper is at night."

"I only ever had supper where I lived."

"Gosh, you grew up some kind of poor," she said, as she wrapped a clean piece of dry cloth around my foot. "How did you not starve to death?" There was a way she talked about terrible things that made them sound like they weren't so bad. Almost like they were even funny.

"I thought I was going to before I ate here today," I said. Talking about that food made me feel my stomach, which I put my hand on and said, "Feels good that I ate. You really eat three times a day?"

"Every day," she said. "That's what a person is supposed to do, Ingram."

"What you mean supposed to?" I asked.

Sinema laughed in a way that the gums around her teeth were suddenly bare and her eyes were almost closed. She only let out one bark of "Ha!" before she shut this laugh up by covering her mouth with her hand. But her eyes were still laughing and she was shaking up and down. The sight of her in this way got my belly to shake, and I could feel the sides of my face pulling way up to my ears and the world got narrow as I knew my eyes were closing like hers. I started to hear the laughing sound coming out of me, "huh, huh, huh," which made Sinema shake even harder. She pressed her hand harder against her mouth and she took her other hand and pressed it on my mouth to quiet my laugh. I was feeling more pleased than ever before in my life as Sinema and I laughed into her hands together on her dead brother's bed. I never wanted it to end but soon the door opened, letting the light in from the hall and I could see the dark outline of Beth Anne's tall body and hair-tails as she said, "They said bring him down to supper."

Sinema led me down to the eating room. This time she was not holding my hand. The sisters were placing the food on the table, but no one was talking. There was only the sounds of dishes and forks touching the wood of the table, feet shuffling, and the quiet voice of Maw in the kitchen sending each girl out to her task. At the end of the table, in the chair where I had been put by Maw, sat a man with a square head and a body that looked covered in muscles. He was wearing an undershirt and black pants. His chest looked like two truck tires were stuffed underneath and pushing his skin out tight. His arms were covered in knotty muscles like black, shiny socks stuffed with crab apples. His mouth was a wide, straight, serious line. His hard-looking jaw was square on the bottom like an iron kettle. The most curious thing about this man, who must've been Pa, was that his face was speckled with brown, black, and red spots, like someone had taken paintbrushes loaded with different colors and flicked them in front of his head. His hair was so short as to almost not be there at all—like a man who hadn't shaved in a day or so, except on the top instead of his chin. His hands were on the table in fists the size of cantaloupes, like my father grew for one summer and never grew again. One of Pa's big hands was clutching a small cup full of a weak-looking coffee with a string coming out of it, which he lifted to his great mouth holding the cup handle only with the tip of a finger and his thick thumb. He took loud careful sips from it as he stared at me standing there in the doorway of the eating room where Sinema had left me as she joined her sisters in setting the table.

The way this man looked at me made me feel afraid. Not that he would hit me, but that he would do something much worse that I couldn't imagine.

"Ingram," said Miss Maw, who was at the door to the kitchen, "come have your supper in here." And she went back to the kitchen.

"Yes, ma'am," I said. In the course of following Miss Maw to the kitchen, I had to walk straight past Pa, who watched me, never looking away from my eyes.

When I reached his chair, something told me to stand and face him. He said, "Yes, ma'am, you say, huh?" and the one side of his mouth curled up in a smile that didn't look friendly. He looked away from me to take another loud sip from his cup and I went into the kitchen.

I sat at a little table near the stove as the girls continued to bring out supper. Sinema walked past me a few times but didn't look at me. The little girl, Charlotte, who had cried at the table, came over and stood real close, looking at my face before saying, "They gonna send you away, out of here, cuz you're white."

"Shut up, Charlotte," Beth Anne whispered and took her away by the arm. Miss Maw put a plate of food and a fork and a glass of lemonade in front of me. "We don't drink lemonade at supper, but I saw how much you liked it," she whispered.

"Thank you, ma'am," I said, looking up at her. She put a finger to her lips and smiled, putting a second plate on my table with butter and a knife. She then took off her apron and went to the eating room for supper. I was alone.

I looked down at my plate, which was crowded with food. There was some kind of stew with chunks of cooked flesh, most likely pork, and vegetables cooked so soft you could just touch them with a fork and they'd fall in half. The stew was poured over a bunch of rice, which I had only had but once in my life and had forgotten till I found that rice in front of me. It brought me back to some day when I sat at the table in our house with a bowl heaped with white rice, which the smell of made me delighted along with looking at this white food—and I remembered saying, "Wowie!" and looking up at my mother who was smiling. And there was someone laughing, which was coming back to remembrance by Sinema's laugh, the same way this rice was bringing back my first remembered rice. Both the laughing and the rice were things I had forgotten.

Next to the stew and rice was a square chunk of hot yellow bread that smelled sweet and had pieces of corn mixed in it. I looked at the plate with butter on it that sat next to my plate of food, and thought it would be mighty good to have some on this hot bread, but I wasn't sure it was allowed for me to take butter for myself. My mother would sometimes put butter on bread for me, but she was awful careful with it and never kept the butter or any food where I could take it for myself. One time, when I was smaller and more adventurous and less understanding of the danger of my father, I climbed up on a chair that my mother left near the cupboard. I found a box of crackers on a shelf, which I sat in that chair and ate. My mother came in and saw me eating the last cracker and she put her hands on her face and yelled my name in fear like she'd found me dead. My father came in behind her, wearing an undershirt just like Pa was wearing now, and slapped my face. I covered my face with my hands and cried. My father pulled one of my hands so far to the side that I felt my shoulder rip in two, like my arm was being tore off. He hit me with the back of his hand on the exposed side of my face over and over again, holding my arm out like a chicken neck ready to be cut as he hit and hit my face again and again till he saw blood on his hand when he drew it back, and then he stopped and went back to the other room, never having said a word or changed his expression. At some point during the beating, which blinded me in one eye for a while, my mother left the room. It was the first beating I could remember and it quickly taught me not to defend myself when my father hit me.

I decided to leave that butter alone.

I began eating the stew, which had flavor that sort of stung my mouth in a way that I didn't like at first but then wanted to keep feeling again with every bite. The rice under the stew was so white and pure at the edges that, as I ate, I tried to keep the stew sauce away from it, because it was so pleasant to put something so simple and warm and white into my mouth. This was a new experience for me, eating a second full meal in one day. Whereas most meals in my life had left me feeling tired as a result of the sudden change from all-day great hunger to an all-at-once full belly. Having sat down to this meal, in Miss Maw's kitchen, already feeling satisfied from the meal before, the food was making me feel something new. The word I would give it was *strong*. Not just full instead of empty but *strong*. I felt my face filling with blood and my chest vibrating with ability. As my fork brought the food from the plate to my mouth, I imagined my arms could someday be stuffed with hard muscle like Pa's. Even though my father was big enough to tear me apart, he never had muscles like Pa.

As I ate, the only sounds coming from the eating room was forks clicking on plates, swallowing of food, clearing of throats, sipping of drinks, and putting down of glasses. Then I heard chairs pushing back and the sisters began bringing dirty dishes into the kitchen, past me and to the other side of the big iron stove, to a deep and long water-sink with a spigot right above it, which was turned on for washing. All the sisters took turns bringing in dishes, washing them, and drying them—none of them looking at me as I cleaned off every morsel of food on my plate.

"Ingram, come in here," said Miss Maw from the door to the eating room. I followed her in there and found Pa sitting with his elbows on the table and his hands together in a twine of fingers in front of his mouth. Miss Maw was sitting in the chair to his side. I came over and stood before them, not feeling welcome to sit down.

"Where are your people, boy?" said Pa.

"My father went off. I don't know where," I told him. "My mother told me to go on my own."

"And you got nothing else?"

"No, sir," I said.

He sat and looked at me for a long minute and then turned to Miss Maw and said, "Well, he can't stay here. Not one single night."

"We can't turn him out into the dark on his own," said Miss Maw.

"It's got nothing to do with can or can't," Pa said, his voice going down deeper and tougher. "It's only got to do with *got to*. This boy don't belong here. He'll bring us nothing but trouble. He's *got to* go."

"Where will he go?"

"That's not mine to answer. It's his. And his people's."

"He's got no people, Richard."

"He's got white people. He's their problem."

"It's not Christian to turn an innocent lamb into the cold on his own."

"Ain't none of them innocent," Pa said.

"I will not send this boy from this house," said Miss Maw, getting bigger in her chair.

I rocked my weight back onto my heels getting ready to step back, knowing that any second Pa was certain to get up and begin beating Miss Maw for talking back more than once and defying his will, and then I was sure he'd turn on me, since he was in a beating way and I was in the room. I wondered what kind of destruction a man so strong could do even to a woman so big and solid as Miss Maw.

"What's the matter with you, boy?" Pa said. I hadn't noticed that he'd been looking at me.

"He's shaking like a leaf on a twig," said Miss Maw.

Pa put his big, big hand on my shoulder, leaned in and looked into my eyes. "Well," he said softly, "this boy has seen some bitter days." Then he got up from the table and walked out of the room, saying to himself, "Where is the world coming to when white folks are turning out their own?"

Miss Maw came around to me and took my wrist in her hand. "Come on upstairs. You'll spend the night in Martin's room. Tomorrow you probably have to go, but not without a night's rest and a breakfast." And she took me up the stairs, in his room, and opened the bed covers, which I slipped into and laid my head, which, I discovered as it touched the pillow, was covered in sweat.

"Shh," said Miss Maw to my forehead and then she kissed onto my forehead the only kiss I have any memory of in my days of being small and new. Miss Maw then turned out the lights and closed the door. As I fell to sleep, I heard Charlotte's voice whisper into the crack of the door, "Goodnight, In-gram."

THE NEXT MORNING, A QUIET hissing wind was blowing through the leaves of a tree outside, fanning the sunlight into twirling ripples and twitches through the window of Martin's room and playing in shapes of shadow and light on my face, which woke me up. I sat up in the bed and looked around the room, which had wood walls painted simple white and the little bed I laid in, which was just the size to contain my body. I felt I'd slept just as much as I needed. My belly felt good. Even my cut foot had stopped the stinging ache of the day before and there was nothing left of the pain in my head that began with the hot hell of fever in the days before that. There was stomping and shuffling of feet going up and down the stairs and voices talking quick, and I heard the porch screen door going *creak, wap! creak, wap!* and the voices of the sisters, being outside, got to be louder and gayer. I laid there listening to them and thinking, *They are a family*—a family was a whole gang of people, living together. My mother and father and I were not so much a family in this way. I didn't even see the two of them the way Miss Maw and Pa were two people together.

My door opened and Sinema walked in wearing a dress like I'd never seen. It was bright, light blue with a yellow squiggling pattern, like a broken robin's egg with the yolk running over the shell. She saw how I looked at her and smiled. "I'm dressed for church."

I didn't know what she meant and she laughed. "It's Sunday, Ingram." Behind her through the door I could hear Miss Maw's bird voice again crying. "In the morning, in the evening, I got Jesus on my mind!"

"Miss Maw is crying again," I said.

"That's not crying, Ingram. She's singing."

"Singing?"

"She's singing a song. Don't you know what a song is? Do you know what music is?"

"I guess I know now," I said.

"You are a strange boy, Ingram," Sinema said, and started to leave the room. "Come on downstairs."

I followed Sinema downstairs and to the kitchen—all of the sisters running back and forth, swishing past me in their dresses, all just as bright as Sinema's. Some red, some blue, and little Charlotte in pure white lace. Miss Maw, dressed in a dress that was dark blue but shone in a way almost like gun-metal, took my hand and led me to the porch. All the sisters were out there now and Miss Maw led me past them to the end of their yard, where Pa waited, wearing dungaree overalls and a cap. Maw brought me to him, turned me by my shoulders to face her, and knelt down. She handed me a brown paper bag and a pair of shoes. "This is your breakfast, and lunch for later. Eat it slow," she said about the bag. "And these should be right your size," she said about the shoes.

"Those shoes are for Charlotte when she gets to size," said Pa.

"This boy needs them now," said Miss Maw, not looking away from my face.

"Those were Martin's," said Pa, sounding like there was too much spit in his throat. Miss Maw looked up at him, with sweetness in her voice. "Martin would want these shoes for Ingram. He was a good Christian boy."

"A lot of good that did him," said Pa, looking away.

"It didn't do him any harm," said Ma. "He may be gone, but at least he's not alone." Then she looked at me. "Remember, Ingram. No matter how lonesome you feel, Jesus is always with you."

"Where is he?" I asked about Jesus.

Miss Maw put her fingers on my chest and said, "He's right here in your heart."

"I don't feel him there, Miss Maw," I said. "How can a whole man be stuffed up in my heart and I don't even feel it?"

Pa laughed low and said, "He's not as dumb as he looks," then took a few steps away and said, "Come on, son. Let these women go to their church. Put on the shoes. I'll walk you out of Black Town."

Miss Maw handed me the shoes and the bag. Her eyes had tears resting inside them but not tumbling out onto her cheeks. I looked at Miss Maw's face knowing she had cared for me and that, like everyone I had known, I would not see her again. I looked at her eyes, her brow, her nose and mouth, and I felt that she was beautiful.

"Miss Maw, let's go!" yelled Beth Anne. Without more talk or looking, Miss Maw stood up, joining the girls as they walked one way. I put on Martin's shoes, which fit my feet just right, and I followed Pa to the other.

Pa and I walked down many *streets*, what I had been calling roads, past houses and buildings and shops, till we got to where the street was dirt instead of that poured and hardened white that I came to know as *pavement*. The dirt roads led to a rusting rail track. I had seen that before, the one time I had wandered the very farthest into the fields behind my house and found the source of the distant rumbling I'd hear as I slept in the shed. A great big lurching metal train on metal wheels on two metal tracks. Here at the edge of this place that was called Black Town, a train track stopped at the dirt road, which started up again on the other side, and I could see that soon after the dirt was more paved roads beyond. Pa pointed in that direction.

"That's your world, son," he said. "You must be careful. You're only a child. You're weak and you're stupid. Like every child on earth." He reached in his pocket and took out a folding knife with a handle like a carved piece of bone. Then Pa took my wrist and held it up, my palm open, and put the knife into my hand. "I would have given this to my son, Martin, if he made it," he said. "Looks like the book is closing on my having another son. Nothing but girls and girls. You take that and keep it where no one can ever take it from you. And don't use it unless your back is against a wall," he said. I put the knife deep in my pants pocket, my hand still squeezed around it.

"You're gonna need to dodge the bullets and rocks of life while you're still small, weak, and stupid. You can't rush getting big, but you can hurry up and get smart. Just learn what you can, don't expect no help from no one, not in this day and age. Feed and defend yourself until the day comes when you're fully grown up. And then you'll be a man. A white man at that. And the world will be yours." And he looked at me in a way like he was thinking of something funny but also I felt like, in that moment, Pa had some liking for me. "You'll do fine."

"But I'm alone, Pa," I said, and watched his face quickly frown down.

"Being a boy *is* alone," he said. "Being a man even more so. In any case, it's yours to be and to bear." And he tilted his head up, showing me the bottom of his chin where I couldn't see his eyes.

"Yes, sir," I said. Pa didn't say anything more, so I turned and walked across the tracks, away from him and away from Black Town.

Part Two

Chapter Nine

The Farm

Martin's shoes made me feel like I could stomp down hard on the road and that I didn't need to keep my eye on every inch looking for sharpness or peril to my toes. The further I got from the city—I was now on the other side of the city from where I entered it—the cars trickled from a storming rush of metal up and down the two sides of the mighty four-deep highway, to a simple, straight road with a yellow line in the middle. Only now and again a single car—its tires singing as it whooshed by, taking one or just a few people from one place to another—passed my walking legs, which could go further now than before without much pain or tiredness. Between the cars were the sounds again of insects, birds, and wind. There were few trees and little shade. The sun was hot.

After walking for I don't know how long, I turned around and looked behind me. The sun was touching down where Houston had been. I wondered, as I often had back home when I had nothing to do but wonder, what it looked like up close to see where the sun sank every night. I imagined and supposed that there must be a hole in the ground, waiting for the sun as it trips across the sky, and another hole that it comes from, on the other side of things, when it rises. When the sun pops out of its morning hole, I figured, its light is cool and weak, as it's only just waking up. Something in the power of the light as it gets more, pushes the sun up and up and it gets brighter and brighter till at noon it hangs in the middle of the sky, burning the world beneath my feet in daisy-yellow heat. Then, when it gets tired, the sun begins to fall down the other way, like a tired old orange, and finally burns itself out into a round, dying red ember that gently drops into its nighttime hole, beneath the ground.

My father's brother, Bert, used to tell him, "It don't matter what I do in this world. In the end I'm gonna burn, down below, in eternal hellfire." I thought that this place he described, *down below*, must be where the sun cooks at night, crawling beneath our feet, in this "hellfire" before it pops out of its morning hole, on the morning-side, all cooked up and ready for a new day. I guess Bert was looking forward to going there when his life was finished and he had cooled down to a dead ember like the setting sun.

I once heard my mother and father talking about dead folks and saying how they'd been *buried* or were *in the ground*. Since all folks who die are put down into the ground—where the sun gets its daily needed heat—that the dead might get cooked into life again, down in that *hellfire*, and that's why, even though folks like Sinema's brother, Martin, and the boy in the hospital bed, keep dying, there's still more people. But that wondering question was soon answered from a gray place inside of me—gray like the skin of that red-eyed creature who slept beside me in my dreams—with a down-inside kind of knowing that when I die I'll be just done, dead, and gone, and that there's nothing below the ground but cold rocks and dirt, and that all that falls stays fallen and that the sun is some far-off mystery, and none of my knowledge or business.

However it was coming to pass, the sun was sinking out of sight, and nighttime darkness began to spread across the sky and smear across the fields around me. I looked for a place to sleep. The farm fields along the side of the road had started to break up with here or there a tree. I walked a few paces off the pavement and found a tree with a thick trunk and figured I could sleep on the far side of it, and it would hide me from passing cars in the night. Then a strong, warm wind started that pushed me on my back with each gust, but the tree was unmoved by it, so I figured the ground at its feet would be as good a bed as any. I laid down, using my shoes as a pillow, and laid my hurt foot, which felt better and better, on top of my good one. I put my hand in my pocket and squeezed my fingers around the knife Pa had given me, hoping I could squeeze it in my sleep. As I drifted off, I made a voice that sounded like Charlotte's and said to myself, "Goodnight In-gram." And drifted into my quiet mind.

My eyes snapped open with a pinching pain on the skin that covers my teeth, right beneath my nose and right above my mouth, where a mustache grows on a man. The tree trunk shot straight up to the boughs and twigs above me, waving to and fro in the early morning wind, the leaves flickering against the dark purple sky. An acorn was cut loose by the wind. It fell, landing beside my head with a hard peck. It must have been one of the same that had hit me on my lip in such a small way but with so much force that it had woken me up.

My back hurt from some rocks and roots I was sleeping on, so I turned on my side and was met with the sudden and startling sight of a man sleeping on his back, his head leaning on a rolled-up woolen cloth. His arms were folded across his chest, which I thought must be tough to do when the body is in the relaxation of sleep. Tucked into the sleeping man's armpits against his shirt was what looked like two shoe soles with leather straps. His skin was a deep red color, like dried blood. His tough brown hair was long to the neck and stuck straight out on top with no curl to it. He had a thick mustache like a brush bristle, but no beard.

I heard a cough from the other side of me. There was another sleeping man laying on my other side and another one beyond him. In fact, the tree was ringed all around by sleeping men, their heads by the trunk and their feet facing out in a circle like petals around the center of a wildflower. Some of the men looked like the first one did, red with spiking dark hair. Two others were black, one with face-wrinkles and white hair, like a cloud, thin and wispy, through which was showing the shiny skin of his black head. Next to him was a black boy, about the age of Jerald who'd taken me to Miss Maw's, but with bigger muscles on his arms.

I sat up. The sky was right in the middle of change from night black on one end to dark blue like denim pants above the tree, and then pale white off the way I'd been walking toward. A faraway sound of a car engine began making its way toward us from the dawn, waking all the men around me, who began opening and rubbing their eyes, as they sat up and scratched themselves. The man beside me pulled on his strapped shoes. I looked down the road and saw a pickup truck slowly appearing from the morning mist. The truck passed our tree, then slowed down, turned full around, and parked on the side of the road. The men were all standing now and gathering their bundles. Feeling like a part of them, I put on my shoes and stood up too.

The man driving the truck opened his door and stood with his head looking over the roof and yelled, "Who's working? Come on!"

The men walked to the truck and they all climbed up and sat in the open back. I stood there watching them. The driver pointed at me and said, "You working or not?"

The man who'd slept next to me called out to me a word I'd never heard—"Muchacho!" And then he said a bunch of words that made no sense to me. The black man with the white hair said, "They gonna drive on, son. Come on now if you're coming." They were all looking at me. The driver quit caring what I did and got in, closing his door and revving his engine. I had a split-quick conversation in my mind where I asked what I should do and the answer came from some part of me saying get in that truck. *There's nothing for you if you stand here alone.* The truck began to move. I ran to the back of it and reached up to grab the tailgate but I could only just touch it as the truck drove off, quicker than I could run. Four arms of four different men reached down and grabbed my arms tight, pulling me up like I was flying, and dropped me on the floor, in the center of the truck bed, where I sat myself in a ball in the middle of all their feet.

My whole body rumbled and shook from the floor of the truck and a constant wind slapped me on the side of my head. I looked behind us. The black road was being spit out the back of the truck, the white line down the middle shooting out quick, *zoom, zoom, zoom*. I looked forward, through the window, at the back of the driver's head, his wrinkled neck, and stiff yellow hat, and I wondered how he got this truck and why he knew how to make it drive. I felt hungry but for a truck of my own so I could move along the road with this box of metal all around me.

The truck pulled off of the road onto no road at all—just driving across a field of low grass, rocks, and mud, the truck bucking up and down, making squeaking sounds and revving and roaring in an uneven way. Every time the truck lurched up, it came down hard and my bottom slammed against the metal bed. A shock of pain went clear up my spine to the top of my head. I felt a hand on my chest as the black man with white hair reached forward to push me back onto his feet. His lower legs and his feet tops became a chair for me. I looked up to thank him, but he was just looking straight outward, his head bobbing around real easy with the lurching of the truck.

The truck stopped in front of a group of low buildings arranged in rows at the top of a gentle swell of grassy land that looked out onto far-stretching fields of corn. The man in the truck got out and talked to another fellow in a stiff brown hat till the man in the brown hat raised his voice.

"Line up, you men, over at the work shack. Let's get started before the damn day's gone," said the man in the brown hat. I followed the other men to a low building where each man went into the darkness of the little door and then came back into the sunshine with a little piece of paper in his hand, followed by the next man who'd take off his hat as he went in.

When the black man with white hair came out he pointed into the door and said, "Go on and get your paper, son." So I went inside to find a fat man stuffed behind a desk like it was growing out of him. He wore a red shirt that was soaked to a dark color to the middle of his chest by sweat that was running like rivers down his face and neck into the collar.

"You worked here before, boy?" he said, as he looked down at something he was writing.

"No, sir," I said.

"You be staying in cabin six. You get fourteen cents a bushel, minus your meals. Smokes and bed is eight cents, you get paid at the end of the week, and if you make trouble you're out. Understand?" I didn't much understand a word of it and I guess my silence called his eyes up to my face, and when he saw me he said, "How old are you, boy?"

I didn't understand the question, as it was the first time anyone had asked me that. So I said, "I don't know."

"You don't know your age?"

"Don't know what that means, sir."

"How long you been alive?"

"I don't know that, sir."

"He don't look nearly ten years old," said the other man.

"Where your folks?"

"Gone, sir."

The man wrote on a little book of paper and said, "You're thirteen. We don't hire under that so you're thirteen years old. Got it?"

"Yes, sir," I said.

The man tore off the piece of paper he'd written on, like the ones the other men got, and handed it to me and said, "You know how to read?"

"I can read an exit sign," I said.

"Never mind that. You're in cabin six. Look here." He pointed at a shape on the paper and said, "That's six. You look for a cabin that got that on it and that's where you stay. Go there now and put your stuff and wait for work to start."

I left the little building and walked amongst the little cabins till I found one with that shape and I went inside. The cabin was one little square room with a small window opposite the door. There was a little bed against each wall except the door side. The beds had thin mattresses that looked dirty and rotten with a thin gray blanket and a thin pillow. A shelf above each bed had a small lamp, a metal cup, and a pack of cigarettes with matches. My father smoked so I knew what that was but I never did it myself. Two men came in behind me—who had slept with me under the tree. Each took one bed as they spoke to each other in the words I didn't understand, putting their stuff on their shelf.

One of them said, "Muchacho," to me, and he continued, "Take your bed." He pointed at the empty bed, which was by the window. I sat on the bed and watched the men open their packs and settle in.

"Oye, muchacho," he called to me again. "Where is your mother?" Something in him asking made me look inside my memory to conjure up my mother's face. The funny thing was I couldn't see it. I couldn't find my mother's face inside my mind. I sat on my bed, looking at my feet. But the shoes I was wearing belonged to a dead boy and given to me by *his* mother. The clothes my mother had given me were long gone. I shut my eyes and tried to make the memory of her face. I just saw a blank. It wasn't a blank like just nothing there. It was a blank like not being able to find a good spot for sleeping.

I was wakened from my thoughts by the smell of smoke. The men had lit their cigarettes.

"Give me your smokes, muchacho," said the man. I didn't want the cigarettes, but I didn't want to give away something that was mine. He spoke to the other man in the strange words, and then said, "Muchacho. I give you one penny for your smokes." He reached in his pocket and took out a brown coin. I gave the man my cigarettes but I kept the matches. He handed me that coin. I had never had money in my hand. I looked at it carefully. There was a faded picture of a fellow on one side and some sort of flower on the other, and some writing. The men watched me look at the penny and they laughed.

Soon after, someone outside started hollering, "Get to work!" as they walked amongst the cabins. We all came out to find two big tractors, each hooked in the back to a long wooden platform on wheels. All the men from the cabins climbed onto the wooden platforms. Somebody whistled a long low whistle that ended with a high screech. Smoke commenced to belching out of the pipes of the tractors and wafted all over us in back as we were pulled along through corn plants as tall as small trees. The tractors in front were pushing the corn down, making a rough road that we were dragged along with bumps that sent us up and crashing down. Many times I almost fell off the platform as there was nothing to hang onto and I knew if I fell it wouldn't matter to anyone.

It was like a whole day in itself that we pushed through the high corn until we reached a clearing and the tractors stopped. We all got down and stood in a line and a fat man with a hat stood in front of us and said, "Tear up all the corn you can and throw it on the flatbeds. Work your way back to camp before dark." And he got into the truck that brought us from the tree and drove back into the road we'd made through the corn. The tractors turned around and started moving back toward camp real slow. I watched as the men grabbed corn plants, clutching them down low and pulling them up, twisting this way and that till they'd crack and tear, and then they yanked the cornstalk up free and threw it on the platform of the flatbed.

There was a man with a hat at the back of each tractor watching the men as they worked, writing on a little paper. I reached for a cornstalk and started pulling at it. I may as well have been trying to pull a house up it was so strong and heavy. I tried twisting it as they had but it wouldn't budge. Some of the men looked back at me and laughed as I was no closer to making this plant do anything but keep living and growing. I watched the black boy who was closest to my size. He kicked the lower part of the stalk with his foot again and again, until it started to crack and then he pushed it hard with his whole body till it lay flat. Then he spun it around by running in a circle and holding it till it came loose. I came to another plant and tried kicking it, but my leg was too weak to crack it. So I leaned my backside against the plant and pushed backward with my whole body's strength until I heard a slight crack. I turned frontward and pushed against the cracking plant until it fell over, then I grabbed onto the top of it and ran in a circle, twisting it till it came loose. I looked around in the quiet after my struggle to find myself alone, the tractors a ways away now. I didn't know how I could do what I just done even one more time, let alone all day long. But I didn't know any better idea than to keep on trying, rather than to go back to trying to live each day on my own on the road. I grabbed that corn plant I'd killed and I ran till I caught up to the tractors and threw it in the flatbed.

"Oye, muchacho!" said the man from my cabin, and then he said something else in his strange chatter that made some men laugh. Thinking how long it had taken me, and how far I'd had to run to catch up, this time I ran a bit ahead of the tractor and started in on a corn plant up ahead, leaning back on it, cracking it, pushing it down frontwards, spinning it round, cutting it loose, and this time I didn't have so far to catch up because I'd run up ahead. I did this again and again, taking just a little quicker each time.

The spot on my backside that I was leaning with was getting sore so I shifted to my other side. My hands were getting red and raw. There was nothing I could do about that, having only two hands and only one way to grab with them. My arms ached. My throat was dry. My head hurt. But the tractor kept on moving and the men kept on pulling, all of them covered in sweat like glass. Again and again I leaned, pushed, twisted, cut and threw corn onto the flatbed, ran ahead, pushed, twisted, cut and threw, ran ahead again. The palms of my hands got bigger and the skin got loose. My hard breathing was scratching the inside of my dry throat.

The bright sky above me was getting suddenly dark. A storm must be approaching. The sky got darker still. But above my head was the naked sun. Then why was all around me turning gray? Then that gray in the air started turning toward black and I realized all that darkness was inside my head. I grabbed onto a cornstalk but I couldn't feel my hands against it. I felt my knees start to give and knew I was about to fall and lose myself again. I grabbed onto the plant harder and a new kind of feeling came upon me, which was that I was mad at myself. I was sick and tired of myself for losing strength and going to sleep right when things got tough. "Hang on, Ingram," I said to myself, and in that moment, the tractor engines shut off and the man standing in the back of ours yelled, "Lunch!"

And somehow all the darkness in the sky flitted away like scattering birds in a gust of wind. The pain in my hands came back to me, the pain in my head, the scratch in my throat. I finished cracking off the plant I was holding, brought it to the flatbed, and threw it in. The men were taking spots to sit, some of them on the flatbed, some in the shade made by the tall tires of the tractors, and they were undoing rag-bundles they'd brought with bits of food. I just watched them eat. A man came around with a tin pail with a spout on the end filled with water. He gave each man a tin cup, tipped the pail into it, and filled it. I got my cup of water between my hands, which were wet from a thin kind of blood that was running out of the skin on my palms which had broke. There was a pink kind of skin showing underneath, like the skin of a brand-new piglet. I didn't care about this or any of my body pain, though, because I had a cup of water in my hands and I drank it like I was a dead man drinking life itself.

"Boy you didn't bring no lunch?" said the black man with the white hair. "You need to bring your lunch."

"No sir," I said. "I can go days without food. But without water, you're dead." The men around us laughed at me and spoke to each other in their strange words. I looked up at the black man and asked, "Why do they talk like that, making no sense?"

"Huh?" he said.

"They sound like they're talking but those aren't words," I said.

He laughed. "They're talking Spanish, son. They're Mexican."

"They're what?"

"They're from Mexico."

I didn't know what he meant. I drank my water until they called us back to work.

Pulling up the corn plants was harder after lunch. The men had more energy from eating their lunch, but me having had none, I felt more than tired. The sun was blasting down onto my head and the back of my neck, which I could feel was turning as pink as my stinging palms, but somehow I put my mind in a place of not thinking or worrying, and I just kept going and kept doing and kept working.

Not too long before dark, the work camp appeared out of the corn, the cabins looking like black boxes with the sun about to drop away behind them. The man on the flatbed, which was now piled high with a heap of corn plants, called out, "Ho! Quit!"

I followed the men to a building, inside of which we found three long tables with chairs on each side. We were lined up at the far end where we took trays and forks and knives and metal cups for water, and waited till each of us met a man with a big pot of stew. I could smell it from my far end of the line. It was making my belly-dog groan with that kind of hunger that knows that food is coming. Like when my mother would say, "I'm cooking supper, Ingram. So stay close at hand." And I'd sit on the porch steps and breathe the smell in real slow and luxurious. The smelling of food you know you're going to have is part of the eating—it's like the meat is coming in through your nose first—so I wasn't in a hurry to get to the front of the line.

The man standing by the pot, who had a big black beard, handed me a tin bowl of black stew and a chunk of hard black bread. I put it on my tray. Next to him was a pail of water, which I dipped my tin cup into like the man before me. I walked around the three tables, now all around covered by sitting, eating men, till I found the black man with the white hair and sat across from him.

"This your first time working, boy?" he said as he ate his stew slowly. I took two big spoonfuls into my mouth one right after the other. The meat tasted like meat, but the rest tasted like water from a puddle with mud and rocks in it, but I could feel it restore my guts, which had felt like they were dried up and flaking away.

"This is my first time," I answered as I bit a chunk off the bread.

"It's not so bad here," he said. "The supper is free. Except they make you go a full week before paying. And the man counts your bushels without anyone to keep him honest. You're likely not to make more than a few pennies, the way you're going."

"I got one penny now," I said, taking my penny out of my pocket and showing it to him.

"Put that away," he said, angry at my penny. "Don't show folks your money. That's how you get your head shoveled."

I put the penny back in my pocket and my hand felt my knife. I squeezed my stinging palm around it.

"I got my penny for my pack of cigarettes," I told the man. "The fellow in my cabin you said was Mexican? I made the trade with him."

"Boy, a pack of cigarettes is worth a dime."

"A what?"

"A dime. Ten cents." He stopped eating, just looking at me, and then said, "Cut a hole in that bread. Put some of that meat in it and stick it in your pocket. You'll have lunch for tomorrow." I did what he told me. The younger black boy that was traveling with him said nothing and didn't look at me. I went back to my cabin after supper and fell asleep as the two men smoked and talked their Mexican words.

The next day we went out and worked the same way again. My pink palms had dried up and turned hard in the night and they didn't hurt so much as the first day. We picked our way across the acres of corn. Then we ate dinner, I saved some for lunch, and went to bed again. After a few days of the same, I picked up my pace with the corn, able to pick more and more. The more I picked, the less hard it was to get each plant out the ground and onto the truck and then go get the next one. I guessed it was getting easier because I was practiced at it, but the truth was my body was building up and getting stronger even just in those few days. Every day was like the last, waking, picking, eating, sleeping. Till Friday came. "Oye, Ingram," said Pedro, the man who had bought my cigarettes. "Sabes que today is? It's payday!"

When work was over, we all lined up outside the little building we first went in when we got there. The same man was sitting at the desk and the fellow who sat on the flatbed, counting, stood behind him. I handed the man at the desk my piece of paper, which I'd saved like he said to. "How many bushels?" he asked the man behind him.

"Ten bushels, boss," said the man from the flatbed.

"Ten?" said the boss, surprised. "Shoot. I could pick ten bushels in ten minutes."

"A combine could do it in ten seconds," said the flatbed man.

The boss got mad and said, "We ain't got a combine, Francis. Anyway combines eat diesel which is mighty pricey compared to the stew you put into these poor bastards." Then he wrote on my paper and said, "Ten bushels times eight cents gives you eighty cents after your keep and bed. I'll tell you what—I'll make it an even dollar if you stay a second week." They both looked at me, waiting for me to say something. "What you want to do? Stay or move on? It's your choice," said the man named Francis. I had never had a choice in anything that I could remember. I never had been asked what I wanted to do.

"Well?" said the boss.

"I'll stay another week," I said.

"Okay, then. You want your dollar in coins or paper?"

"Coins," I said. And he reached in a tin box and gave me ten small, shiny coins. I looked at those coins sitting in my hand. "These ain't pennies," I said. The men laughed at me.

"If those were pennies you'd have a hundred of them, dummy. Those are dimes."

I remembered what Marshall said. Marshall was the black man with white hair, whose name I knew by then. Marshall had told me that first day that a dime was ten pennies. I didn't know what a hundred was but I knew dimes were more than pennies and that I had ten of those, so I was satisfied.

"Go on and take your dimes to the canteen, son," said Francis. "You know how to work now, best learn how to drink." The men laughed. I put my dimes in my pocket next to my penny and my knife and went back to my cabin.

"Oye, muchacho," said Pedro. "How much you get paid?"

"Ten dimes," I told him.

"Where do you keep it?"

"In my pocket."

"You gotta find a place to hide your money, you know?"

"What for? My pocket is fine."

"Sure. Your pocket is fine." And Pedro smiled. That made me remember what the mountain said: "Watch out for folks who come at you with a smile."

"Hahaha. You such a serious hombre, chiquito. You gotta get some fun outta life. Come on, let's go to the canteen, hah?"

Pedro and I left our little cabin and walked through the camp. All the men walked toward a shack at the end of the camp that had some metal sides and some wood kind of lashed together, and it was leaning over looking ready to fall. Coming from inside the shack, I could hear the singing of the Mexican workers. They sang every day in the fields. Their songs were in Spanish. Marshall had explained to me about languages and different countries. It was one of those things I had to learn piece by piece, having been told nothing at home, like about the Mexicans using a different way of talking with different words and ways of putting them together, and when they sang, they'd repeat the same words over and over, which is how a song generally goes. I even started to learn some of them songs, and along with that, a little bit of what Spanish words mean. Sometimes I would sing along with them inside of my mind.

"La mujer en la calle tiene verguanza de monton! Su esposo tiene tetas y su hijo es maricon!"

Enrique, the other man who lived in our cabin, sang, and he told me that the words in that song meant, "The woman in the street has a lot to be ashamed of. Her husband has teets and her son is a homosexual." Which I didn't fully understand, though I knew they found the song to be funny. Enrique laughed when he told me. I liked Enrique. He was the tallest of the Mexican men. Everything about him was tall and long. His fingers were long and even his toes, which hung over the ends of his open-strap shoes.

He had no beard but he let his mustache grow long and down, past his chin and down his chest like a weeping willow, and his hair was stringy and dry and it hung down his back.

"Oye, chaparrito!" Enrique was standing at a long, high, and thin table covered in small glasses filled with what I knew to be whiskey because I had smelled and seen it when my father and uncle drank it down hard, though they rarely poured it into a glass.

My father would come home with one of his pockets heavy with a bottle, and his brother and him would come into the shed where I slept and sit on two tin chairs my father would bring in from the porch, and they'd crack off the top of the whiskey bottle and start drinking. I would sit on the dirt floor and keep quiet, like any time my father came near me since he'd put me in that shed. They would sit on the tin chairs and drink like I wasn't there. My father would clutch on the bottle and tip it up and I'd see his lips tight around the neck of it and that gas-smelling brown water would go down into him and turn his face all red, and then my uncle would have a turn and there was something dirty about the air around them as they'd breathe it out. Something about that smell made me want something, I didn't know what. I would wait till the whiskey got them talking loud and I'd crawl out the door and end up sleeping in the grass that night.

The men in the canteen lay coins on the high long table, which I soon came to know as the bar, and then grabbed the glasses and threw the whiskey into their mouths, which were pointed up to the ceiling like baby birds. Enrique slapped his hand on the bar and said, "Lay your dime down, chaparrito. Time for you to have a drink!" All the men standing near there cheered. I was confused. They laughed at me. "Que pasa, joven?" said Enrique in this way he had of looking sad and joyful at the same time. "I was small like you when I had my first. Come on and put your dime down. It's ten cents a glass."

"I only got ten dimes," I said.

"So what you gonna do with those? You get your food free. This is what the money is for, chaparrito. Drink it down. Sleep tomorrow. Church on

Sunday. Life don't cost a dime. But whiskey does!" With that, he threw a dime down and it clinked on the bar as he threw his whiskey back so hard and fast I thought he'd drink the glass. Everyone cheered and did the same and they all looked at me with a kind of excitement like they wanted to see something they never saw before. I felt a struggle inside because I liked the feeling of all the men, who were so much bigger than me and stronger than me, all looking at me now and smiling and waiting, like buying a whiskey and drinking it was something I could do for them. Like they needed one more man or else they didn't have enough.

"You can't rush getting big, but you can hurry up and get smart," Pa had said by the train tracks that cut Black Town off from the rest of Houston. And I didn't reckon that drinking a glass of whiskey would make me smarter any quicker, but the waiting smiles on the faces of these men told me that at least it would make me one of them. Anyway, Pa could be wrong. And he had sent me away. It was just me here with a pocketful of dimes. So I fished one out, reached up to the bar, put it down next to a glass of whiskey, picked it up, threw my head up to the ceiling with my mouth wide open. And the whiskey fell straight down, burning the back of my tongue and my throat like the green sludge burning my skin in the river that carried me into Houston and away from my clothes.

Chapter Ten

Jackson

Nights on the farm were all short, like a blink of an eye, and were never enough to rest my body for the working day. Each day of each week had a different purpose, but they were the same when they came around again the next week on each side of a payday.

Mondays were the start of workweek, after the arrival, on Sunday, of new men who, like me and Pedro and Marshall and Enrique, had been found like fallen fruit under the tree on the highway.

Tuesday was the second day when you'd work while feeling all the tired from Monday, when the food would start to feel like not quite enough to run the working body.

Wednesday was the day you got used to it all and the hurting turned to no feeling in your arms and legs, like you could have hacked them off as if they were corn. And I would have just watched you do it and felt no regret except maybe when it was time to eat, which would be a chore with no arms. On Wednesdays, nothing occupied your mind but pulling up corn and putting food in your mouth. No one talked much on Wednesdays. No one sang. The Mexicans I met that first week were gone but new ones always came and they sang some of the same songs and some new ones.

Like "La pinata tiene caca, tiene caca, cacahuates de monton." Which was about some strange animal made from paper who, when he shit, peanuts would come out instead of crap. Something like that. But Wednesday we were silent. No singing, No talking. No thinking, no feeling, no waiting, no remembering.

Then Thursday would come and we would start getting lively and thinking about payday and the end of the week. Some men talked about where they'd be headed next if they were moving on—others just sang songs about whiskey and sunsets.

Friday was a quick day. Wake, work, get paid, go drink whiskey.

That was a week on the farm. How many weeks I was on that farm, I don't know. It was enough to begin forgetting what life was like before I got there, which I didn't mind.

I WAS WORKING FASTER NOW and earning more. The more dimes I earned, the more whiskey I drank. I had hated the way whiskey felt going down that first time. But once I started to feel how good it was to be drunk, that feeling taught my tongue to love the burn it brought coming down from the glass. Every week the new men that came crowded around to see me drinking. They liked seeing a child shooting back whiskey like it was breathing air. And I liked their liking it. But best of all I liked the feeling of that warmth on the skin of my face, in my chest, and with each dime gone and each glass down more and more of me would feel that warm—a warm that made my body not hurt from working and made me forget till I was swimming through air like it was warm water all around me. And the Mexicans sang and I waved my arms up and down like I could fly and sing, "La vida tan bonita quando tengo mi chiquita."

Sometimes singing that song made me think of Anna Lee, because "chiquita" meant "girl." I'd close my eyes and lay back against the wall and start seeing things like they were swimming in the warm water of life all around me. I saw the animals that used to sit around with me in the dirt who had been slaughtered and rotted. I saw my father's face and wondered if I ever got big enough and if I ever drank enough whiskey could I slap him in his face? I still couldn't see my mother, but it started feeling easier not to try to see her either. Then I'd see Anna Lee sitting there by my side, watching the chickens peck, and I'd get a feeling about looking at her and the warm water of life would get to be a flood and I'd get sort of scared of how big the feeling was coming up. So I'd throw down my last dimes and fill up on so much whiskey that I'd forget so much that I'd wake up the next morning in all sorts of places. Sometimes on the floor of the canteen, sometimes outside of my cabin, knowing I must have tried to crawl back but didn't make it. My head always hurt like someone beat me up in my sleep and my pocket was always empty except for my knife.

Saturday was "sleep it off" day, and the men who were leaving packed their bundles and got back in the truck that brought them.

Sundays, a woman named Gloria, who was the wife of the man who paid us, would come in a car with a man called Preacher who gathered us in the eating tent and we sat in chairs facing him as he talked about Jesus. I never could put two words that he said together in my mind enough to understand him because of the way he talked. He wasn't talking Spanish—it was English. But it made no sense except that he would get excited when he'd say "and JESUS" in the middle of it now and again. But boss said we had to listen so I sat there and pointed my head at his with my eyes open but I never heard a word that I could repeat outside of "and JESUS," and I wondered why everybody always talked about Jesus like he was there when he wasn't.

After Preacher left the trucks would come and bring new men. Sometimes a lot, sometimes only a few. Monday we got back to work.

Monday was always the longest day of all, with the sun taking its time and burning hotter and meaner than ever. "How come some days are longer than others?" I asked Jackson, a man who had come a week or two after I arrived.

"Every day is the same length, except in the winter they get shorter, in the summer they get longer," he answered.

"I'm not sure that could be true," I said. "Today is definitely longer than yesterday. By a sight."

Jackson cleaned his spectacles on the end of his shirt. We were working together because while I was smaller than the rest, Jackson was weaker.

"This day only *seems* longer to you," he said.

"Seems?" I didn't know that word.

"'Seems' is the way you perceive something. It's what your own mind contributes to your experience of the outside world."

Jackson wasn't like any of the other working men on the farm. There was something *same* about all of the other men.

Jackson lived in my cabin. He told me he was a writer. The first time he said it, I thought he said "whiter" because he was not only white but red on the cheeks from burning by the sun and he dressed in a wrinkled suit that had maybe been white but for the dirt and yellow stains under the arms from sweat because he even wore it when he worked.

He slept in the bed Pedro had been in. No one had Enrique's bed that week. Jackson would smoke his cigarettes and read books, which were like magazines but smaller and with no pictures. "What happens when you stare at them pages with no pictures on them?" I asked. "There's nothing to look at."

"I'm reading the words," said Jackson.

"What for?"

"To see what was written. Someone writes a book. Like this one. It's a story. They tell a story and I read it, see? Just like you might tell me a story and I listen to it."

"A story?" I asked.

"Holy hell, Ingram." Jackson shook his head. "You don't know a single thing, do you?"

"What is a story?" I asked again.

"Something that happened. Told to a person by another person. You have stories. Everything that's happened to you. You could tell me a story right now."

"How?" I asked.

Jackson put down his book and sat up on his bed facing mine and he said, "Think about something that happened to you. And tell me what it was."

"Why?"

"To tell me a story. So I'll know what happened."

"Why'd I want to do that?" I asked.

Jackson laughed and lit a cigarette. "Telling stories is a way of connecting."

"Connecting?"

"Like meeting another person but inside. Like the way you see each other with your eyes closed."

I thought about that.

"Okay," Jackson said, "I'll tell you a story. Do you want to hear a story?"

This was the second time someone asked me if I wanted something. I looked at Jackson sitting there smoking, his white shirt dark around his neck and chest from sweat. He was waiting for me to answer. He was giving me a *choice*. The first time I had one of those, I had said yes. And I thought if I say yes again, then these aren't really choices.

So I said no. Jackson's eyebrows shot up. He smiled and put out his cigarette and went back to reading. I went to sleep. I liked sleeping when he was still up reading. I wondered, as I felt my sleep coming, what could be in those books? And I wished maybe I'd said yes to hearing his story instead of saying no. But most of all, having Jackson in that room kept me from seeing the gray creature of my future death and I fell asleep more peacefully.

I liked working a lot more when Jackson was there to talk to. He was sort of weak for a man and he couldn't pull up much more corn than I could. Sometimes we worked at a stalk together.

Jackson had a strange sort of voice when he talked. He told me it was because he was from "Massachusetts."

"What language do they talk in that nation?" I asked him.

"Massachusetts is a state—not a nation," said Jackson. "It's part of this country. And we speak English there, but it sounds different because, among many reasons, life there is very different from down here."

"How is it different?" I asked.

"Well, for one thing it's a lot colder. Down here in Texas you don't have much for a winter. Up in Boston the whole ground gets covered in snow." Every day Jackson told me about things I never heard of like snow, which he said was like a white cold blanket made from drops of rain that had frozen in the sky on their way to the ground to become like cold little feathers floating into a big pile that you could jump into or shuffle through and you could even pack it into balls and throw it at a friend.

"Why would you want to throw it at your friend?" I asked.

"We call it a snowball fight," he said.

"Why are you fighting with your friend?" I said.

"It's playing, Ingram. It's a way of playing." I stopped working and looked at Jackson, confused.

He stopped working and said, "Ingram. Tell me you know what playing means."

"I know what it means," I said, and went back to work. I did know the word "playing" but I couldn't remember where I'd heard it. Trying to remember touched something that I didn't want to think about, so I went and pulled up my own corn plant and quit talking to Jackson, who let me alone.

One Friday, after many weeks of Jackson living in my cabin, he went with me to the canteen for the first time. He didn't drink any whiskey because he said, "I can't drink anymore." But he sat against the wall and watched me drink with the crowd of cheering men and he looked at me with that face he made that was serious and thinking a lot of thoughts inside his head. I just kept on drinking till all knowing flew out of my head.

The next day I woke up in my bed. Jackson was packing his stuff. He must have brought me back to the cabin the night before. I realized he was leaving on the truck and I wouldn't see him again. He finished packing his case and lit a cigarette and sat on my bed next to me.

"Ingram," he said, "I'm leaving. I have a minute, though, and I'd like to talk to you."

"Where are you going?" I asked him.

"I don't know," he said. "Just going."

"Why?" I asked him. "Why don't you stay here?"

"I got something catching up with me," he said. "I can't stay anywhere too long."

"What is it? What's catching up to you?"

"Reality," he said.

"What's reality?"

"It's the way things are. It's what can't be avoided but is too much to look at. At least for me."

"Like what?"

"Remember I told you that I'm a writer?" he said as he closed his suitcase.

"Yeah," I said.

"I haven't written a word in five years."

"So you're not a writer anymore?"

"I wish. But I am a writer. And I can't write. It's a damn joke."

"How come you can't do it anymore?"

"If I knew that, Ingram . . ." Jackson took a much longer pull off of his cigarette, smoking almost half of it at once as it glowed bright, making the bottom of his nose red. "Writing is something that comes into your life and you fall in love with it. Every story you have in you starts coming out through writing and it's such a good feeling. That feeling of connection. Even if no one reads it, you get this feeling while you're writing. A great connection with all people that are and ever were. I met writing when I was about your age. And I made it my life. And then writing just left one day. I woke up and it was gone." Jackson's face started to change into a kind of sad that was almost hard to look at. Then he shook his head quick, like getting a fly off of his face, and said, "Listen, Ingram, I want to talk to you."

"Okay, Jackson," I said, getting up on one elbow. My head hurt like always, but the hurt didn't mean much anymore. Somewhere underneath it, knowing Jackson was leaving gave me a strong feeling. It was so strong and bad, I pushed my hand into my pocket, which was funny because I realized I was reaching for a dime, so I could drink again. But the dimes were gone and it was morning. With no whiskey to put inside me I couldn't push away the feeling that was coming up like a burp and the feeling was that I didn't want Jackson to leave. I was tired of seeing folks leave me, which was funny because before I came to the farm it had been folks making me leave them.

"Ingram," said Jackson. "You just can't keep drinking like that."

"You mean the whiskey?" I asked. "But I like it. It's just about the only thing I do like."

"I know that. I get it. But you're just a kid. And it's going to kill you before you get a chance to live. These people here, they want you to drink. You work hard on this farm and they pay you, but you give them the money right back for that cheap whiskey. And if you don't stop that drinking, your money will keep going straight out of your pocket and you'll never leave here."

"Why would I want to leave?" I said. "They feed me and I have a bed. And they give me money for whiskey."

"Listen, Ingram. Don't drink anymore. Just don't do it. When the next payday comes, keep your dimes and go to bed. It'll hurt the first time, because your body will ask for whiskey. But you're a kid and you should be able to kick it pretty easy."

"But all the men drink," I said. "They're my friends."

"You're not like them," said Jackson. "And they're not your friends."

"You mean because they're Mexican?"

"No," Jackson said, "because they're lost. Their chance is all gone. Like me. But you're too young to be lost just yet."

"What do I do with my dimes?" I asked.

"Find a place to hide your money and save it up. If you save money, you can do something with it."

"Like what?"

"Well, what do you wish you could do? Or what do you wish you could have?" he asked. I thought about it for a second and it just popped into my head.

"A truck," I said. "I would like to have a truck of my own. So I could move down the road quick when I want to."

"That's good, Ingram," Jackson said. "Save your dimes and find yourself a truck and you buy it and you get out of here. Otherwise, you'll die here."

I thought every day on the road I was going to die for all the danger I'd faced. But this farm was safe and I had a bed and food. But I took from Jackson's face that what he was saying was true. More than anyone who had ever told me anything.

"Okay, Jackson," I said. He got up from my bed, picked up his case and left. I watched him go out the door of the cabin. I fell back asleep and didn't wake up till supper.

The next payday after Jackson left I walked a little out of the camp where there was some trees. They all looked about the same as each other except one that went up only a little before it turned its trunk to the side, like it forgot which way to grow, and then it turned straight up. This strange curve in the tree made it bob and bend more than the others when there was wind. I chose a soft spot of dirt close to the trunk of the bent tree to dig a hole with my knife, and in that hole I put my dimes and buried them. I walked by the canteen and heard the singing and hollering from the quiet of the night outside.

Chapter Eleven

Girl

I guess it was owing to my not being in the canteen to drink anymore that I didn't get to know any of the new men coming to the farm after Jackson left. I didn't sing with the Mexicans anymore either, though I had started to know their language. The only people who stayed around were the boss and Francis, who would give me more work to do around the farm, since I stayed longer than any other man. Sometimes I served food in the tent.

Days and weeks went slipping one into the next, on and on. I wasn't sure how long I'd been there for. I didn't expect much beyond that I would probably live on that farm the rest of my life. I'd started growing out of my clothes.

"You're too big for those britches, boy," said the boss one day. And he threw me a pair of coveralls. "You still ain't much good picking. But keep helping in the kitchen and such. And keep learning to talk Mexican. That'll come in useful." Which is something I had been doing, helping the boss talk to the Mexicans that didn't know English.

"Why don't you learn Spanish?" I asked the boss.

"Why don't you watch your mouth?" he said back, pointing at my face and walking away.

I went to my cabin and put on the coveralls. They were much too big but I could roll up the pant legs and tie the straps in knots to make them shorter. They had a little blood on them on the back of the bib and I wondered who they belonged to before the boss gave them to me. Many nights in the canteen men fought, just like my father did with his brother, except it was different when they didn't know each other. Something would happen like a man pushing against another man when the place got crowded. The man who got pushed would turn and say, "Watch it." And the man who pushed might just back away, or if his face was hot with whiskey and excitement, he might say something like, "Watch what?" Or if he was Mexican he might say, "Oye, gringo." And the other men would get quiet and the two men would keep their eyes on each other like there was no one in the world but them and they'd make little moves with their feet and shoulders, and their hands would start slowly balling up as they said things like, "You better step back, you dirty Mexican" or "Vayate, pincha cabron." Until one man would do something he couldn't take back like stepping on the other's foot. And then the fists flew and there'd soon be blood and teeth on the floor till the boss would come in with a wooden club and crack one of them on the head. There was one time where a man took the blow from the boss badly and someone said he died the next day. It could have been I was wearing the coveralls of a dead man.

Martin's shoes, too, had become too tight on my feet. I traded those shoes with a Mexican man who gave me an extra pair he had of sandals. He took my small boy's shoes and for some reason he just looked at them kind of sad and after that he'd keep them tied together and slung around his neck when he worked in the field till about a week later he moved off, like most men did.

"Ingram," the boss said to me one Monday morning, "come on with me." I followed him back to the office and there, standing in the dark spot in front of his desk, was a girl with a Mexican face. She wore a man's clothes—a striped shirt with sleeves rolled up so it made big balls around her wrists with a sweater over it but the neck of it was so wide it could almost fall off her shoulders. The shirt and sweater were tucked into suit pants with a belt that was tied in a knot instead of buckled to keep it all closed around her. Under her ripped straw hat, her eyes were the first thing that said "girl" to my mind. Her cheeks were smooth and beardless with girl's lips in the middle. She looked at me, ready to fight, like she was mad that I could see how soft her cheeks were.

The boss man pointed to her and said, "Tell her she can't work here." He stood with his hand on his hip, wiping sweat off his brow with a white cloth and looking impatient. "Go on," he said, waving from her to me with his cloth.

I turned to the girl and said, "Tu no trabajo."

"Si, trabajo!" she spat. I saw that both her hands were making fists. "Yo trabajo aqui!"

"She said she works here," I told him.

"No, she doesn't," said the boss man. "This is a men's camp. Men. No girls."

"Muchachos," I said to her, "no chiquitas." This girl's eyes flashed wide open.

"No soy chiquita! Soy mujer! Yo trabajo muy fuerte!" And she started squawking out and shrieking all kinds of Mexican words I'd not heard before. The boss watched her yell and curse and he smiled a little. She finally quit and stood there breathing hard like she'd run around the room in circles.

"I don't know what she said," I told him, "but she's mad as hell."

"I can see that for myself," he said. He went around to sit at his desk and began writing on his small paper. "She can stay in your cabin," he said. "She only gets five cents a bushel. I'm not gonna get out of her what even you can pick and she'll cost me more in food. I've seen a girl eat twice as much as a grown man. But hell, if she wants to work, she can work," he said, looking at her and at me. "Hell, I got nothing but children and girls left to work this place. Hardly got any men this week. They come less and less. I guess folks are dying out there in larger numbers, least ways the grown ones. Less men to work. Less men to buy the grain. Guess it works out in the numbers."

"Why are folks dying so much?" I asked.

"Why? What the hell kind of question is that?" he said. And he ripped the paper and handed it to the Mexican girl. She took the paper and looked at me. I didn't know how to say all that. "Go on, now," said the boss. "Settle her in and get to work."

"Viene," I said to the girl, which means "come," and she followed me to the cabin. I pointed at the two beds and she took the one furthest from me. The other one was empty. Like the boss man had said, there weren't many workers the last two weeks. I sat on my bed waiting for the call to come and opened my weekly pack of cigarettes. On Mondays a man called Terry came around and dropped new packs by the beds. I had learned to smoke when I was drinking and the taste of it helped when I felt that bite inside that asked for whiskey. It was like my hunger dog had a new pal in my stomach who wanted me drunk. The girl watched me smoke as she picked up the pack on her bed and looked at it. I took a dime out of my pocket and held it out to her. "Comprar tobacco?" I said to her, which was what men said when they bought and sold cigarettes. I figured if she didn't want her smokes, I'd buy them and sell them as singles at lunch, which some men would pay up to two cents for, and that could add up to profit, which meant more to bury under the crooked tree. The girl opened her pack and lit herself a cigarette. She put her bundle under her bed and we sat there filling the cabin with smoke until the call came to get to work, and I took her outside.

I took my seat on the flatbed. The girl climbed up beside me. All the other men were looking at her, smiling like you do at a cooking piece of meat. The tractor pulled out and rumbled us through the corn. When we got out to pick, the girl followed me as I grabbed for my first stalk. I had gotten to where I could yank them out of the ground without twisting and breaking first. I'd squat down like a frog and grab real low on the plant, then spring up my body and it would come loose. It didn't hurt my hands anymore because I had pads of hard skin all along my palms and fingers. I was making five dollars a week, when I'd started with one. I was bigger and stronger.

The girl watched me pull up the corn and then went to the next stalk. She grabbed at it and turned toward the flatbed and just started walking with a face full of anger and that stalk just came with her. I didn't know how someone with soft skin and small arms could pull so hard except that this girl had such fire in her that I started to suppose she could pick up the tractor and throw it at the moon.

When it got to be night, the girl and I went to the cabin. I got in my bed, laying on my side, watching her get ready. I'd never seen a girl or a woman get ready for bed and something made me wonder what I would see. She took off her broken straw hat and set it on the shelf above her bed. She had strings in her hair which she untied and let her hair tumble down her back and shoulders. It was dark and heavy like mud. Then she took out a brush like my father used to have for brushing the bugs off the horse and she pulled it roughly through her hair like she was pulling up the corn. She had her lip set tight against her teeth. She was hurting herself with that brush.

Then she pulled off the sweater and unbuttoned her man's shirt and pulled it off her shoulders. At that moment, the lower half of my body twisted away from her and my upper part and my head followed with it, turning my whole self to the wall. I saw something under her shirt, some part of her that I couldn't look at and started forgetting on purpose the second I found myself staring at the wall beside my bed. I rushed through things I'd seen before to put it in front of that part of her in my mind. The animals in front of our house. The dog. The hogs. The chickens. The fence at the end of our field. The river when it was full after a rain. The water falling down. The hog when it lay on its side, its belly pink and almost naked of hair toward the center. Getting punched in my face by the boy in Houston. By my father. My mother slapping my face. Taking that man's meat my first day on the road. I kept forcing one thing after another through my mind to cover what I'd seen. Pa's voice again came into my mind. "You can't rush getting big, but you can hurry up and get smart." So why was I looking away from something new, something to learn and get me smarter?

I heard the girl's body get into her bed. I reached down into my pocket and clutched onto the knife Pa had given me. "This is my knife," I thought. "Pa gave it to me and it's mine." I didn't know why it was important to me to think this thought so hard but I said it in my mind over and over again. And I squeezed that knife so hard, if I didn't have the pads of rough skin on my palms I might have cut my hand from it. The girl turned off her light and then it was dark except the electric light that stared down from the pole over the cabin and came in the window. The wood on the wall in front of my face was gray in the light. I touched the wood thinking that it would be warm, as it always was at the start of night from the last of the day's sun beating down on the outside of the cabin. But when I touched it, the wall was as cold as it was gray and instead of the soft wooden feeling it was wet and slick, or my hand was, and I knew it to be the skin of the red-eyed creature who had been gone from my dreams. I pressed my hand against it hard, wanting it to sap away my natural warmth, relieved to be touching the only thing that had been with me all of my life. I would rather be dead than so alone, I thought. And I wondered why having that girl breathing in the next bed made me feel more alone than ever.

The girl stayed in my cabin the whole week she was at the work farm. I never learned her name because she didn't speak a word to me or to anyone else. The men said things to her in Spanish, using words I hadn't learned, but she never talked back to them. She stuck by me at meal times, worked by my side, pulling up about as much corn as I did, and every night I'd get in bed quicker than her so I could face the wall as she got into hers. I thought about things I wanted to ask her and say to her but they never came clear in my mind and a mighty force of fear kept me from ever looking straight into her eyes. When Friday came the girl got her pay, and instead of waiting for a truck to take her back to the highway, she simply walked away from the farm.

I watched her go till she was too small to follow with my eyes and I went back to my empty cabin. Something about her leaving and not wanting to know who would next be in my cabin made me feel all at once that I couldn't stay in that farm any longer. That night when all the men went to the canteen I went to my bent tree and dug up my dimes. There was an awful lot of them. Enough to fill my pockets front and back and both my hands. I walked to my cabin in the dark and laid the money on my bed and wondered how near I was to having enough to buy a truck of my own. My mind was making my body tired by thinking what it would be like to walk and walk, the way I had done on the road all those days before the farm. It'd been hard. But the bed I sat on was mine as long as I chose it. Why would I ever leave? It hurt my head to think about it. I had to sleep. I didn't want to sleep on my dimes, so I went to the girl's bed and got in it. Her sweat was in the sheets. The smell was sweet but going, like ripe crab apples turning brown.

I woke the next morning to the sound of clinking dimes. I looked over at my bed. A man I didn't know was picking up my dimes and putting them in a scarf.

"Those are my dimes," I said. He turned and looked at me and said nothing. "Those are mine," I said again. The man was white and skinny, wearing a full black suit, tie, and hat but dirty all over, with his hair looking like he had just been swimming, combed back from the bright red burn on his forehead to the blood-red burn on the back of his neck. I had come to know this as "road burn," which men would have on the day they arrived from walking into the bright sun in the morning and away from the dark sun in the evening. After working in the fields for a while, twisting your body this way and that, the sun left its mark more even all over your face, hands, neck, and shoulders if you left them bare. So this man must've just arrived and thought he'd got lucky getting a bed full of dimes.

"This is my bed," the man said. "I was told come in here." His voice was low down and muffled like he had a strap of leather in his mouth.

"That's my bed," I said.

"You're in your bed, boy," he said, standing over me like the way I had seen men move their bodies before a fight. He was angry and dirty, like a crow who'd been pushed in the mud and wanted revenge.

He had me scared. I had never been in a fight. I had been hit and punched, kicked, and otherwise beaten but I had never struck another person in the face, which is what fighting required. And this man was so tall I'd have to jump in the air to get my fists anywhere near his face. Then I remembered the knife that Pa had given me. I reached in my pocket, which the crow couldn't see me do because I was still laying under the covers, which no longer smelled like the sweet sweat of the girl.

"You better just set tight, boy," said the crow. "What's mine is mine. And ain't nothing yours on that bed."

All at once I jumped out of the bed and to my feet, holding the open knife up in front of my face. "Those are my dimes," I said. I was breathing so hard it was shaking my head and his body was going up and down in my vision.

"What you going to do with that knife?" he said. He was breathing hard too. I guess the idea was to stick him with the knife if he didn't let me have my dimes. Pa had given me that knife to *protect* myself but now I was fixing to hurt a man to protect my dimes and to protect a truck I wanted to someday buy but didn't have. None of that was making my hand want to push the knife into his skin.

I looked up at his face to see if I'd see something there that would change my mind. He had the front of his mouth open, showing his teeth that were clenched together and his eyebrows were pushed down in a knot over his nose. To me, he looked like a man who wanted to look angry. But in his eyes was something different. I recognized it as being hungry. Looking down at his belly, where my knife was ready to plunge, I could see it quiver. I wondered if he had a hunger dog inside him. I sure didn't want to open up his guts with a knife and have that dog come out.

"Why don't we split it?" I said. His bunched-up eyebrows shot up in surprise.

"Split it? You mean the money?"

"You take half, I'll take half," I said.

He looked over at the dimes, then at me, then bunched his eyebrows back up and said, "I ain't have to split it with you. I can just take it all."

"Not without trouble," I said. "If you want all of it, you gonna have trouble. You want half, no trouble."

The man looked at me, my knife, and his own fists. Then he went and stood over the pile of dimes in his kerchief. He sat down, rubbed his spiky chin, and then started thumbing through the dimes, making two piles of them. I put my knife back in my pocket and came over, watching him shifting one or two dimes from one pile to the other. Then he put his hand on the back of his neck and looked at me, his face square with mine now that he was sitting, and he said, "You know how to count?"

"Only to ten," I said.

"There's more than ten there." He seemed relieved that I didn't know more than him, and with what he said next, he sounded more like he knew me, which was, "Goddamn numbers. I hate 'em."

I sat on the bed, across from the hungry crow, and pushed the dimes into two piles. "These look like about even to me," I said.

He looked them over and said, "Well. You choose one, since the money was yours till now." I picked a pile of dimes and scooped them up with my hands. I was glad to realize that the problem was gone of how to carry so much, since it all fit my pockets. The man rolled up his half of dimes into his scarf, which he then tied around his neck. That was a right smart way to hide his money, I thought. I took my pack of cigarettes and my saved-up supper from the night before and I headed out of the cabin. "Good luck," said the crow as I went outside, leaving that farm for good.

Chapter Twelve

Tornado

I woke up laying on my back. The sky was nothing but white. Not clouds, but one big sky of white. At home I used to lay on my back and watch the white clouds float by, like leaves in the river, and I'd figure the sky must be like a river, moving and pushing with a current, and the clouds must be like the white babble and churn that the river made when it ran harder or crashed around some rocks. The sky being a river made even more sense to my mind when the clouds got dark and angry and rained on my face. I'd try to keep my eyes open to see way up high where the drops were falling from.

The white sky was the same all around except where I could see the round yellow bottom of the rising sun peeking out from under the giant flat bottom of the cloud, on its way up and over. I got up and shook myself, stamping my feet, waking up the bugs that had slept in my pants, letting them fall to the ground. It had ceased to bother me that bugs sometimes wanted to crawl on a sleeping person. If I was a bug walking around at night, and I found a warm body, I'd think it a good comfort to crawl up and sleep between their flesh and clothes like it was a bed.

I had only a bit of food left, having eaten most of it during the walking the night before. I ate what I had as I started to walk toward where the sun had set the night before. It was already up hiding behind the white. I lit a cigarette. It felt good to smoke but quickly made me thirsty and I got mad at myself and said out loud, "Damn it, Ingram. You got so used to water when you want it and now you got no way to get none." It was just at that moment that I heard the low, hard sound of thunder in the distance. "Well here comes a big ole' drink," I said. It was funny to be talking out loud like I was two people. I had been around folks for a long time on the farm and talked to so many—more talking than I had ever done in my life. It was a kind of relief to be back with just myself again—just me walking in my sandals that let the air get at the tops of my feet and kept them cool, though I sometimes wished I could have kept Martin's shoes, which were snug and tight, making my feet feel kept in a way I liked. But by then I could have never got them on. Thinking of his shoes made me think of Miss Maw and Sinema, and since I was already talking, I decided to talk to myself about that.

"I wonder what Sinema would be doing right now," I said. "Probably eating some breakfast. Cornbread with butter. Probably her sisters are arguing. But she's not. She stays silent or saying things agreeable. She's helping out Miss Maw. Maybe they're taking in another boy who's lost." I liked remembering their home and the little time I had there. I didn't care if all my memories of that farm just blew away like dead leaves—though I'd been there for very long. No one needs dead leaves for anything.

I reached down and patted the outsides of my pockets, feeling the hard lumps of the dimes inside. That's all I needed to carry away from that place. The dimes. I wondered how many it would take to have myself a truck. "Must be more than two handfuls," I told myself. "Can't be two handfuls of anything that's worth a whole truck. Two handfuls is just a drink from a stream. To be truthful, I'd take that now over a truck."

The rolling thunder got louder and the air around me started getting thick with wind whipping around and blustering. I knew a storm was coming. I wondered how big. It didn't matter much since there was nowhere to go for cover. My mother and father and I hunkered in the fruit cellar when that storm came that bashed in the new roof my father had built and that sent him back to drinking. We were all three of us down there hearing the awful, howling wind and loud thunder like gunshots right next to your ear and the crashing of trees falling down and breaking on the ground as the rain came in hard through the cracks between the cellar door-boards over our heads, which my father was holding closed, by its rusty handle, shutting out the storm with the weight of his body. It was perfect dark in that cellar except when lightning would strike and I could see everything and then nothing. My father's undershirt stained yellow under the arms, his neck muscles straining as he looked up at the door saying, "I just put that roof on. Just put that goddamn roof on." And my mother's face as she stood against the cellar wall, looking straight ahead, same as she looked when the kitchen was clean after dinner and there was nothing left to do.

A loud and nasty crack of thunder that came from directly above me stopped my feet and told me to look around. The sky above my head and to all sides of the world was fast going from white to black and the wind had started not just to blow but whip and whistle. The thunder was instead a constant rolling. Lightning flashed, lighting things up so bright you couldn't see, like a white night instead of a black night. The wind rippled my clothes and hair and even tossed my arms around, whipping in jerks and circles and I knew this was going to be a vicious storm.

I looked around in every direction, foolishly, as if I expected a tree or a house or a root cellar to appear where I hadn't seen it already in all this time of walking past nothing. My feet didn't seem to understand there was nowhere to go and they sort of darted from this way to that way. Faster than I could think, the black sky above me sent down a hard sheet of water, not in drops but just dumped down all at once like a bathtub just broke in half over my head. Next came hail. That's what my mother had called it. Hard white balls crashing down onto the road, hitting my head and hitting the backs of my hands when I raised them to protect me. The storm was on me.

Again, like a fool, I looked around me for somewhere to go or something to do. There was nothing. The black from the sky was now twisting around in the air around me and all around, picking up dust and dirt and chucking it around, and water and hail was falling and then being swept around in shifty circles by the wind. A gust of wind punched me on my chest so hard that it pushed my breath out. When it let up, I took a deep drink of air and water both, through my nose, and then I pushed it out with a long breath that, for some reason, came with a sound.

"Aaaaaaah!" I said out into the wind, which took my voice and whipped it around to the back of my head. "Aaaaah!" I yelled loud, knowing that if someone was standing close enough to hold my hand, they wouldn't hear a peep, because the whipping air was closing me in like a tight blanket from head to toe like the one time I'd seen someone, I couldn't remember who, but someone, with a blanket wrapped around their body from head to toe and they were dead. The wind got tighter around me and I yelled out, again, as loud as I could when all at once everything stopped. Everything that was hanging in the air dropped to the ground, all was quiet, and there was a shift in the air above. The black sky turned itself in a slow circle, like a wheel spinning on its side, and the air in front of my eyes had a color that was green. My guts told me, and I knew they weren't lying, that this green was a bad thing. There was a rumble from under my feet, like thunder coming from the ground. The rumbling came harder and closer and my heels told me that it was coming from behind, so I whipped around to see something that just couldn't be, but was. It was a giant, walking tree of gray, black sky, that started on the ground and shot way up, twisting like a dirty wet rag being wrung out into a bucket. It was a moving, changing, big, black, jerking, dancing tree—its top, instead of branches ending in leaves, was the whole entire sky and its roots were dancing along the ground. It picked up dirt in great chunks and sucked them up, leaving a trench behind like the fastest craziest farmer that ever sowed a field, and this tree of destruction was headed right for me, like it knew me and it hated me or loved me or wanted to eat me and it was moving at the speed of wind and there wasn't one single thing I could do about it. I felt my feet lift off the ground as I saw a big chunk of pavement from the edge of the road crack and go up into the root of the tree and explode up into the sky in tiny pieces and I realized this was going to happen to me. I threw myself on my belly and pushed my hands into the earth, digging and clawing with my fingers, trying to hold onto the world in any way I could, digging my toes down and my fingers and pushing my cheek against the dirt. The earth around me shook so hard and before anything else could occur to me, the earth was whipped away and I had nothing around me but black-gray swirling sky. I wasn't standing on anything and nothing was against me but whipping wind and I flailed my arms and legs, trying to run in the air as bits of dirt and sand whipped me all over, filling my ears with mud and grass and cutting my face and I tasted salty blood in my mouth.

Something was hitting me all over my face and arms, something small like hail but harder. There were shining twinkles scattering around my head and I realized it was my dimes being sucked out of my pockets and dancing around me in the black wind. I closed my eyes and mouth tight to keep the dimes and sand and rocks and grass from getting in and blinding or choking me. Without seeing, I felt myself being whipped around and up, lifting up and up till I only felt clean wind and then suddenly there was no force on my body at all, and I opened my eyes and saw bright blue sky. Then my floating body tumbled over, facing a blanket of black cloud beneath me. Faster than I ever ran, faster than the truck had carried me on the road to the farm, I fell through the cloud that went gray then black then white and then the whole world opened up beneath me—the road, the flat plains, and far in all directions. As I fell toward it all, I flailed my arms and legs, hoping the sky was a river as I thought and that I could swim and keep myself up, but all my dangling and jerking around just made me tumble, end over end, the world making circles around me as I fell, sky, then earth, sky then earth, all I could do was try to pull myself into a ball and close my eyes tight as I fell. I just wanted to stop thinking and stop being and stop knowing and then it ended with a hard SLAP.

My first deep, gasping, waking breath was stopped by a pain in my side. The road, which had been way down far below me, was now right up to my eye, laying against my cheek—or my cheek was laying against *it*. The pavement was pressing against my chest and hurting me when I breathed. I rolled over onto my back and opened my eyes and saw clear blue sky over my head. The storm was gone.

I didn't know how long I'd been laying there. The pain was bad on my head, face, arm, and leg, all along the side I was sleeping on, which must have been where I landed after falling from way up high in the cloud tree. I tried to push myself up, but when I put weight on my arm, I got a pain like being stabbed by my own bones from the inside and fell onto my back hollering out a big loud scream, clutching my arm. The pain echoed through my body like my screaming voice coming back to me. "I can't hold that much hurt in my mind," I said to my body. "Some of y'all pain needs to get in line and wait."

I laid there on my back, panting like a dog in the summer, till I could breathe deeper and think better. "Can't use that arm no more," I said to myself. So I tried putting my weight on my other arm. It had no pain. With that one good arm, I was able to push myself up to sitting. I kept on hefting my body up and up until I was standing in the middle of the road, my hurting arm dangling down, feeling like it was on fire. My leg on the same side hurt, but it was just plain hurt. The arm was something much worse. I kept on walking. What else could I do except to keep going the way I'd been before the storm? I walked along that straight road that never changed and never went anywhere. I might have thought I'd come to the end of all things and seen the last place where people ever lived, except the road stretching out ahead must have been put there by someone.

I needed water. There wasn't any. I needed food. The night came quick and all went black around me. I stopped walking. I stood in the road, looking to where the sun had dropped, and then the other way, to where it would rise tomorrow. Then a new light came from over to the side, over the land. It was the moon, white and bright, starting to rise.

"Follow the moon, Ingram," said a voice inside. I wasn't having any luck walking the way the sun went, rise and set, following the sun from one bad day to the next.

I turned myself to the side, walking off of the road, into the night, against and across the way the day comes and goes. I walked toward the moon, its bright light coloring the dead grass white, like an old man's hair. The pain in my arm got dull and quiet and then it disappeared. Without the sun's heat, I wasn't hungry or thirsty, as long as I stared at the cool, white moon. The moon got higher and higher in the sky until it was right above my head and I figured I'd come to where it brought me. So I laid down on my back and stared up at that moon until my eyes closed. Somewhere inside of me I could hear laughing.

Chapter Thirteen

The Pond

I made up my mind to keep moving with the sun to my side instead of toward or away from it. I figured that was the way of the moon. I walked in this way for many days and nights, across burnt, short grass on flat land, nothing changing from day to day, place to place. Nothing to look at, nothing to notice. At night I'd just drop onto the grass and try to sleep, but I never could much before I'd roll onto my hurt arm, which would jolt me with a pain that made me yowl so loud I'd wake myself up and I'd keep on yowling. Anyway, there was no one to complain about the noise I made because I might as well have been alone in the whole world. I had no one to talk to. I got so I didn't care to think, the way thinking is talking on the inside. There was nothing to think about. Nothing to notice or wonder about, in the same way there was nothing to eat or drink. My mouth was so dry it hurt to close it.

I was less walking from one foot to the other and more just falling forward and just catching myself with each foot at a time, so the going forward was just by-the-way. On account of the strange, bobbing around way I was walking, my head was sometimes dangling down and sometimes flopping back and I'd see the sky and the world flipping up and down and back. My thinking and my thoughts quit coming in words or ideas and had started to slip and slide around like water sloshing in a glass. I couldn't feel what my legs were doing, but I guessed I was still moving because I never felt myself fall and more and more I felt that I was walking through a dream.

Sure enough, I started to feel things get dark in the middle of a cloudless day and then I started to hear a wind that also sounded like a car—that sounded like it was coming behind me except I didn't feel a wind at my back or anywhere else. I wondered if another tornado had come to finish me off and I almost hoped it would, though not quite. As frightening, confusing, and painful as that walking dream was, I didn't want to die during any of it. I wanted to see it through. I wondered if this was all happening because I'd decided to follow the moon. Maybe it was taking me to the end of the world, where up is down and dark is light. I decided it was time to try to see better what was really going on so I stopped my walking and tried to hold my head straight.

I saw a line of darkness in the grass that was moving ahead of me and I realized it was a shadow of some kind. I looked up at the sky, where the sun had last been. My head was light and swimming like I'd drank fifty whiskeys, and I might as well have for what I saw up there, which was like a bird with wings that don't flap but I swore to myself it could not have been but a dream because it was bigger than anything I had ever seen in my life. It was bigger than a house, the tornado, or the tallest building in Houston. It was so big I'm not sure it could have fit in the great hole Ernie and the men were digging in. And it was just hanging in the sky and making a noise that hurt to hear it. I didn't know what this thing could be, but I hated it. I hated that it was loud, that it was big, and that I had begun to feel a heat pressing down on me from the underneath of the great black and silver bird, which was slowly coming lower and lower as my head went back and back and I fell hard on the grass and the next thing I knew it was night, and quiet, and the bird was gone and I was covered in sweat, laying on my back. At least I had gotten some sleep. I laid like that, not wanting to do or decide anything more, until the sun started creeping up and I did the only thing I could do. I got up and walked again.

The walking was getting tougher and tougher and I was breathing harder from each step and I thought it was from me dying of hunger, thirst, and no sleep, but I started to realize that I was walking on an up-slope, which I couldn't tell from looking because there was nothing to see except the sky and ground. But soon I was walking in a hunch and having to push myself up and up and then I was needing to lean forward and put my good hand down on the ground to push myself. Then I was outright climbing. It was hard with my hurting, mangled arm still on fire. It was swollen now and red and even black down by my elbow, which bulged way out like I had an orange under my skin. Even just the moving up and down of my body was making it hurt worse even if it wasn't involved in the work.

All of a sudden, I was coming up and over the top of the world and now I was looking down at the dry grass sloping down and down ahead of me, and as down it went, so did it get greener and greener. Further on it stretched out flat, and further on there were trees and amongst the trees and grass I saw a great big pond of water. I took off running—or just falling faster—feeling the wind against my face and feeling less and less pain as I ran down and down from brown grass to green, through trees and tall weeds and wildflowers along the edge of the pond and I threw my whole self into the water. My hurting arm took the water with a shock of pain but every single other part of me was so happy to be cool and wet. Soon I was drinking and bobbing up and down and hollering and laughing and feeling my whole body thank the cool water for being there and for getting in me and on me and cooling even my hurt arm and setting all the parts of me right as could be. I didn't care that my clothes were wet. I wasn't about to take them off to swim. Never that again.

I floated easy in that sweet pond, my arm clutched safe to my side, singing and laughing and not caring if it was my last day living, till I could feel my clothes getting heavy and wanting to drag me down, so I swam to the shore and laid in the grass.

I wasn't long in enjoying myself before the hunger dog bit me on the inside and reminded me I hadn't eaten in days. Maybe there was a fish in that pond but I had no string or pins to catch it. Figuring it couldn't be too different from the pond behind the house back home, I walked along the edge, looking for bullfrogs. Sometimes when my mother didn't have food to feed me supper because my father would be drinking in town instead of bringing anything home, I found bullfrogs by the pond and killed them. I'd get two or three, catch them by the leg, and smack their head with a rock. Then I'd put a stick through their body, coming out of the mouth, and beg my mother for a match so I could cook them over a fire of long dead grass and twigs. And then I'd eat alone on the edge of the pond as it got dark. As I walked around that pond, away from home and away from everything else, I realized it was the first time since I'd left home that I felt a wish to see my mother again, just so she could give me a match. So I could cook up a frog and eat. And I wondered why I had never brought the frogs I had caught back home so I could share the meat of them with my mother.

I could hear bullfrogs singing all around me. I knew the best way was to catch one as it hopped into the water for a drink. I took off my sandals and stuck them in the front of my coveralls and I walked, all the time looking down at my feet sinking into the muddy grass, along the edge of the pond. I soon walked full around it and I sat on the grass where I'd started. I gave up. "If a man don't eat, he dies," I said to my feet. And I wondered how I'd come to know that for sure.

I laid back in the grass and I remembered the eggs that had hatched one time back home, and how one chick had only one foot and when my mother spread feed out in the dirt the other chicks pecked him away. He couldn't hold his ground. He'd be pecked in his side and just fall over. That little chick soon turned brown from the dirt he kept falling in, while his brothers and sisters stayed white and yellow. After only trying a few times, he got so weak and skinny and tired, that he laid on his side, his tiny eye closing, and by the end of the first day out of that egg he stopped breathing and just lay there dead, only to be eaten by bugs while the other chicks grew up and didn't care one way or the other. I could have fed that chick and made him a pet. But I just watched him die. And he wasn't the first thing I'd seen die. I couldn't remember what was the first. Here I was about to die from hunger myself, except I was alone. That baby chick had me watching over him as he died. So did someone or something else. Here was only the bullfrogs hiding in the high grass, laughing at me as I died. Well, I thought, at least I'd had a drink and a swim. I closed my eyes, figuring the gray creature of my death would show his face in my coming dream. I expected that this time he'd sap away all the warmth I had and I'd join him in cold gray darkness. And I'd have red eyes just like him. And I'd become someone else's coming death. But as my vision went black, I didn't see him. There was no one there. And I felt a bitter sadness that dying is alone.

"WELL, GOOD MORNING," SAID A voice that scared me harder than anything in my life. I sprung up on my feet, whipped around, looking for who said it. But there was no one in sight. "Up here, kid," said the voice again. I looked up and saw a man sitting up in a tree. He was a white man. I had started to notice if a man was white, black, or a Mexican. His hair was white too, though he didn't look old. He wore a thick jacket of leather like an old saddle taken apart and sewn together, with no shirt under it. His pants were dark blue with thin white stripes down the sides. He wore a black hat that was round over the top of his head. He had something about his face that made me like to look at it. Even though he was way up in the tree, sitting in the crook of a bough against the trunk, I could see his face from far below him. His shoes were brown and white with black bottoms.

"When did you get up there?" I asked him.

"Up where?" he said, looking confused.

"Up in that tree."

"I always been up here," he said. "How'd you get down there?" I started walking along the pond's edge again.

"You hunting for bullfrogs?" he asked me, as I heard the sound of him scrambling down from the tree and following me.

"Yeah," I said. "Hungry."

Now the man was walking beside me. He was not much tall for a man. In fact he was just my size. But his face showed him to be a man for sure. He walked with his hands in his pockets and watched me have no luck finding a bullfrog.

"Best to scare them outta the grass and into the water," he said. "I'll stomp around and you catch what comes."

I said, "Alright."

And the man started stomping and shuffling around in the grass and saying, "Ha bullfrog! Ha now! Come on now, bullfrog! Ha now!" And out of grass came hopping, almost flying, a big fat bullfrog, which I caught right outta the air, my hands coming together around it so fast that my hurting arm hit me with a pain like a hammer to the center of my mind. I screamed and fell to the ground on my bottom, my elbow feeling hot like a fire.

"Holy hell, buddy," said the man. "Looks like your arm's broke."

"Feels like it's full of knives," I said.

"You managed to hang onto that bullfrog, though." He pointed at how I had caught hold and kept that frog's foot between my fingers. The man took it from me and he swung that frog in the air by its legs and brought it down on a rock by the pond's edge and a little blood spurted out, showing it was dead. "Tell you what," he said. "You do the flushing, and I'll do the catching."

We commenced to catching bullfrogs together. I stomped around in the grass and I made noises just like he had. "Ha now! Hey, frogs! Ha ya go!" More frogs came out hopping and he caught them, killed them, and stuck them on a stick that he cracked off of the tree he'd been sitting in. I plucked some dead grass and found a few pieces of wood dry enough and he lit them up with some matches he kept in a bundle in his pocket. Just as the sun fell all the way, we had us a little fire to light our faces and arms all orange-colored as we took turns holding the stick of frogs over the flames. As soon as their skins began to sizzle, we sat down in the grass to eat them frogs.

"What's your name?" he said, and it was the first thing either of us said since we started hunting together.

"Ingram," I told him.

"Hm," said the man with the white hair as he crunched through the bone of a frog leg. "How'd you get your arm broke?"

"Big storm came. The sky twisted up into a black tree of wind that caught me up, shook me around, and then threw me back down where it'd got me from."

"Dang," he said, "you got caught up in a tornado."

"Tornado?"

"Can't be but ten people in history ever got sucked into a tornado and lived to tell the tale. I'd call you a liar if I hadn't seen that storm myself from a distance and if you didn't have the busted arm to prove it."

"It happened," I said.

"I believe you," he said. "Gonna need to splint that arm, boy. The bones are cutting it up inside. It'll never heal without some help."

"How do I do that?" I asked him.

"I seen it done once," said the man.

"Where?" I asked.

"Prison," he said.

"I heard of prison," I said.

"Yeah? What'd you hear about it?"

"My father's brother, named Bert," I told him. "I heard him tell about a man who stuck a knife in someone and went to prison. He said it's a place where once they put you in, you can't never leave."

"I did," he said, commencing to chew his frog again. "Took a shovel to a bull's head and run off. I'm wearing his jacket."

"How come they put you in prison?" I asked him.

"For doing about the same thing to a cop on the outside," he said, and he chucked a frog bone into the pond. "Well, come over here. Let's set that arm."

I had finished the frog I was eating so I came over and stood next to where he sat. The man searched through the pile of sticks I'd gathered and put two of them against my hurting arm, saying, "Yep. These ought to do. Now, let's get the sleeve off that shirt." And he took a big knife out of his jacket pocket, unfolded it, and cut away at the sleeve of the bad arm. I wasn't concerned about this man hurting me and I didn't see a reason to stop him from cutting up my shirt. I just stood there and watched him rip my sleeve into strips. "Come over here, Ingram," he said. "Sit with your back against my chest." I did what he said and he folded his legs over mine, crossed his arm in front of mine, and with both hands he took gentle hold of my hurting arm. I could feel the warmth of his strong body firmly holding me against him. I was letting him do what he liked.

"This is gonna hurt like hell," he said.

"I thought you were gonna fix it," I said, looking up at his chin above my head.

"Sometimes fixing hurts," he said. I just nodded. He locked his legs around my waist, held his elbow hard against my chest, and all at once he squeezed hard around my arm and twisted it. I heard a crack and like a lamp being switched off and my mind went blank.

The next time I opened my eyes, it was morning. I knew I was sleeping in the grass but I felt like I was in a bed because I was covered on top by the man's leather jacket. I sat up and found that my hurting arm was tied up between the two sticks so I couldn't bend it. It felt snug and had less pain. I heard splashing and looked around till I saw the man on the edge of the pond washing himself. I propped myself up on my good arm and watched him bathe. I had never seen a whole naked person before. His skin was white as the moon, like the white of his hair. As he stood in the grass, shaking off the pond water, I looked between his legs and saw his spigot, which is what my mother used to call it. "Don't forget to wash your spigot," she would tell me when I bathed in the pond behind our house. This man's spigot was long and dangling, closer to the size of a horse than a man's. He put on his pants and two-colored shoes and took his leather coat off of me and put it on himself.

"I'm gonna set out," he said.

"Where?" I asked.

"Can't stay here. Good luck to ya." He started walking away.

"Can I go with you?" I asked. He stopped and turned around. He looked surprised that I asked him, and I was just as surprised that I asked. I had been told to go, or been left behind, by my father, my mother, the mountain, Pa, and Jackson. I had never thought to ask someone if I could stick with them. It seemed just like my mouth opened and did the asking, without asking me first.

"Well now," the man said, coming back and hunkering down on his haunches beside me as I propped up on my elbow. "Like I told you, I'm a wanted man. You understand? I'm a criminal. Lifelong. Just like my daddy."

"Why are you a criminal?" I asked.

He pulled out a handful of grass, looking at it as he continued. "I reckon you gotta be something. But let me tell you, if you're gonna go with crime, you can't do nothing else. There's fellows who try to live honest and do just a crime now and again to get an inch ahead. They end up getting squashed between two worlds. Not me. I never earned an honest dollar in my life. Nothing I got is rightfully mine except I took it. These shoes and pants are prison issue. Stole them when I busted out. This hat is the only thing I got that was ever given me, fair and square."

"Who give that to you?"

"My daddy," he said, and he smiled wide. "He was the world champion thief and bad man. House robber by specialty. Up in Canada, he stole us a whole house outside of Toronto."

"He stole a house?"

"Stole it. Stole my mama too, from another man. My daddy would go off nights, prowl the big fancy houses in town and he'd come home with silver and gold, clocks and china. He'd give my mama all the fanciest things and the rest he'd sell off for all we needed. He was a great man." The man took off his black round hat, turning it in circles in one hand while smoothing the velvet of it with the other. I liked listening to this man and hearing about his life. It made me not care where I would be going next or where I'd find to sleep that night. "Had me a brother once," he said as he shifted off his heels and sat down beside me. "He was my half-brother."

"How can someone be only half a brother?" I asked.

"Well now, his mother was my mother, but he had a different daddy, a rich man who my daddy was robbing one night when mama got up in the night to feed her child and walked in on him putting all her house valuables into a sack. She's standing there looking at him, holding my brother who was a baby. And she's scared as hell. But she didn't holler or run or nothing. Because she didn't want to disturb her baby boy. Well now, my daddy saw this all at once and said to himself, 'That's the kind of woman I want raising my children.' So he stuck a gun in Mama's face and put her in his truck, baby and all."

"He took your mama from her house?"

"He damned did!" he said, slapping his hand down on his knee. "Took her at gunpoint. That was up in Alaska, where Daddy was born. He took her for himself and he run off southerly, robbing his way down to Toronto where he stole her a house and dedicated his life to setting her up the way she was properly accustomed. She had me by him, and then we were a family."

"Why aren't you still there?" I asked.

"Well, sir," he said, running his hand through his white hair, "the thiefing life has its qualities. You do what you please, you take what you want. But it's short-lived. My daddy got walked in on again, this time by a man with a gun, who shot my daddy right in the back as he rummaged his drawers. We went to see him in the hospital. Mama was crying. My brother'd been dead already. I was sixteen. Daddy told Mama go back to Alaska, tell her husband she'd been his prisoner, and recommence her former life. And he told me, 'Go on south. You're an American by birthright.' And he give me this hat and made me promise never to be a thief like he was."

"Did you promise your daddy?"

"I did. He give me this hat and said, 'Boy, go to America. And promise me you won't be no thief.' And I looked in his eye and said, 'I promise, Daddy. I never ever will steal a thing in my life.' And he died with a smile on his wicked face. Because he knew he'd raised me right. To be as good at lying as I am at stealing!" And he laughed at his story, a big laugh that filled up the air around us.

"Let's get goin'," said the man with white hair as he hopped up and took my good hand, pulling me to my feet beside himself.

It was funny to walk beside a man and have his eyes nearly the same height off the ground as mine. "What's your name?" I asked. The man with the white hair laughed, stopped walking, and turned to face me.

"Well, I left my name a while back when it got no good for telling. Tell you what, Ingram. You can call me Bull, after the frogs we ate at dinner." He put his hand out and I shook it. "Good to meet you, Ingram."

"Good to meet you, Bull," I said.

We didn't say much for a while. Then Bull took out something funny from his pocket. It looked like a fat coin. When he pushed a button on its side, it popped open, and he looked down into it while peering around us, his mind working.

"What's that, Bull?" I asked. I liked using his name, which he had made for himself just for me.

"This is a compass. It tells you which way you're walking."

"How does it tell?"

"Look here at the needle. See, it's pointing north. I'm looking for us to go south by southwest until we find the road that heads to the Gulf of

Mexico." He clicked his compass closed and we walked some more. Sure enough, we found a road, and alongside of it was a low building with a lit-up sign outside.

"What say we go in that diner and get us a couple of burgers?"

"What's a burger?" I said.

"Ingram," said Bull, putting his hand on my shoulder, "you're about to make a great discovery."

Chapter Fourteen

Bull's Run

Bull showed me how to order food from a waitress and how they come and bring it right to you with a smile. We had two burgers, which were sizzling, watering, piping-hot clumps of mashed-up meat set between two pieces of fluffed white bread, the top one having a brown, round, smooth top like the top of Bull's black hat. On top of the burger were pieces of tart vegetable called pickles and cheese that got all gooey from sitting on the hot burger.

"Love a damn burger," said Bull, as he smelled the one on his plate. "World might be going to hell in a hot car. But at least we got meat back in it."

"Amen, brother," said a man sitting on Bull's other side. He was wearing a hat that looked like it was made of metal. "I was about ready to pick up a gun and go to town when they outlawed the meat."

"Shut up, man," said Bull. "I wasn't talking to you." And the man went back to eating his stew. Bull turned to me and smiled. He reminded me of Tab, back at the hospital, the way he could be unfriendly to one person one minute and friendly to me the next. "Eat your burger, Ingram."

"How?" I asked.

“Just pick up the whole damn mess like this,” he said.

I did like Bull did, picked up my burger in its bun and bit into the side and I could taste all the wonderful things, the bread, the cheese, the pickle, and the meat, all at one time.

“How about a Coke for your little brother?” the waitress asked Bull.

“If you’re buyin’,” said Bull, and he shut his one eye and opened it, which made the waitress smile and turn a red color as she put a tall glass that looked like a tulip under a spigot which she pulled on to make black water come out of it into the glass which she put in front of me with a piece of plastic next to it.

“This water’s all dirty,” I said to Bull.

“Dirty?” the waitress said, confused.

“Marion, you’re about to serve my brother his first Coca-Cola,” said Bull. He had asked her name as soon as we sat down at the counter, which was like a bar but for food instead of whiskey. He had a way of talking to her, kind of like how he talked to me—friendly and knowing you right away.

“He ain’t never had a Coke?” said Marion.

“He ain’t never even drank with a straw,” said Bull.

Marion’s eyes and mouth all opened wide and she looked at me. “My, my. These country boys are sure shut-in. You don’t know how to use a straw, kid?”

“No, ma’am,” I said.

“Why don’t you show him how it’s done, Marion?” said Bull.

Marion’s face turned red again and she looked at him like he made her mad, but then she smiled and she picked up the little piece of plastic and held it between her fingers, which had long fingernails like tiny knives painted red like the side of a car. She put the long piece of plastic he called a straw up to her lips, which were painted the same shiny red as her nails. Then she bent down and put the other end of the straw into my glass, put her lips around the straw and sucked that dirty water up into her mouth. Then she tipped the straw toward Bull and said, “You have some.”

And Bull bent over and both their faces were right in front of me and they were staring into each other's eyes with a sort of frozen excitement. Bull took the straw in his mouth and sucked in all the dirty water until there was a slurp sound at the bottom of the empty tulip glass, which made him and Marion laugh, their faces still so close together and so close to mine, I could smell their laughter.

"Hey, get to work," said a sharp, angry voice from behind the counter. Marion went to some other people to ask what food they wanted and Bull and I went back to eating our burgers. Later, she came back over and put another Coke and straw in front of me, and Bull said to her quietly, "My little brother and I need a place to kip tonight. Any ideas?"

"I might could," said Marion. She was wiping the counter and talking in a way where her mouth almost didn't move. "I live in the motel behind. I cop the room next door."

"Sounds fine," said Bull, in the same quiet talk, which he was hiding with his hands. She looked at him in a still and careful way like she was trying to decide and then she said, "What's your name?"

"Bull," he said, and she showed him all her teeth.

"Meet me outside at nine thirty. The Cokes and burgers are on me," Marion said, and shuffled away, pouring coffee for folks. Bull's big smile and bright eyes faded back to normal. He leaned into to me and said in a secret voice, "See that? Free meal. Free beds. That's something you'll learn down the line, Ingram. You make an ugly girl feel pretty, there's not a thing she won't do for you."

"Ugly?" I asked.

"Her face, brother. Just look at that face." I looked at her face. It was longer from forehead to chin than some others. Her nose was thin and long in a way that sort of fit the shape of the face it sat in. Her eyebrows were thick and came together in the middle in sort of a knot. Her lips were red and kind of juicy and thick. They stuck out front like she was always making an "ooo" sound. On one of her cheeks, sort of up by her eye, she had three dark red spots and also one right under her mouth, before her long chin started. What stood out the most about the waitress's face was her eyes, which were a green color that didn't seem human. They were bright like grass, but not natural. I liked looking at her face. Every part of it was interesting.

"Drink your Coke. You'll love it," said Bull. He put the straw into my glass and slid it to me. I took a sip through the straw like they had and I couldn't believe what flooded into my mouth. It was a cold, sparkling, sweet water that tickled the inside of my mouth like lemonade that got hit by lightning. The Coke went down my throat, waking up my belly. It was a shock like whiskey, but instead of putting you to sleep inside it woke you up. I closed my eyes and kept sucking through that straw and gulping down that good, good Coke until the slurping sound came, waking me out of my joy. Bull laughed at the sound, like he had with Marion. I laughed at the sound with him, like she had. I learned, and never forgot after, that laughing at the slurping was part of enjoying a Coke.

Bull and I hung around in the weeds behind the diner after our supper and waited for night. As different types of trucks pulled up to the pumps by the diner, he told me how they were there to gas up and he told me about *fuel* going in the *engine* and being sparked at so it can explode like pops of fire in little metal boxes that push off the pistons, which then turn a cam shaft, which turns a drive shaft, turning a differential, which turns the wheels. He drew little pictures in the dirt with a stick showing me how it all worked and I couldn't get it all in my mind, but I listened as close as I could and I started to get a sense of it.

"You smell that fuel?" he said, as a truck was filling up close by, and he breathed in deep through his nose, waving to me to do the same, which I did. "That's diesel. Diesel is thicker like a syrup and it burns slow. They use that for trucks and big ships in the ocean. Cars use gasoline, which is pink and slick and pops real quick. A truck or a ship, they want to carry far as possible. While a man in a car wants to put his pedal down and go, go, go, baby."

Just then there was a loud, low growling sound behind me. I turned around and saw the biggest truck of my life. Instead of a box in the back, this truck was carrying what looked like a long shiny tin can, laying lengthwise across eight wheels behind the truck's head.

"What kind of truck is that?" I asked.

"That's a tanker," Bull said.

As the tanker slowed down to pull up to the pumps, it made a sound like wheezing wind, which Bull said were the air brakes. "Takes as much work to stop a tanker like that as it does to move it. And when it's time to stop it needs to stop, boy. He's hauling about ten tons of pure octane gasoline. If he wrecks, it's boom coyote! Goodnight and good luck!" Bull laughed as he tore a tuft of grass and dirt next to where he was laying and flicked it into the air, to resemble a great explosion.

"Why would that happen?"

"Cuz it's full of fuel, boy. That tanker come up from the oil fields in the Gulf of Mexico. That's what I come here to find. You ride one of them back where it came from and you'll find where all the money in the world is. Which means rich folks. Which means big houses full of what to steal."

We stayed quiet, watching the business of the pumps and the diner till it got dark. Then the lights went out in the windows of the diner. The folks eating and working there all got into cars and drove off, and then Marion come out and Bull shot up onto his feet and said, "Come on."

Marion took us to where she lived, a place behind the diner they called a motel.

"I got two rooms put together," she said as she opened the door, which was bright red, and let us in a room that had a big bed in the middle and another door inside that led to another room with a bed. "Your little brother can be in there," she said.

"That okay with you, little brother?" asked Bull. I said okay and went in the other room. They shut the door behind me and I laid on the bed, which bounced up and down under me and made a squeaking noise. I sort of lifted myself up and dropped myself down a few times to feel the bounce and hear the squeak again. Bull and Marion were talking but I didn't know what they were saying. Bull would say something and then she would laugh, and I heard their bed squeak and then squeak again, and she was making a sound like she was being slowly slaughtered, and I remembered when my mother and father made sounds like hurting each other as they lay in bed at night and soon I heard Marion moan long and low and then it was quiet.

I laid there for I don't know how long before Bull came into my room, closing the door behind him. He had the spread from their bed wrapped all around him and he sat on the bed beside me looking tired.

"Are you married to her now, Bull?" I asked him.

"What?" he said with a laugh. "Aw, hell no, Ingram. All we did was screw." He looked down at me and said, "You know anything about that, Ingram? Sex?"

"I seen animals do it," I said.

"Then you know most of it," he said. "Except a woman, unlike a cow, when you fuck her, she don't never forget it." I laid there and listened to Bull as he went on. "Look, here. You're too young to do it just yet, but it'll happen before you're old enough. Nobody gets it right on time. You know what you call that thing between your legs?"

"You mean my spigot?"

"Spigot, huh?" He laughed. "Yeah, sure. Your spigot. Well, between her legs, a woman got a mouth. You lay on top of her and you ease your spigot in there."

"In her mouth?" That sounded crazy to me. "Won't she bite it?"

"Well, that's the trick, see? You gotta ease in there, pull out, ease back in—you gotta trick and tease her till she loses her right mind and then get out before she knew you were ever there. Otherwise she will eat your life." Bull was looking out the window as he talked and all of a sudden his face got a worried expression. And he said, "Aw, shit."

Just then, some blue flashing lights started glancing off his skin and flashing on the ceiling above him. I heard car doors opening and closing and men talking. Bull reached over and closed the curtains as Marion came in the room. "Bull?" She sounded scared.

"Listen up, honey," Bull said. "They're gonna get me now, but it's a short rap. Six months at the top. Will you wait for me?"

"'Course I'll wait for you, Bull," said Marion.

"Good girl. Now listen, take my little brother and clear out of here tomorrow. I'll run round the back and take them on a chase."

"Bull, why don't you just give up?" She worried, "If you run, they'll shoot you."

"Aw, naw," said Bull. "They don't like when you surrender. Takes the fun out the chase for 'em." As Bull talked fast, he was hopping from this room to that, getting his clothes and pulling them on. "I'll take them on a little run and make them feel some pride in their work. You wait till morning and go south. Look for a job in another diner right on this highway, wait there with my brother. Tell everyone you're his ma. I'll come join both of you right quick and then we'll find a place to all be together. How's that sound, honey?"

"Yes, Bull. I'd like that," Marion said. She was smiling.

"Okay. Go in your room and start packing for morning so I can talk to my brother a little bit," he said.

"Okay, Bull," said Marion and she went in the other room.

"Is it true, Bull?" I asked. "Are we going to live together like a family?"

"Hell no, Ingram. That's just a fable I told Marion. Women need fables. The truth to a woman is like poison. They spit it out. But they never get enough of bullshit. They live for it."

"I'm not going to see you again," I told Bull.

"Nope," Bull said back. And we looked at each other. I didn't like that I wouldn't be seeing him again. And I don't think he did either. But it was just true. Just like a tornado is true. Or a dead frog on a stick being cooked and eaten.

Bull handed me his leather jacket. "Take this, Ingram. Should fit you as good as me. They'll give me a whole new suit of clothes where I'm going."

He laughed. "The only thing I keep is my hat." He smiled big and put his round black hat on his head. He looked funny just in his pants and hat. "Now listen to me. You stay with Marion and let her take care of you, which she will with her head full of all that bullshit. You stay with her till your arm gets healed. When you're healthy, leave her while she's sleeping and jump on a tanker truck like we talked about. And you ride that tanker back to the oil fields. But don't do no stealing there. You're no criminal. You get yourself a job. Plenty of jobs down there."

Bull went to the door and opened it, then turned and said to me, "So long, brother." And he ran out the door and shut it.

I heard a man yell, "Hey there!" I peeked through the curtains. I saw Bull running past a car with the blue flashing lights on top of it and I saw men chasing after him.

I heard Marion yell, "Oh my god!" from the next room, and I knew she must be watching from her window. Bull ran this way and that as the men dashed after him, yelling and hollering. He looked just like his name—a naked, hairless white bull with a round black head, up on his hind legs dashing and darting till finally Bull was stopped by one great big fellow wearing a blue suit and hat, like the man in Houston who'd made me quit sitting on the curb. And this man had a hand torch that was long and black and he brought it down on Bull's head so hard I could hear through the window and across the distance that it hit him like a hammer on a fence post. Bull's hat toppled off as he fell to the ground. He looked dead. They grabbed him by the arms and pushed him into the back of the car with the blue lights and drove off. I heard Marion crying.

Chapter Fifteen

Reading and Writing

I slept that night on the floor of the motel room, the bed being too bouncy to settle on. I got woken by the waitress, Marion, with a plate of eggs and sausage and bread smeared with butter and a cup of coffee, which she had carried from the diner where she'd gone to work while I was sleeping. Marion told me to come to her room, which I did. Her clothes were laid all around the room. They were all soft and colors like pink and light yellow. There was a light blue kind of dress or shirt laying across her bed, looked like foam or like soapsuds. I sat at a small table to eat what she brought. She watched me eat, meanwhile smoking a long cigarette which was colored red on the tip of it from the paint on her lips.

"What you gonna do now?" she said to me. "Who's gonna take care of you? Your big brother is gone."

I used my tongue to push the toast and sausage to the side of my mouth and said, "He wasn't my brother."

"'Course he wasn't." Marion laughed. She watched me eat a little longer and then stamped out her cigarette, getting up and saying, "Well, what you gonna do?"

"Bull said stay here till my arm is healed," I told her. "He said then to leave you while you're sleeping and catch a tanker truck to the gulf coast to work the oil fields." Marion looked down at me, hands on her hips, then suddenly she looked up at the ceiling and laughed.

"Oh that man was a beautiful bastard," she said. "Well, you can't stay here without some rent, honey." I didn't answer, not knowing what she said. She went on, "Lookit. I get this room for myself for working at the diner. That's my deal, see? You get things for doing. I work, I get a salary, which is hardly better than shit. But I also get this room which means I get to keep what I earn, so I can someday go where I want to go."

"Where do you want to go?" I asked.

"That ain't any of your business." She pointed at me with one of the little red knives on the end of her fingers. "Your business, for the time being, is that you can't stay in that room. I had to pay money for that room next door. Regular rate. Which I gladly did to stow you aside, so Bull and I could have some fun. For one night. What I won't gladly do is pay for it ongoing so you can live there doing nothing for no reason. I'm guessing you have no money."

I reached in my pocket and put my few dimes I had left onto the floor by her bed. Marion looked down and said, "Oh brother. How much you got there?"

"I don't know," I said. "Can't count more than ten."

"Aw, hell," said Marion, and she squatted down and picked up every dime I had left and poured them into the front of her waitressing apron. "Okay," she said, her arms folded and her eyebrows folded almost just the same. "You can stay in the room till your damn arm heals. But don't ask me for nothing else." As she left, she took my plate, which still had on it some eggs. I learned after that to eat quick when Marion brought me food, which she did every day, on her short breaks, twice a day, breakfast and supper. Breakfast was always eggs and toast, sometimes sausage, sometimes bacon, which I liked. Dinner was different every night. Meat loaf, hamburger, and something called a pork chop.

I had new people to look at every day—different kinds of faces and clothes, different-sounding voices, some wearing hats of shiny metal and bright colors, like the man who Bull told to shut up in the diner had worn. And there were cars of many colors and shapes. One time I saw a tiny car that was fast and loud with no roof on it. Everybody who happened to be around watched the man in the tiny car as he filled it up with gas.

The only thing that came regularly were the giant, shining, tin-can trucks that went and came in both directions each day. I knew one day I'd jump on the back of one and go to work in the oil fields like Bull said. I tried to picture in my mind what a field of oil looked like and what I'd do working there. I wondered if the oil would be laying on the ground like a swamp and if we'd scoop it out with buckets or maybe with something like a straw. Each day I'd practice lifting my arm up and down, feeling the pain get lesser and lesser. I knew that one day, as Marion told me, I'd take off the splint and my arm would work as good as ever.

"You're a damn boy," she said. "You can always fix a boy. Good as new." She would shake her head when she said it like it was a shame. "You can't break a boy except you kill him. Your arm will be fine. You will be fine." And she'd take my plate away and go back to work.

At night, Marion would come into my room for a while before going to bed in her own. We didn't talk much. Often, she read a book she had, with a picture on the cover of a man with a torn shirt grabbing onto a woman with few clothes on. Marion said things to the book like, "Oh my. What in hell?" And I'd just lay on my bed on my good side and watch her read. Then one night she came home and threw a book on the bed beside me, saying, "Here. Tired of you staring at me. Have yer own."

I picked up the book. It had a picture on the front like hers but it was a man sitting on a horse with a shotgun across his lap. I opened it up and on the inside was just words up and down each paper, paper after paper. I flipped from the front to the back and then I just looked at the cover again, at the face of the man. He looked brave and ready to fight. His horse had a face almost like a person. "Oh, lord." Marion said. She always sounded mad at me. "You white trash. You don't even know how to read, do you?"

I looked at her plainly and said, "No, ma'am."

"Don't know when you're being insulted either," she said. "Goddamn country going to hell with illiterate hungry children running around like rats." She came over to my bed and sat beside me, yanking the book out of my hands and looking at the words on the cover. She said, "Mighty Mike. Showdown in Silverado." Then she opened the book and read out loud.

"Mighty Mike was a cowboy from Texas. He had a horse who he named Hector, after a great Greek hee-ro he'd heard of in a thee-ater show back in aboleen." Then she looked at me, all angry, and said, "Well I can't read my book if I'm reading yours. Lookit. Come here." And she pulled me closer to her so we could both see the paper inside the book. She pointed at the first words on the first paper with her long red fingernail and slowly said, "Miiighty Miiike" as she ran her finger across the words. "You see that? Miiiighty Mike. They both start with an M and an I. See that? M? It goes up down, up down." And she made a motion in the air in front of my eyes with her finger going up, then down, up then down and then she pointed again at the words on the paper and said, "Look. Look right there. See?" I bent my head in close so that her hair was hanging on the side of my cheek and I looked where her red nail was perched on the paper and right above it was an M. Up down, up down. And she said, "There. That's an M. It makes this sound like 'mmmm.' I mean you know this sound. You talk. You know words. All this is is like pictures of talking. See? Mmmmmiiii. That's an I. And a K and an E spells MMMiiiike."

As she took me from one letter to the next, I felt my brain hurt like it was boiling on a stove. I put my hand over my eyes and groaned. "I guess Mike is enough for today." Marion laughed.

The next morning when she came with breakfast, Marion brought a little pad of paper and a pencil. "The rookie waitresses use this to write down their orders," she told me. "I never needed it myself. I remember what folks tell me. You know why? Because I listen. I take notice. I don't mind telling you I have a good brain. Not that it's done me any good. I'm stuck in this place. But at least I know why!" She laughed, and then stopped laughing when I didn't. And then she chucked the pad and pencil down in front of me.

"Here. You can use it to learn how to write. You'll learn a whole lot quicker how to read words if you learn how to make them." And she sat me down at our eating table and she stood above me, leaning over my head and shoulder, and she used the pencil to make the lines. "Up down, up down. See? That's an M? Remember?" I looked down and saw it was an M just like in the book. "Then we make an I, which is easy. See? I, easy as pie." She made all the letters till it said MIKE. Then she put the pencil on the table in front of me and said, "Now you do it."

"Do what?" I said, looking down at the little pencil.

"Write."

"But I can't write," I said.

"God sakes, kid. You need to know how to read and write, or you'll end up a dirt boy your whole damn life." She was almost yelling, mad at me. "You want to end up dead in a parking lot like Bull? I guarantee you that man couldn't read, write, count, or nothing else. That's how he ended up a criminal. How he ended up dead."

"Bull was a criminal because his daddy was. He was proud to be a thief," I told her.

"That's a load of shit," she said, bending down and looking in my face. "Ain't nobody a criminal except they can't do otherwise."

"I thought you liked Bull."

"Yeah, I liked him. I'm a grown woman. I can like who I like."

"Bull said women need fables. That you need to feed them bullshit."

"Well. He ain't wrong," she laughed. "We women do enjoy a man's bullshit. Especially when they make it pretty like he did." Then she pointed at my face. "But we don't believe it. It's men who need to believe their own bullshit. And because we love them, we let them. But only a woman will ever tell you the truth, Ingram. Because the truth is what we get stuck with, like I got here in this nowhere place. And like I got stuck with you! Now pick up that pencil and write."

"But I can't write, Marion." I was afraid to pick it up, which was funny to be afraid of a little piece of wood. But I was.

"You can't YET. You need to LEARN. Didn't you never learn nothing?" I thought for a minute, and mad as she was, she stood there, hunched over, looking in my face, patient, waiting for me to think about it. So I did.

"Yes," I said. "I learned how to pull up corn."

"Good enough," she said and she picked up the pencil. "Now you're left-handed or right?" I looked at her, not understanding. She said, "Well, you only got one good wing anyway, so I guess that makes you a righty." And she put the pencil in my free hand, took it inside of her hand and together we put the pencil tip on the paper. Her fingers were cool and skinny against the backs of mine and she made them hug down onto the wood of the pencil and underneath her MIKE she guided my hand, saying, "Up down, up down, I easy as pie, down across and kick over for K, and then E all the way." And like that she wrote MIKE with both our hands and the pencil. "There. Now you do it on your own."

Without her hand on mine, I found my grip on the pencil to be uneven and wobbly as I tried to go up down, up down, and my M came out just all shaky lines. I felt embarrassed but she said, "Not bad, Ingram. Not a bad start. You keep going. I gotta go get back to work."

Marion left the room—leaving me alone with the pad and pencil. I practiced making the letter M till I could make it better and better, and then easy and quick and it gave me no head pain. The letter called I was sure easy, and I actually enjoyed the way that K was a little tougher with the up, over, kick it out of the pencil.

After that I spent my days trying to write words I saw around the motel, on the sides of trucks. There was barely a place in the world that didn't have writing on it. I copied the shapes of the letters into my waitress pad, and at night, Marion helped me read them in my own hand.

"Caution. Toxic materials. Breakfast lunch and dinner. Ice cream and pie. This area reserved for people of color. No beer on Sundays or breakfast." I got to where I could do one word of it at a time, easy words like PIE and IN or NO. It was harder to read a whole sign like "DO . . . NOT . . . FLUSH . . . TAMPONS OR . . . G . . . G . . ."

"Generative products!" shouted Marion from the next room.

When I tried to read my book, the words were so tiny and there were so many that it was too hard to even read one. I'd run my finger under the first word, and try to say it out loud. "Mi. Mig . . . Mighhh."

"Goddamn to hell, kid," Marion yelled one night. "Bring your book in here." I went in her room to find her laying on her side in bed. She was wearing the light blue soapsuds-looking dress. Marion opened the covers and scooted back, saying, "Get on in here and I'll help you get started."

I got into her bed sideways facing out the same way as she was. The bed was so warm inside from her body that it was like I was cheese slipping into hot toast to melt it. "Don't get any ideas, neither," she said, and she put her arm over me and took my book, holding it in front of my face the way I might hold it for myself. "Now I'll read a part out loud while you follow with your eyes. Then you read a part. Okay?" She put her fingernail, which on this day was painted white, under the first word, and traced along as she read, "Mighty Mike was a cowboy from Texas. He had a horse named Hector, after a great Greek hero he'd heard of in a thee-ater show back in aboleen."

"What's a Greek hero?" I asked. And I was about to ask what "thee-ator" and "aboleen" meant, but she smacked the side of my head like she sometimes would, and said, "Now you can't be asking questions. The point ain't to know everything about what's in here. The point is learning to read." She went back to reading: "Mighty Mike and Hector traveled the trails of Texas from town to town, looking for adventure, work, or trouble, whichever came easiest. For he was a cowboy by nature and never knew anything else." She stopped reading and said, "Now you go. Start here." Marion tapped her finger under a word and did me the favor of tracing along as I slowly read . . .

"Mike always c. Caaaarried a pic. Picct."

"Picture," she finished it for me. "A picture of Angeline."

"Angeline," I went on reading. "She was his O. ON."

"His one true love and he had promised someday to return to her where she did live in Abilene, home of the toughest men and the softest women in Texas." I looked up and back at Marion's face and said, "Where you think Mighty Mike is now?"

"He's not real, dummy," she said. "It's fiction."

"Fiction?"

"Yeah, dummy. It's made up."

"Why?"

"For the fun of reading is why. Look, nobody is named Mighty Mike. It's a name they made up cuz it's fun to say. Mighty Mike. Hector Horse. See? Traveled the trails from town to town? See how they make it sound like singing almost? It's nice. Puts a little sugar in your mind."

"Who made it up?" I asked.

"The author. Look, Ingram, I can't explain the world to you tonight. I need some sleep."

"I won't ask questions, Marion. Can you just read with me a little more?"

"Okay, I'll pick up where you stopped." And she dug into the bed a bit more, pulling me down and in, a little closer to the front of her warm body, and went back to reading. "On one occasion, Mighty Mike was working on a ranch, wrangling and branding a herd for a rich rancher named Robert M. Montgomery Jones of Wichita Falls." The next thing I knew she was bringing my breakfast. I'd fallen asleep in her bed.

Every night Marion and I read together like grilled cheese as I would fall asleep in her bed. In the daytime, while she worked, I stopped setting in the dirt and watching the cars. Instead I sat at the table in my room and read about Mighty Mike and I copied the words down on the pad of paper, writing as small as I could because Marion said, "I can't keep stealing those for you." And sometimes she added a reminder that, "You can't keep staying here either. Your dimes ran out long ago, and I'm not the department of child sanitation." I started writing in the pads with much smaller letters so that I would need less paper, since she was saying I might not get more pads.

I liked reading the words I had copied more than reading the book. I would pick a paper from the middle of the pad and read what was there. It didn't matter the order I was reading in. "'Draw your pistol,' said Mighty Mike, 'and see how long you live to tell the tale.'" I read my own words aloud: "Red Jerry stood with his hand hovering over his pearly white pistol but it was shaking with fear, for Mighty Mike was known in Texas all over, for his speed and ice-cold nerves."

Marion was right that the words and how they were put together put a little sugar in my mind. I tried not to read out loud too much when she was around because I liked when Marion read out loud to me and I didn't want her to know that I could do it myself.

I liked the way things felt living in that motel with Marion, eating meals with her, listening to her talk. She would tell me things about her life and how she got herself "educated" hoping it would take her someplace better.

"My momma raised me and my two brothers on her own spit and muscle. She worked in a convalescent home, cleaning and feeding and caring for dying men. It was a bitter job and it made her a bitter woman. She would tell me and the boys that life was all divided up into the rich and the damned and that the only way to cross the mountain in between was *educootion*. Ha. That's what she called it from her side of the mountain. My father had drunk himself to death and both my brothers followed right behind him with those new chemicals. Sucking every man in town down into the grave like a great hoover. That left me to go to school and I believed what she said. That if I got myself smart I could change my life. Turned out to be a load of bullshit. She died herself from something she caught from the men she was caring for. I was only eighteen. I wish she had taken the little time she had to teach me the truth, that the only hope a woman has in this world is to find a man that drinks a little less than the others and hitch on to him and ride him as far as you can go. All I got out of my *educootion* was that I love reading. And I will say, that ain't nothing."

At some point, Marion would quit remembering and telling and she'd look at me listening and say, "You don't want to hear all this." But I did. It was something about hearing someone else's life that made me forget my own. It was a comfort.

My arm had started healing better and better and I wondered if that meant I'd have to leave, like Bull said. But I remembered that Marion had said Bull was a criminal and a liar and how men need to believe their fables and their bullshit, which I knew meant lies. I thought about all these words that meant the same thing. Fables, bullshit, lies. Fiction. Things that weren't real. What Marion said men "need" to believe, or what she said puts "sugar" in your mind. Then there were other words that come together like what Jackson at the farm called reality and Marion called the truth. What you get stuck with. The way things are and can't be avoided and are too much to look at. The way they talked, everything that was real was bad and sad. Everything that a person could want was fables and bullshit. I wanted to stay there living with Marion. That was a fable. Which meant I would have to face the truth—that she was not my mother and I didn't have any money to pay for the room next to hers and neither did she if she was going to save enough money to move out herself. Sure enough, and too soon, I was right.

"Look, Ingram. You need to go," said Marion one day. "I met a fellah and he's coming over tonight. And, if my stars are lining up, he might be interested. But he ain't gonna be if he thinks I have a kid. You understand?"

"Okay, Marion," I said. I didn't understand about the *fellah*, but my part in it seemed simple to me.

Marion looked at me and suddenly got mad. "Well, what do you expect me to do? I'm not your mama. Go get one someplace else." It didn't bother me that Marion was yelling like she was mad. That's how she talked to me all the time, and all the time she did nice things for me, like taking the splint off my arm and showing me how to move it around easy so it would heal right. I didn't mind that she was making me leave, either. I didn't figure I could stay there forever any more than I ever thought I could stay forever anyplace else. It was reality and there was nothing I could do to change it.

Part Three

Chapter Sixteen

Oil Truck

"Where are you headed?" said the driver of the silver can truck who let me into his cab and took me south, which I knew was south because of the compass Bull had left in his jacket, which had belonged to a prison guard, which was now mine. The driver picked me up because I was hitchhiking, which I'd been taught to do by Marion.

"Walk backwards with your arm way out and your thumb pointing the way you want to go," she said into the mirror, as she cut my hair down to shorter than I ever had had it. "You got to be presentable, Ingram," she said as she yanked tufts of my hair up tight between her fingers and snipped it away. "You walk around looking like a mop and nobody will want nothing to do with you. Now your arm is all healed, and you can read and write better than some folks, you need to look like you live indoors."

"I'm headed to the oil fields," I told the driver. "Are you going there?"

"Where else would I be going?" he said and pointed with his thick hairy finger to the seat beside him. I climbed up and shut myself into the truck with the heavy metal door. The driver worked the levers and pedals of his truck, pulling at the big wheel to turn it out into the road, and as we started moving, the roar and rumble of the machine made my whole body shake. "What's your name and where you from?" he asked me, looking straight forward. We both had to talk loud for the engine noise.

"My name is Ingram," I said. "I guess I'm from home."

"Where's home?" he asked without the sound of interest in his voice.

"I don't know what it's called besides home," I said.

"How far from here is it?"

"I don't rightly know except I walked for two days from it and then I was in Houston."

"Where's your folks?"

"My father's gone and my mother sent me away," I said.

Then there was some silence until the man said, "Well, keep telling."

"Telling, sir?"

"Lookit, son. I need someone to talk so I don't fall asleep and wreck this truck into the side of the road, or worse. So you talk, or you walk."

"Yes, sir," I said. I didn't want to walk.

"Your mother sent you away, and then what?"

I began telling that man everything that happened since I left home. His face showed no interest or concern and he made no comments. The only sign that he was listening was that if I paused, even for a moment to wet my lips, he would say, "Go on." And I did. Because it was good to be moving so fast in such a big loud machine, knowing I could soon be working the oil fields, something fixed in my mind as what I wanted.

I told that driver of walking on the road and falling in the ditch, waking up with a mouth full of bugs. I told him of the road rising up to fearful heights and how I was just as fearful to look up at that road from the darkness below it. I told him of the mountain and what he told me about the world being black people and white, to which the driver simply made the sound "huh" with his mouth curled up at one side only. I told him of swimming naked in the river and losing my clothes, my skin being scorched by the sludge from the pipe. I told him of waking up on the pavement and climbing the metal ladder and watching the men work below. I told him of being chased around the high wall and of the man who took me in his truck to the hospital. I told him of being sick and feverish and of the boys in the hospital who told me to run when the nurse got mad and I told him about cutting my foot in the busy streets of Houston. I told him of being hit by the black boy in the street and he said "huh" again and I told him of Miss Maw and Sinema and Pa taking me to the edge of Black Town and giving me the knife meant for his boy. I told about walking away from Pa . . . and it was then that I started to feel sad at the hearing of my own voice.

I leaned back in my seat, needing to rest my voice and mind for just a spell. I guess I started to drift off to sleep when suddenly the man stepped on a pedal and the truck made a sound like a groaning cow and I was thrown forward, my body chucked against the front of the cab, as he pulled the wheel to the side and then we were stopped. The engine rumbled low and the driver turned to me, only the side of his face lit by the light coming off the front of the cab and he said, "What I tell you, boy? If you're gonna shut up, you can get out. Talk or walk."

The sharp anger in his voice scared and alerted me. I didn't want to begin walking in the dark, so I sat up in my seat and said, "Yes, sir." He got that truck rolling again and I went on telling, about the tree I slept under, about waking up surrounded by men and the truck that took us to the farm and I told him about my time there working and how I learned to drink whiskey, which made him say "hah" like only one piece of laughter. I told him about the girl who came to stay in my cabin, but when I came to the part where she undressed I stopped in hesitation, to which he asked his first question in many hours. "Did you make it with that girl?"

"Make what, sir?" I asked.

"Never mind," he said, waving his hand at me. "Go on."

I told that driver all of my story, from leaving the farm to meeting Bull at the pond, Bull getting knocked on his head and how he gave me the jacket I was wearing and the compass in the pocket, and about Marion teaching me how to read and write and how my arm got mended and how I'd taken the splint off, ready to go to the oil fields to work and earn some money so I could someday buy my own truck.

"That's about it, sir," I said. I had told him everything that had happened to me to the moment I climbed in his truck. "I don't know what else to tell about."

"Tell about before you left home," he said. "Before your mama done sent you away."

So I started telling about life at home. It was a different kind of telling and remembering. Instead of going along a line, telling what happened and then what happened next, in the order that they happened, I just sort of wandered around my memory, picking and touching at this and that, here and there, as it came to my mind. I told him about the animals that I spent my days watching and how my father had said he didn't have enough money to begin a proper farm but raising a couple of pigs, hens, and whatnot could bring in a dollar here and there when they get beefed and slaughtered, with eggs and milk in the meantime. And I told about how the cows, with not enough to graze on, the grass on our land being dry and dusty, they had got skinny and died and laid on the ground till their insides blew up in the sun. I told about Anna Lee, how my mother had said to "look after her" and about walking around in the grass with Anna Lee and sitting on the porch. I told about her naming the chickens and I told about watching Anna Lee and her mother leave for the last time I saw them.

"What did she look like?" he asked. "Was she good looking?"

"What, sir?" I asked.

"Your mother's sister, dummy. What did she look like?"

"Well, she was a woman," I said.

"Never mind. Goddamn kid is all you are," he said, sounding grumpy. "Keep telling, now."

I told about having to stay outside of the house for most of my days and how I slept in the shed at night.

"Why was that?" asked the driver. "Why'd your folks make you sleep in the shed?"

"I don't know, sir," I said.

"Well, why do you think they did?" he asked.

As I searched in my mind for an answer to his question, it gave me an awful feeling. I felt stuck. There was something I didn't want to think or talk about, but I knew that if I couldn't keep up talking, I'd be put out on the road.

The driver said, "But why'd you have to sleep in the damn shed? That ain't normal for a child."

"I used to sleep upstairs in a bed," I said, remembering as I said it. "They kicked me out of there. Then I was in the shed from then on."

"Why?" the driver demanded. Wanting to do what he said so that he wouldn't stop, I tried to remember. But it was in a haze. I sort of walked to it, backwards, in my mind but I couldn't remember the events of it all. I could sort of tell what the feelings were.

"They were mad at me, I think," I said. "It was one morning when I woke up in bed. My mother was crying. Screaming. My father was hot mad. He grabbed me by the hair and dragged me out of bed, down the stairs, and threw me in the shed and slammed the door so hard it opened up again. I can remember that," I said.

"Why? What did you do? Shit in your bed?"

"No, sir," I said. I searched back for what happened right before that part. Then something happened to me in that truck, in that moment, which I struggle to this day to remember and describe. As I looked back, to right before my mother came in and discovered me in my bed, I remembered that I wasn't alone in that bed. There was something horrible. Like the gray creature. Or what the creature was before he became my greatest fear. Whatever it was, it was worse and more fearful than anything in all the world. It was so awful to think about that instead of remembering what it was, I took a deep breath, until I had no more room for air, and I held it, my throat shut tight so I couldn't breathe it out or breathe in. I grabbed the sides of the seat I sat in and I began shaking worse than the shaking from the engine.

"What the hell, boy?" said the driver. "What the hell's wrong with you?" All my muscles and joints were locked up like frozen or rusted tight. I couldn't stop shaking and my mind was like a white light inside and I couldn't let out that breath. I could feel myself suffocate and I could feel the truck lurch to the side of the road and stop again. The man took me by the shoulders and began shaking me. "Hey!" he yelled into my face. "Stop that! Hey!" He shook me and shook me and then let go with one hand, reared it back, and slapped me hard on my face. The sudden burn of his tough skin and the strike of his hand bones against my cheek pushed the air out of me and knocked the white light out of my head and now he was holding me up by the shoulders. I was soaking wet.

"Goddamn it," said the man. "You done pissed yourself. Get out my truck, boy. I can't have no invalid in my truck pissing on my seat. Get the hell out!" And he reached across me, popped open his door, and pushed me out onto the road. His silver truck roared off. I stood there on the dark road watching the two red lights on its back go away and away and away until I was alone and wet between my legs.

Chapter Seventeen

The Boy

More silver can trucks went roaring by as I walked, but I didn't stick my thumb out. I didn't want to have to tell any more of my story to anyone. I had no reckoning of how far away the oil fields were. I had an idea in my mind that working there would be a place I could stay long enough to grow up to a man. "You ain't ready to be a man yet anyhow," said the mountain's voice in my mind. I knew it was true. My body was still small. I had more muscles in my arms but they were nothing compared to the thick limbs of that driver or Bull or even Marion, though she was a woman and they are weaker. But I knew working the farm had brought me along and grown me up, and that learning to read had made me smarter. I knew pulling oil out of the ground would grow me up all the more.

I walked until I saw a sign on my side of the road. The sign was painted white with black letters but it was rusting and old-looking. It said "Tannersville."

The small road that curved off the highway stretched out between two long fields, stacked high with corn plants that were charred black and burnt.

After a while, the black corn gave way to black grass. There must have been a terrible fire. The grass had wisps of smoke coming off of it, being twirled up by a light but gusty wind. The fire that consumed all that land must have been pretty recent.

I walked until I reached what must have been Tannersville. It was just a few stores and restaurants and a brick building that said "Town Hall." But there were no people. No one on the streets. No cars or trucks. And the buildings all around were quiet and felt empty. I could hear my own footsteps and my own breath and even the sound of my pant legs rubbing together, like the buildings on each side of the street were hugging my sounds close to me instead of letting them twirl out into the fields and sky. Then I saw a diner.

I went inside. It was empty, but it wasn't cleaned up. Plates were on the tables and on the counter. I figured the kitchen, which was behind the counter just like Marion's, was not working, because there wasn't heat coming off it from the grill. I sat down on a stool at the counter. There was a plate sitting in front of me with a burger on it, unbitten. I touched the top of the bun and found it to be hard like a box-top. I lifted it off and there was the meat. I was hungry but it didn't look right. I knew that eating old bread is not as bad as eating old meat, so I bit into the hard bun. It was tough, but it was food, so I chewed it down till it got moist and tasty. It felt good to be eating. And soon I needed a drink. I heard the sound of a tin can dropping back in the kitchen.

"Hello?" I said. I heard shuffling. Someone was being sneaky. I thought about turning and running out the door, but there was something in the sneaking sound that told me it wasn't coming from anything or anyone dangerous. Just in case, I reached in my pocket and held my knife in my hand as I walked around the counter, slow and cautious, back to the kitchen. There on the floor was a boy. He was littler than me by a half. He looked up at me. I would have thought his face was covered with red blood, if in his lap he hadn't had a big open can of ketchup. His hand was red from sucking the ketchup into his mouth and getting it all over his face. He looked up at me, not moving, and I looked down at him, not moving either. The boy's face was round and his skin was like cream, laid smooth over his head bones, with only a small bump of a nose, like an acorn with two holes. His eyes were blue like the sky, but angry instead of gentle like the sky. He looked at me with those angry eyes for a while, while I looked at him and then he gave up waiting for something to happen and reached his hand in, scooping up more ketchup and catching it into his mouth with a slurp.

"Is that all you could find to eat?" I asked. He looked up at me, saying nothing, and went back to his ketchup. "Where are your folks?" It was funny to ask a thing I'd been asked so many times myself. Seeing this little boy without a mother nearby felt missing. That must have been what folks thought when they saw me. "Where is your mother?" I asked him. Still the little boy said nothing. I looked around the kitchen a bit till I found the sink and poured two glasses of water, squatting down in front of the little boy. "You can go days without eating," I said, "but you need to drink water every day."

"I'm dranking thiss kaychup!" he said, in a funny way of talking which I hadn't heard before with all his words having a big "AY" sound in the middle sounding like saying "ate." "Kaychup tastes bayter than dayam water."

"Just because you can drink something don't make it water," I said. "You couldn't live on that no more than you could live on gasoline. Have some of this water."

"Don't WANT none," said the little boy. I sat down where I was squatting and drank from the glass I'd poured for myself. He kept slurping ketchup till he seemed to get sick from it and then put the can down and looked sad.

"Want some now?" I said, holding the glass out to him. He gave up and took it and gulped from the plastic glass, the water running down his chin, cleaning off the ketchup and dribbling it all down into his shirt, which I could see was about the size for a man, with the sleeves rolled up so much they made big lumps of checkered wool around his little elbows. The whole look of him and the way he talked and acted made me want to laugh, but I kept it to myself. "What's your name?" I asked, and I put a little bit of force in my voice, like the way men talk who are in charge.

"M' name is KYLE," he said, "which is none uh yore dayam bizniz!" His face, which started out pink, turned so red with anger that it made his hair glow like gold on top of it.

"How'd you end up in here all alone, eating ketchup, Kyle?" I asked him.

Upon hearing me say his name, little Kyle made a little red fist in front of his face, squinted up his bright blue eyes, and said, "Ah told yew ma name ain't NONE uh yore bizniz!"

"Well I know your name because you told me it," I said. Kyle leaned over to the side until he was laying on the floor.

"A'm tired," he said. And in no time he was sleeping. I don't remember how long I watched Kyle sleep before I laid on my own side and fell asleep myself.

"Ah wuz a miner in tha diner and a cooker in tha mines!" I heard Kyle singing as I woke up to a smell I knew to be pancakes, from breakfast specials on Sundays at the diner with Marion. I heard the sound of frying on a griddle along with Kyle's voice singing up high like a songbird. "An' I cooked me up some grayddle caykes and dug me up some daymonds!"

I figured someone must have come in while we slept and opened up the diner, but when I sat up I found Kyle himself standing on a wooden box in front of the sizzling griddle. He had a ladle, with which he was scooping batter out of a big metal bowl and drizzling it onto the hot griddle. I got up, my bad arm stiff from sleeping against it.

"How'd you learn to do that?" I asked him.

"Dew whut?" he said, returning back to his angry voice.

"Turning on the griddle and making pancakes?"

"Frum ma paw. He's the cooker heyar."

"He taught you how?"

"Naw. I juss wotched hee-um."

"How come you were eating ketchup when you have real food here?"

"Cuz ah lack ketchup! Whut?" he snapped at me. I couldn't help it but I laughed out loud. He didn't seem to mind it.

Kyle and I ate pancakes at a table by the window as he told me, in his funny voice and mouth full of food, what had happened to make that town all empty, leaving him on his own. First there started to be fires all over the land outside of town. Kyle said during the fires the night sky would be all red and black with smoke in the day. Nothing in the town had caught on fire. "But they wuz a bad smell what made a heap o' folks sicker than hayal." Then he said that men came in trucks with red lights on them and they hollered all around the streets, telling everyone to leave because there was a bad cloud of fire coming from outside town. "Some folks had said that a freight ship had flew by near and dumped somethin' it shouldn'ta."

"What's a freight ship?" I asked.

"Hell I know for?" he yelled. And then he went on telling how folks were scrambling into the trucks to get out because the men said to get out because Tannersville was shutting down quick and for good. "My daydee said he won't go," said Kyle, "and Mawma got angry as hayal and they hallered at each other and she told me wait and she was gunna git her sayster and she ran off an' ma daddy gawt sick," he said. "Lack udder folks had, he dun got sick and storted throwin' blood out the mouth and fallin' on tha floor." Kyle said his father died an "ugly dayth" and the men put him in a truck of dead people while Kyle hid in the closet because all the commotion had him so scared and because he was waiting for his mother.

"But ma mawma nayver did come. So she must be died too," he said. And he didn't seem to care much about that fact, or the fact that his father died in such a terrible way. It was just the way it had gone. It was reality for him. He didn't die. And since all that happened, he was living by himself in this kitchen, cooking and feeding himself, for I don't know how long before I met him.

"I got a feeling this is no good place to be staying," I told him. "I'm going to get moving and I reckon you should too, Kyle."

"Whut I tell yew 'bout ma nayme?!" he said, pointing his table knife at my face, which made me smile a little bit.

Chapter Eighteen

Me and Kyle

I had never thought much about how fast or slow I'd been walking on the road until I started walking it with Kyle, who just about had to full-on run to keep up with my slowest stride. He was huffing and puffing and scampering, his tiny feet clap-clap-clapping on the pavement, his fists pumping up and down, his face red and his mouth never stopping.

"Mah mawma always wonted ta go to the moon, but mah daydee sayd it cost too much. And Mawma said, well, my sayster got to go to the moon, and Daydee sayz it cost too much. And Mawma sayz you never give me nuthin'. And Daydee sayz it cost too much. And Mawma said . . ."

His story went on like that for miles and miles with his little legs running and his feet clap-clapping and his arms swinging and his face all red and sweating and I don't know how he wasn't exhausted because I sure was just being next to him, having to keep my pace slow and listening to him talk.

Just as I was wondering what could break this boy down, he all-at-once sat on the pavement and said, "I caynt walk no moe." We had only just gotten about half way across the burnt grass I'd crossed before arriving in Tannersville. It didn't make sense to stop there on the side of the road with the sun blaring down and nowhere to take shade and it too early for sleeping.

"Come on, now," I said to the back of his head, which he had hanging between his knees. "We best keep walking." Kyle picked up his head and hollered up to the sky like a coyote. "AH SAID AHM TAAAAARD!"

I took out the compass from my pocket, flipped it open, and read it. It said we were headed east. I snapped it closed, the sound of which got Kyle's attention. He looked up and saw the shiny compass in my hand and demanded, "Whut's that?"

"It's a compass," I said. "It tells you where north is."

"Layme see it." He reached out with his little hand.

"You can see it while I hold it," I said and I opened it up and faced the dial toward him.

"Layme hold it!" he shouted angrily. This boy's rage was almost something like my father's but as if he had a tiny body that couldn't make so deep and loud a shout. And unlike when my father got mad and my mom and me had to do just exactly what he said or get hit, I was free to stand there and do nothing as Kyle shouted, "LAYME HOLD IT!" His face was about going from red to purple, from mad to crying. I didn't like upsetting Kyle. I didn't like the way it made me feel.

"I'll make you an agreement," I said. "You get up and walk a little more and I'll let you hold the compass."

"How far?" said Kyle.

"As far as those high corn plants down there," I said, "so we can catch some shade under the corn. Then we can rest. It's no good resting here in the hot sun."

Kyle put his hands on the pavement and commenced to pushing himself up to his feet, but his body wouldn't go. All at once, the rage and toughness went out of his face and he started to cry. "Ah can't," he cried softly. "Ah juss can't walk no moe."

I watched him cry for just a little, then I handed him the compass, which he took, still crying, and I got on my knees with my back to him, took his little hands and put them round my neck, and stood up. I don't know why I knew that this was a good way to carry him, but he must have known, because he hooked his legs around my waist, digging his heels into my sides, and in this way I carried that little boy, while he looked at the compass, all the way to the tall black corn.

"Can you tell me a story?" Kyle whimpered as he lay in the black soil beneath a corn plant.

"What?" I said.

"Ma mawma use ta tell me a story so I can slape."

I reached in my pocket and pulled out the waitress pads I had copied Mighty Mike into and I read out loud.

"Mighty Mike came riding into Laredo, Texas, which, at the time, was no more than a dirt road with a saloon, a blacksmith, a barbershop, a jail, and another saloon. Folks used to say that two saloons in one town can only lead to fighting and what they said was true. The owner of one saloon was named Red Jerry, and the name of the other was Black Jerry, on account of the color of their beards. Half the men in town, who was mostly ranchers from the empty miles around Laredo, drank at Red's as it was called, and the other half drank at Black's. And just as it goes with folks when they drink, they would get mean and violent. You put two saloons on one road, you can bet a handful of silver dollars that the men in one saloon will take to fighting against the men in the other."

"Whuts a sa-loon?" asked Kyle in a dreaming voice as his head tipped over the side and he began the deep breaths of sleeping. I stuffed the waitress pad back in my pocket and wondered what I was going to do.

Traveling and walking with a smaller boy was something that had to be learned how to do, because it wasn't easy. The way I liked it was that I had less to think about my own self being hungry or unsure what to do. All

I had to do each day was keep Kyle safe and to figure ways to keep him from getting upset and complaining too much.

I had come to understand that when Kyle said, “I can’t walk no moe,” he really couldn’t walk anymore. I often had to carry him and we had to stop to rest many times. At night we slept a little away from the road, using Bull’s jacket for comfort from the ground. He liked hearing me read. Often he would ask things that I didn’t know, like, “Whut’s a cri-now-leen gown?” after a description of a fine lady wearing *crinoline.*

“I don’t know,” I said. “I figure from the story that it’s a fine fancy cloth, that makes a lady look fancy and pretty.”

“Ma mawma wore a fancy dress when Granmaw died. It was shiny and purty and all black! Yew think cri-now-leen look like that?”

“Maybe it does,” I said. In this way, we were sorting things out together.

Kyle only made a fuss when he was feeling tired. I started looking for places to rest before he would start talking about getting tired. Kyle never complained about stopping too soon. Getting him to some resting shade before he knew he needed it cut our arguments to nothing. I also learned that if he was tired, it was no sense trying to tell him something he didn’t know or didn’t understand. I got better and better at these things and Kyle started to feel better every day, be more often in a cheerful state. And I started to enjoy being occupied with what he needed.

“How come we reading this part again?” he complained one night as I read from the early parts I’d copied of Mighty Mike.

“We come to the end,” I explained. “Got to start over.”

“Aw, but ah know what happens. Mahty Mike shoots Black Jerry an’ Red Jerry dies at the hand of his own woo-man. Then Mahty Mike mosies outta town to his next adventure. But whut haypens after thayt??”

“I don’t know,” I explained “That’s the end of the book.”

“Wayal, what you think happened nayxt?”

“I don’t know,” I said. “Probably he rode out in the prairie for a while.”

“What yew think he dun ayfter thayt?”

"Probably he made camp, started a fire. Cooked his beans and his supper."

"And thayn?" Kyle reached over and shoved me, trying to make me keep telling.

"How do I know, Kyle? It ain't in the book. I'm just making it up."

"So keep own makin' it up!" He punched me in the chest with his little fist. We were sleeping on the ground close, facing each other. "TAYAL MOO-ORE!" cheeped Kyle.

"Give me a second to think on it!" I barked back. I closed my eyes and pictured Mighty Mike eating his beans. And I started to tell what I saw. "Mighty Mike ate his beans by the fire. Then he cleaned out his cup and leaned back on his saddle, and began playing his guitar. His horse, Hector, made a sound of satisfaction."

"What kinda sound?" Kyle asked, sounding sleepy.

"The kind of sound a horse makes when he's doing alright," I said.

"I never heard a horse make no sound!" He punched me again. "Whut's it sound lack?"

"It sounds kinda like this . . ." I said, and I made the sound my father's horse used to make when he'd got lots of grass to eat and had a good drink by making my lips loose and fat and blowing out of my mouth, making a sound like farting. The sound made Kyle laugh, and his laugh made me laugh. Then he made a horse-fart sound just like mine, only a higher pitch, his mouth being smaller. And I made another and we laughed at each other's sounds and laughed, two satisfied, laughing horses, till we both fell asleep.

"What do it say?" Kyle asked, stretching his neck way back to read the sign that hung high over the road with electric lights pointed at it from under and it lit it up bright green with the purple sky above it.

"Austin, Texas," I read it to him. "It says we get there in twenty miles."

"How fur is thayt?" he asked.

"A long way," I said. Behind the sign, way across the darkness to the side of the road, I could see bright lights. Houston had looked the same from far off, I thought. I knew that must be Austin. But the road wasn't leading in that direction. "The road must bend way down south," I said. "We might save a whole day walking if we walk across the land, off the road."

"Ain't it batter to stay on the road?" said Kyle. I thought he might be right. But then, hanging in the sky above the city lights, I saw the moon. It was only half of it, but there it was.

"Let's go," I said, grabbing Kyle's arm and pulling him up onto my back. He didn't argue, always liking when I carried him, and we walked off the road into the darkness.

We walked until we found a grove of trees standing in the moonlight. The road was far enough behind us that we couldn't hear its traffic anymore. Kyle and I slept on the ground, under the biggest tree. He slept closer to me than usual, his mouth breathing almost into mine. I had a dream that night that Kyle was a possum and I was an elk. I'd seen an elk one time walking across our yard, and never saw one again. My mother had called out from the kitchen to where my father was sleeping upstairs. Meanwhile this brown animal, at least twice bigger than our horse, with great tree branches coming off of his head, stood and stared at me and the pigs with dark green eyes. I stared back and all was silent between us, till my father come running out, barefoot, his overalls dangling by his feet, cocking his shotgun and fumbling with the trigger as the elk ran off.

In my dream, that night in the tree grove, I was just like that elk and Kyle was hanging from one of my head branches and screaming. He was mighty upset. The gray creature with the red eyes was nowhere in the dream. I hadn't dreamed about him nor thought about him for a while.

The next morning, we woke up to find that the trees around us had oranges growing from their twigs. "Those is rainges!" said Kyle. I picked him up by his waist, lifting him over my head so he could reach up and pick some down. Oranges don't quite kill hunger, but they were good for tearing apart and sucking on. I showed Kyle how, if you bend over at the waist, the juice don't go down the front of your shirt when you bite into it.

I kept us heading east by Bull's compass since I couldn't see the city lights now in the daytime and that's where they'd been coming from. There was more green grass, which gave back cool to your walking feet instead of dragging them down into scorching hotness of pavement. Kyle was skipping and sort of gliding in almost a dance, coming up over easy hills and then tumbling down their sides, then swooping back up and then back down again, all easy, green grass, with enough trees to keep us shaded when walking and safe when sleeping nights, and enough empty blue sky to let the sunshine touch us on our faces and shoulders. "Can yew tell me 'bout Mahty Mike whilst we walking?" asked Kyle.

"Sure," I said. I liked when Kyle asked for stories about Mighty Mike, because I got to hear them myself and be surprised by my own made-up story, which was pleasurable. I never knew what was going to happen next to Mighty Mike. I just sort of reached inside of that part of my thinking, made to do so by knowing Kyle wanted the comfort and distraction, and the story of the lonesome cowboy would simply come to my mind.

"Mighty Mike had found himself surrounded by many bad men," I started.

"How many?" Kyle interrupted.

"It was seven bad men," I told him, knowing it as I said it.

"How many is sayven?" growled Kyle, mad that I picked a number a bit higher than his understanding.

"Seven is . . ." I said and I stopped walking, and put my hand on his shoulder to stop him. "Look here around," I said, and spun him slowly in a circle, in the small patch of trees we happened to be walking through, and pointed out some of the bigger trees surrounding us as I counted them: "One. Two. Three. Four. Five. Six. Seven. See that many trees around us? Now fix your mind on just those trees and that's how many bad men was surrounding Mighty Mike, just like these trees surround us. All guns drawn. All mean and ready to fire. And Mighty Mike with his gun belt hanging off his saddle, out of reach, and him naked, out of even his britches, having just taken his morning bath in a creek. And looking up to find himself surrounded by: One. Two"—I pointed at each tree again as I counted—"Three. Four. Five. Six. Seven bad men armed and ready to gun him down." Kyle looked from tree to tree, seeing in his mind the bad men with guns drawn, seeing himself as Mighty Mike, naked and unarmed, and all at once he tore off running out of that grove and across the sunny hillside we'd been heading to. I stood there and watched him run, watched him get smaller and smaller, and I knew I'd told a good story, especially since it got him running right in the way we needed to go, saving me time carrying him on my back.

Chapter Nineteen

Austin, Texas, and the Road South

The buildings in Austin were as tall as the ones in Houston, but pale, light, cheerful colors: pink, yellow, green. Kyle and I woke up and stood in a wide field of yellow grass looking at those buildings, which had been rows of lights when we stopped walking the night before. The city looked peaceful in the daytime, peaceful as dead trees, from far away. The only sound around us was soft wind and the chirping of waking insects. But I reckoned that when we got closer to that place, it would show itself to be loud, ugly, and dangerous. I could feel my chest getting tight, like if a hand of warning was reaching from there, across the grass, over the soft hills and was pushing on my heart, telling me to stay away. A city is full of cars, trash, broken glass, and people who punch and move fast and try to put you into bad places. But the natural land around us didn't offer much better. There was something that looked like a pond nearby, but the water was brown and thick. The oranges I had put in the pockets of Bull's jacket tasted good going in and quenched a thirst for a moment, but they left my mouth feeling stingy and dry and my stomach about the same. Probably it was the same for Kyle, I figured. A city might have a place like Miss Maw's house where a boy with no place to go can get something to eat and a bed to sleep in at least for a night. So we walked to Austin.

The grass we walked through was the kind kept short by gusting winds, blowing sand, and the killing light of a dry, hot sun. Every tough little plant of that grass was like a knife cutting into my feet and toes, which were uncovered by my sandals. Kyle and I walked without talking till the sun got to the middle of the sky.

The sharp grass simply ended where began the city of Austin, which to my big surprise, didn't get any louder from close up. We were looking up at what seemed like the back sides of the tall, bright, colorful buildings. But we were still hearing only the bugs, now louder with the sun being brighter in the world of empty grass we'd been walking across. I wondered if Austin was a dead place like Tannersville. I wasn't sure how to come into the city because the buildings were all stuck close together and there wasn't a highway leading in. But where the grass ended, which was in a straight line right where we were standing, was a road as flat as an indoor floor, with a kind of pavement that was almost pink in color. Looking down at it, I couldn't see the tiny rocks you usually see trapped in the hard black of a road. It was just a pink-colored soft, with a yellow line down the middle. Kyle was still saying nothing. I think the sight of that place had him scared and confused. As I stood there thinking of what to do, I felt his hand come up and grab mine. Without deciding to do it, I felt my fingers squeeze down onto his fingers. Kyle and I held hands as I led him off the grass and onto that quiet road, which seemed to be curved. I thought it might be going around the city in an outside circle.

The pink road was smooth and a bit cool to our feet as we walked along its side. We still didn't talk and we might have gone on not talking, walking in a confused circle forever, if there hadn't come, with no sound of warning, a fast red car, which whipped right past us with no sound of an engine or a horn. Just the squeaky hissing of tires on the pink, as it disappeared in the distance and around the curve.

"Whut the HAYAL was thayat???" shouted Kyle, whipping his hand out of mine and pointing with it at the vanishing red dot.

"Some kind of damned car," I said. I had started to use the cursing words that Kyle used. When men at the farm and other grown people had used words like "damn" and "hell," I'd kept myself from using them because I knew, even though I didn't remember learning it, that children ought not to curse. I never thought to curse around Marion. But Kyle and I were children together, and his spicy sort of angry talk made me smile and I learned that using it myself helped me make a feeling better known.

"I don't know where the hell that came from," I said. "I didn't hear it till it was gone." We walked closer to the edge of the road now that I knew there were cars driving on it, and a few more went whipping past, silent as the first, and all bright colors. We walked on the road, looking up at the backs of the tall buildings and, sure enough, we were going in a long circle.

We finally reached a place where the road went between two buildings into the city. It had a sign which was glowing with light. It said "Welcome to New Austin," then those words vanished all on their own, and a new page of words appeared. I had never seen anything like that happen before, but I was more interested in reading those new words than trying to figure what was happening on that sign. The new words read, "New Austin is an independent, stage-two city." Then those words vanished and a new page appeared, saying, "New Austin population is mixed between the hours of 9:00 a.m. and 7:00 p.m." Then the next page showed a picture of two people with no faces. One was black and the other was white. They were holding hands, like Kyle and I were. Under the picture the words said "Work together. Live apart. Get along," and then the next page said "Gas powered vehicles prohibited in New Austin." Then: "Next exit: Austin, Texas."

Kyle and I followed the road the sign was on. The road turned from pink into almost a white color. It led between two light blue buildings that seemed tall enough to be part of the sky touching down to the ground. I couldn't see the tops of them. We took the white road straight into town.

The quiet cars coming off the white road all pulled off into great paved squares that had signs like "Parking 1A" and "Parking 2C," and all the cars were parking there and folks were getting out and walking. Past the parking squares was all green grass cut like a man's hair-top fresh from a barber, lined with sidewalks like in Houston but no cars were driving where the people walked, which was all quiet and orderly and clean. The people were all dressed in clean and pretty, bright, colorful clothes. The ladies' dresses were kind of like the straight white dresses that the nurses wore at the hospital except colored bright, with shiny paint like the cars or like Marion's fingernail paint. The men's suits were also bright colors and looked more round on the edges and some men had on skirts and even dresses and some ladies had beards. Everyone was walking and talking even if they didn't have a person next to them to talk to. It was strange to be around so many people and only hear the quiet of easy talking, with no machines and no trouble.

Kyle and I walked the way they were walking, like we were going with them to some place but we didn't know where.

"Whut tha hay-all ais dis playce?" yelled Kyle. Lots of folks walking near us turned and looked at him, then at me, stopping their gentle talk. Everyone was silent and standing around us. Something about the way their eyes looked made me feel like we were dirty, which we were, from sleeping on the ground night after night. But you don't really notice dirt on yourself till someone else sees it.

"Say, boys, are you alright?" said a voice behind us. We saw a man in blue, with a blue hat, and a yellow shiny button on his chest, like the one in Houston. And the men who beat Bull on the head with their sticks. This *policeman* didn't have a stick and he was smiling, and I didn't like it.

I grabbed Kyle, slung him on my back, and ran. "Hey!" the man yelled and ran after us. I ran us off the pavement and across the grass. Almost everyone I could see was watching us be chased by the policeman as Kyle squeezed around my neck with his little hands. Out of a pink building to the side, another policeman ran out and now there were two chasing us and

I ran in zigzags trying to get away but Kyle was feeling heavy and suddenly in front of me I saw a blue and white car with a red light on top like the one that took Bull away and I thought it must be time for me to die.

I put Kyle on the grass and told him, "RUN!" He ran off and I ran the other way but there was another police car and another and there were clean and colorful people everywhere standing and watching. There was nowhere for us to go. I wondered if they would crack our heads and kill us like Bull. I felt Kyle reaching up and tugging my hand, wanting to be lifted onto my back. I reached in my pocket and took out my knife, opened it up, and held it in front of me. "Leave us be," I said in a growling voice like Kyle would make. We were surrounded. There was nowhere to go.

Then another police car drove up, but this car was loud, heavy looking, and dirty, like the cars I was used to. Folks around us were putting their hands over their ears like this car was the loudest thing they'd ever heard. The door opened and a man got out in a gray suit, and I could see he was a boss. His clothes weren't shiny or colorful. He was smoking a cigarette. None of these other people were smoking. This boss man looked like a regular man from Houston.

He said to us, "Okay, boys. Get in the car." And he said to me, "Put that knife away, son. You ain't got no use for that here." I knew we had to do what he said. So I folded the knife, took Kyle by the hand, and we got in the back of the man's car and it drove us across the grass, all those people staring at us through the windows, and out of the pretty, quiet, clean part of Austin and into another part that had normal streets, loud cars, and people wearing normal tired-looking clothes, most of them black people, Mexicans, or regular whites—all who I could see through the window.

"Way thay tayking us?" asked Kyle. I didn't answer him because I didn't know. But soon the police car stopped in front of a building with a big green light out front and a sign that said "Austin City Police Department," and they led us inside, where Kyle and I were told to sit on chairs at a desk. The boss man in the gray suit offered me a cigarette and I smoked it as he asked us questions like, "How'd you boys end up in New Austin?"

"We walked into it," I said.

"Walked? From where?" he asked, all his questions coming quick after my answers.

"From the west."

"From the west where? Where'd you start?"

"We were going south on a road from Tannersville. And . . ."

Another policeman, who was in a plain suit, stopped me. "Tannersville? Ain't nobody in Tannersville."

"That's where I found him," I said, meaning Kyle.

"And who's he to you?" said the policeman.

"He's a boy I found in Tannersville. I walked there from up north. He was living in the diner where his father worked." The men all turned and looked at Kyle.

"What's your name?" the man asked Kyle. I smiled a little because I thought Kyle would start getting mean and tough with them. But instead Kyle spoke softly and said, "Ma nayam ais Kyle Dunnigun, sir."

"Check that," said the boss to another man, who then left the room.

"I thought they got everybody out of Tannersville after that ship dumped there," said the policeman in the plain suit. "All them people were dead or brought here. Wasn't nobody left behind. You sure you're not making up some bullshit, son?"

"It ain't some bullshit," I said. "It's reality." They all looked at me when I said that.

"Where did you come from?" asked the boss.

"Doesn't matter," I said. I was trying to answer as quick as they were talking and that was the answer that came to my mind.

"You looking for trouble, bub?" said the boss.

"I'm not," I said.

"What were you doing in New Austin?"

"Looking for someplace to eat," I said, "and maybe sleep."

"New Austin ain't a place for someone like you," said the man in the plain clothes. "Don't you know that?"

"I don't know nothing about anything going on around here," I said.

"That's clear," said the boss. "Anyway, they don't tell anybody anything anymore," he said to the other man. And then back to me he said, "Where did you come from, son?"

Something in how he asked made me want to answer, so I said, "I walked through Houston and across some farmland. Then since I got a compass I know I've been going west, a little north. That's how I got to Austin."

"Yeah, out to Houston is still old world," said the boss. "I guess you must feel pretty lost around here. Where are you trying to go?"

"Down to the oil fields," I said, "so I can work. Make money."

"Well," said the boss. He slid his cigarette pack to me with his matches on top. I lit one. It made me feel a bit calmer with all those men looking at me and asking me questions.

"What they need to do," said the man in the plain clothes, "is build a road from out in Houston straight to the oil fields."

"Better they just dig a big ol' pit and let them all walk down into it," said the boss. Then the man who had left the room came back and gave the boss a piece of paper. The boss man read it and said to us, "Okay, you two, come with me." And he put us in a little room where he had us sit in chairs and he gave me a cup of coffee and another cigarette and they gave both of us some kind of yellow cake to eat, which we did. We sat and waited for a long time.

"Whut yew thank they gunno dew?" asked Kyle.

"I don't know," I said. I really didn't know and I didn't like the feeling of being inside of a big building where I didn't know where the door was or where the road was or how to get out of there. I wondered if they were going to put me in a reform school. I was trying to think of Kyle and what might happen to him, but worrying about myself like I hadn't since I met him made it hard to think about him at all.

After a while the boss man came in the room with a woman. Kyle yelled, "Mawma!" and he ran to her arms. Kyle's mother cried and hugged him tight and picked him up off the ground till he was wrapped all around her front side, the way he'd been wrapped around my back on the road.

"I guess that closes the case on Tannersville," said the boss man.

"How can I thank you?" asked the mother to me, and I just looked at her not knowing what to say.

"Okay," the boss man said to me, as he led me to the front door and out of the building. "You done good bringing that boy to his mom. Maybe you'll be rewarded. In the next life." He reached in his pocket and took out a five-dollar bill and put it in my hand with a pack of cigarettes. "Go on now," he said and pointed at the side pavement, which I went and stood on as he said, "Stay out of New Austin. Around here is Old Austin. And it's still Texas. You'll do fine here." And he walked back inside.

A moment later, that woman came out with Kyle in her arms. She got into a police car and was driven away. I looked at Kyle for the last time, through the window of that car, and realized that I had never told him my name.

Kyle and I had come in that place together. Now I stood outside by myself. Nobody had tried to find my mother. That man gave me some cigarettes and money and sent me off. Pa had said, "Being a boy is alone. A man even more so." And I wondered if I had, somewhere along the way, become a man, and quit being a boy. I wasn't sure how to figure how long it had been since I left home, or how long it took to grow into a grown man. Was I the same as my father already? I didn't feel different enough to think so. I thought I was more a boy like Kyle. But those policemen sure hadn't thought so.

I WALKED AROUND THE PLACE the man had called Old Austin. It felt something like Black Town in Houston, how it was quieter and a bit run-down with less to go around. Except in Old Austin, whites and blacks were all mixed in. Through the window of a diner, full of eating folks, I saw cornbread and grits, steak and potatoes. I saw apple pie and Coca-Cola and cheeseburgers. I saw folks piling food in their mouths and slurping their Cokes while they talked, as if there was nothing in the world to say that could be more important than eating that good hot food. I felt in my pocket at the five dollars and the cigarettes.

"Ingram?" I heard a voice say from next to me. I looked and there, standing beside me, looking at me right in my face, was Sinema.

"Sinema," I said. "You look different." And she did. Her face was wider than when I met her at Miss Maw's house. Her lips were bigger and came further away from her cheeks, closer to mine. Her hair was brushed back behind her ears, and caught up at the top of her head, showing her neck to be longer and stronger. Her yellow sweater swelled out in front, in two hills of breasts, and she wore a gray skirt that hugged her hips and her legs coming out the bottom of the skirt were thick like iron posts, but small at the bottom with brown shoes that showed her toes, and they were not the toes of a little girl.

"Of course I look different," Sinema said with the same smile she showed me in Houston. "So do you. I barely recognized you."

"Why do I look different?" I asked her.

"Ingram," she said, all of a sudden serious, but tender, "it's been three years since I saw you. You don't look like you're doing much better." Then she laughed. "Come on inside," she said. "I'll get you something to eat."

Sinema let me order a cheeseburger and a Coca-Cola and she got the same for herself. We sat across from each other.

"Why is everyone in here looking at me?" I asked, because they were.

"Because, Ingram. You're all country. You're wearing old dirty clothes; your face is dirty. Nobody like that lives around here."

"I don't like them looking at me," I said.

"If you're not looking at them, how do you know they're looking at you?" she said and she was smiling from behind the straw that stood up in her Coke.

"How come you're here now?" I asked. "Did your family come here from Houston?"

"Nope," she said, sipping her Coke, "just me. I came here to work and go to college."

"Just you alone?"

"It costs a lot to go to college, Ingram. I got picked to go because I had better grades. Pa said at least one of us can learn enough instead of dying in the oil fields or in Black Town."

"What about your sisters?" I asked.

Sinema looked down at her nice brown arms that were on top of the table, behind her food. She said, "They got mad because I got picked to go. I write home all the time but they never write back. Even Maw doesn't write back. I know it's because she doesn't want to vex my sisters. But. Anyway."

I saw that she was maybe about to cry. I didn't want her to. I said, "I got picked up into the sky by a tornado."

She looked right up, showing me all her bright white teeth, and she said, "What? Tell me about that!" So I told her about walking on the road, and I told her about the tree of black wind that sucked me up into the sky.

"A tree of black wind?" she said, laughing.

"That's the way I saw it," I said.

We finished our burgers as I told her some more things about the farm, about Bull and Marion. Sinema laughed and found interest in many of my stories, but the more I told, the more she became serious.

"But, Ingram," she said, "how can you just walk around like this? What are you going to do? Aren't you lonely?"

"Lonely?"

"Being alone. Doesn't it hurt?"

"Hurt?" I said. "Getting my arm broke hurt. Being alone doesn't hurt. Being alone is just reality."

"I mean hurting on the inside," Sinema said, putting her hand on her chest. "I know I hurt on the inside from being alone here. But at least I have back home to think about. What do you think about to keep from hurting when you're alone? Hurting on the inside?"

"I don't think about nothing except what is happening to me," I said, which wasn't true. There were many times when I was alone that I thought about Sinema. I didn't want to tell her that as we sat in the diner. Something told me that if I did, she'd tell me to stop it. Then I'd have nothing.

Later we were walking in a quieter part of Old Austin, where it was more houses than stores or places to eat. Sinema told me how she could only go to school three days a week because she needed to work at a library to pay her way.

"What's a library?" I asked.

"Ingram. Didn't you learn anything yet?"

"Well, I don't know what a library is."

"It's a place full of books for people to read and borrow."

"How many books?"

"I don't know. Thousands."

"Is that a lot?"

"Ingram!" Sinema laughed and took my hand.

"I read a book," I said as we kept walking. "It was called *Mighty Mike, Showdown in Silverado*."

"I haven't heard of that book," said Sinema.

"It's not a real story," I said. "It's fiction. About a tough man who wanders across the prairies and desert, from town to town."

"Well, I'm glad you're reading," she said.

"What are you learning in school?" I asked.

"I'm going to be an engineer," she said.

"What's an engineer?"

"That's a person that designs or works with machines and other things that are technical. I would rather be studying literature."

"What's literature?" I asked.

"Holy moly, boy," she said, and she got up closer to me and put her hand in my hair, sort of scratching underneath it. "Literature is books, Ingram. Books and reading and writing is literature. And it's what I would study if I could. But I need to learn something that will get me a job in New Austin. That's why Pa wanted me to come here. He said"—Sinema made a face like she was trying to look like Pa, and she dug her voice down low to sound like Pa—"'Those new-striped people are going to go off to the moon some place, and they'll take the future with them. At least one of you won't be stuck here in the old dying dirt.'" Then she smiled like herself and said, "He don't know much about what's going on himself. But I do need to get a practical job so I can at least work in New Austin."

I didn't make much of what Sinema was saying because everything inside of me was feeling her hand and fingers in my hair and her face closer to mine than she had ever come, closer even than my mother's had been, and I looked at Sinema's face knowing that this face I would not forget. Not ever.

"I gotta go home now, Ingram," Sinema said, and stopped walking. We were in front of where she lived, the upstairs of a row house. She said she lived there with four girls. "One is from Kansas, one from Florida, and one from California. I like the Kansas girl. Her name is Henrietta. We call her Henry. She acts more like a boy than a girl. She does all the boy stuff, moving heavy things around and fixing. She's studying astronomy and propulsion science."

We stood in front of her house together with no more to talk about.

"Where are you going to go?" she asked.

"I don't know," I said, letting her take her hand away even though I didn't want her to. "I'll do something."

"You can't stay here with me, you know," she said. "Only girls allowed here."

"Can I come see you tomorrow?"

"Tomorrow, I work in the morning."

"Okay," I said.

She looked at me, made her eyes kind of small like she was mad or something, and then she said, "I can't take care of you, Ingram. Nothing like that. I got to look after myself and get my education. You got to figure your own self out, just like me."

"I know," I said. "I will. I'm fine." Then we were quiet and just standing there. I figured she was getting ready to turn away from me and go inside of her house and I wouldn't see her anymore after that. But as long as she was standing there, I didn't want to leave.

"Well, okay, Ingram. It was nice to see you. Goodbye." And she quickly turned around and went in her house.

I stood there for a little while looking up, watching the dark shape of her appear in an upstairs window and then the lights went out in that room, killing her pretty shadow. I walked a little way away from her house, but then I just stood there in the street, which was all dark now, and I was tired. The day had started way out in that orange grove and now here I was. I'd had a nice meal and I'd seen Sinema. That was over now. Kyle was gone. I didn't know where to go next. On the road I could always just walk a little away from the pavement and sleep on the ground. My body and my mind hurt something awful. The house across the street from Sinema's was dark, the lights out in all the windows. I walked around behind it and saw some trash cans against a dark wall. I figured I could just catch some sleep there and then look for south on my compass in the morning and keep walking.

I laid down between two garbage cans. There was a foul smell but it didn't bother me. I put my arms around my chest and closed my eyes. It was the first night in a while that I didn't have Kyle's little face just in front of my chest at sleeping time and I didn't have him now to tell stories to about Mighty Mike. I wondered if I could imagine one for myself. I sort of let my mind wander to where I knew the stories of that cowboy, but there was nothing there. Like an empty room. All I could imagine was a room with nothing in it. Somehow that was the most frightening thing I could think of. I curled up trying to get my head down further into my chest as I felt myself getting upset and more sleepy all at once.

Soon I was drifting in my mind, dreaming of an empty place with no floor and no walls or ceilings or air to breathe and I hated knowing that it went on and on for so far and so wide and up and down that I'd grow into an old man if I tried to walk along it all the way. And I knew he was there. I couldn't see him or feel him. I didn't have to. I could feel his cold. I could feel his killing and his dying and I hated him. I had always been just shaking and afraid of the gray creature and maybe there was another feeling, like excited. But laying between those garbage cans in Old Austin, after saying such a quick goodbye to Sinema, knowing she didn't want me around her, and knowing I wanted to be around her more than anything else, made me feel something new inside of that big room of nothing. Which was that I wished I wasn't alone and I wished reality was something else. I wished I could make up a story, that I could live in fiction, in literature. I wished my life was some bullshit that I could believe, where I had someone that didn't go away or send me away. And I wondered why I'd been born alone. And yet somehow I knew I wasn't. That something had been taken away. I didn't know what it was, but as I felt the gray creature of my every dream coming closer and closer, I began to hate him for the first time in my life, for what he'd taken from me and what I hated wanting because it wasn't the reality and I'd never have it. And I wanted the gray creature to keep on coming and swallow me up whole and make me just like him, so I'd be dead. And I knew if I kept dreaming that dream, I would never wake up and I'd be found dead between those trash cans. I felt my breathing about to stop when a dog was all at once barking right into my face.

I opened my eyes to find it was morning and I was looking right at the dangling tongue of a dog whose spit was falling onto my cheeks and nose as he barked it onto me. "What the hell you doing here?" I heard someone ask, and I would have been sure it was the dog, but for that I knew that dogs can't talk, and even if they could, they couldn't talk and bark at the same time.

"Get off him, Pucky!" said the voice a few times till the dog backed off. There was a man standing there. He had a plastic bag in his hand. "What the hell you doing here?" he said to me. "You can't sleep there, man. You gotta go. I'm to clean this up. Go on. Get out of here."

I got up. My whole backside where I was sleeping was wet from the muddy ground. I stepped away and the man took the bag out of the garbage can I was sleeping against and put the new one in. His dog was calm now, watching him. And I watched as the man switched the bags on all the cans, talking to me while he worked. "Why don't you get yourself to a men's home, if you don't have a place?" he asked. "Don't you have a place to stay? People don't sleep in the street in Austin, man. They got all kinds of shelters." While he talked, I looked across the street and saw Sinema come out of her house. She was holding some books against her chest and started walking down the street. She didn't see me.

"I need the road south," I told the man.

"Oil?" he asked.

"Yes, sir," I said.

"Yeah, oil. Sure," he said, and he pointed down the street, the way that Sinema didn't go. "Take this all the way," he said. "No need to make no turns. It'll take you to the interstate. You'll see signs south. Can you read?"

"Yeah, I can read," I said.

"I don't care, man. They won't care down there either. Work you to death or till you burn up. Go ahead now. Follow the signs that say south. Go catch the road and get out of here. You don't belong here, man," he said.

I walked away the way he pointed. I got pretty far down the street before I looked back and saw that he and his dog was still watching me go. I couldn't see Sinema anymore.

Chapter Twenty

Bart's Yellow Shirt

A white car with lots of dents and rust along the sides pulled up close to me just as it was getting dark on the road south. The engine made a noise like someone had thrown a handful of rocks into it. The windows were all wide open. Later I'd learn they were broken. The man driving the car leaned across his seat and said to me, "Where you going?"

"South. To the oil fields."

"Same here, buddy. Get on in." I got in the car. He put out his hand and said, "What's your name?"

"Ingram," I said, and I gave him my hand.

He pumped it with a strong grip and said, "Name's Bart. Short for Bartholomew. You looking to work the oil fields?"

"Yes."

He pulled back on the road. "Same. Same. You been down there before?"

"No," I said.

"I was down there drilling for 'bout two years. Left with my life and swore I'd never go back. Yet here I goddamn go. Haha, oh man." He laughed and shook his head. “I done made myself a solemn promise,” he went on talking, “that I would take the money I earned drilling and make myself a life and never ever go back.” He had to shout to be heard above the wind rushing into the car through the open windows. I let him talk, turning my face to the wind coming in from the darkness. He didn't seem to care. Like maybe instead of needing me to talk, to stay awake, like the truck driver did, he needed to talk himself.

“Man, I guess I'm gonna die where I'm destined to die,” Bart went on. “No getting out of it. Better to die doing something though, I guess. Least I'm not dying in the Army like a plug idiot, haha, oh man. I got stuck outside Omaha? Saw a whole army marching down the middle of the highway. They had tanks, trucks, and about a thousand guys on foot, walking like cattle, right down the middle of the interstate. Meanwhile traffic was piled up behind them, all the way back to Iowa. I'll tell you what. I wouldn't join that army for all the money in the world. Uh-huh.

“Goddamn Army,” he went on, starting to push his voice like it was getting blocked in his throat. “A bunch of hired killers. That's all. Hired killers dressed in green. Like my brother . . .” He stopped talking. I looked at his face, lit up by his car's inside lights. There were tears coming out of his eyes. The wind coming in the window was pushing the tears back, into his ears. “My brother joined that army,” he said. “Doris, his wife, had a baby coming. ‘I got to make some money, Bart!’ he told me. ‘Plus I got to get out of this house full of kids. Anything but all that hollerin'.’ Ha, ha, ha.” Bart slapped the steering wheel as he laughed at what his brother had said. “He joined up. They sent him to fight in California. Made him kill like an animal. Not killing no soldiers neither. Just house to house cutting regular folks down. He would never had done a thing like that before they got him wearing that green. ‘They ain't American anymore,’ is all he said about it. I tell you what. He ain't my brother anymore. He ain't nobody.” Bart had to wipe his eyes to see where he was driving. Then he looked over at me, like he realized someone was in the car seeing how upset he was.

"Hey man," he said to me, "where are you from?" I just looked ahead, out the window.

"What, 's it a secret?" said Bart. "Where you from?"

"Where I'm from is none of your damn business," I said, my voice coming out kind of loud and fierce. "Why don't you let me sleep?" I turned away from him, wrapped myself tight in my arms, and hunkered lower in the seat to get my ears out of the wind. I felt Bart looking at the side of my face for a while. Then he left me alone. I didn't sleep but I found it restful and sort of safe to be just quiet with my eyes closed, with Bart saying nothing because I'd shown my displeasure. I'd made it quiet for myself in that car, had made that man leave me alone, with what I'd said and how I'd said it. I don't know how I came to doing it, but that's what I had done.

Bart drove all night and into the light of the following day before he got tired and pulled over, which woke me up. "You want to take over for a while?" he asked when I opened my eyes and looked at him.

"Take over?"

"Yeah, can you do some driving? I gotta rest my eyes too."

"I don't know how."

"Aw, it's easy," he said, getting out of the car, running around the front of it and coming to my door. "Push over," he said, shoving me to behind the wheel and sitting where I'd sat. My body and my mind came awake quick, with being scared and excited, sitting on that side of the car, a whole new place. "Put your hands on the wheel," he said, and I did, just like I'd seen him and other people do. The wheel was shivering with the rumble of the engine. I felt like I was holding a scared chicken by the throat.

"See the pedals down there?" said Bart. "Feel them with your foot. The one on the right is go, the one on the left is stop. The wheel points your way. There's no traffic and this here Dodge is an automatic, so it's easy. This lever here. Step on the brake, pull that lever toward you and down till right there the red line goes from P, past the R and N, to D, which is for drive. But you gotta have your foot hard on the brake, the stop pedal. As soon as you get in drive the engine connects to the wheels and it's ready to go. It's only your foot holding us. You got it?"

I did like he said, stepping down on the stop pedal. I took a breath and pulled back the lever till the red line pointed at the D. I felt the car jump a little forward and I knew I was keeping it still with my foot which made my ankle shake.

"At first, you'll do everything too much but it's okay. Nothing here to hit. The idea is let the brake go, you'll feel us roll. Ease the wheel over to the road, got it?" I nodded. "Okay, let up the brake a bit. Just ease off the pressure." I did and the car began to roll. I turned the wheel and the car pointed into the road. We rolled back onto the pavement but started going too much to the left. I scrambled my hands around to go back to the middle and went too much the other way. "Okay, now go back to the middle with the wheel. Always point it back to the middle. Doesn't take much." I did like he said and now we were rolling slowly in the middle of the road. "Now keep your heel where it is but just tilt the tip of your toe to the gas like this," and he showed me with his hand, like he was waving hello in the air. I did that with my foot and touched the go pedal, which I guessed is what he meant by gas. "Ease down onto it," he said and I did. The car woke up and shot forward. "Easy, easy, easy, you're doing great," said Bart. He had me go faster, then slower, then fast and slow again, then he told me to pull over and stop, which I first did so hard that it sent me lurching into the wheel, but not him because he had his foot on the dashboard, knowing what would happen. He just laughed a little and said, "Let's try that again."

It made it easy that we were just on a straight, unstopping road. When other cars started coming by and passing it made my head and hands tingle, but that got less and less. I got good enough at driving that Bart fell asleep. It got so my foot and hands just knew what to do. Pushing down the gas a little to get up a hill, or tilting the wheel just so much to take a curve. It was like walking down the street or washing my face.

Some folks were walking on the side of the road like I had been for so many days, nights, and, I guess, years. I looked over at Bart sleeping and I thought about how he had been driving, seen me walking, and decided to pull over and take me with him. I felt a feeling toward him I later learned to be *grateful*, which is a word I found in a dictionary, a book that Bart bought for me the next day at a truck stop, along with a book called *Moby Dick*. He had woken up as the sun went down and took over driving again and this time we talked more. He asked me about my life and I didn't mind telling him where I came from and where I'd been, and I had told him I was learning to read.

"Good you're learning to read," said Bart. "Reading is all you need to learn everything there is." And he found that book at the truck stop, which had a picture on the cover of a fish with a boat full of men on its back.

"How could a boat full of men be smaller than a fish?" I asked.

"It's not the boat that's small," he said, "and that's not a fish. It's a mammal. An animal, like a giant cow that lives under the ocean."

"What's the ocean?" I said, and that's when he reached for that book called a dictionary, which was fat, but small enough to hold in my hand.

"Every word in the English language is in that book," said Bart. "It lists them and tells you what they mean. Look up *ocean*." He showed me how to find a word by its first letter and I found it. It said *the whole body of salt water that covers nearly three-fourths of the surface of the earth*. I didn't know what to think of that.

Bart and I sat down to eat at that truck stop. I told Bart I had five dollars, which the policeman had given me in Austin. He said, "Keep it. You pay next time."

We had something called spaghetti with chili and orange soda. The spaghetti made a stinging hot feeling on my tongue and the orange soda cooled it off while pinching the sides of my mouth with a different kind of flavor than

Coca-Cola. Bart let me order a "Trucker *Portion*" 'cause I hadn't eaten in a while, and that spaghetti and chili with orange soda set in my stomach like a warm ball of mud in a way that put me right to sleep as he drove that night.

The next time we stopped at a truck stop, which was the same as the one before, and after I ate another spaghetti with chili and orange soda, Bart showed me how to do a *map* check. There was a picture hanging between the two toilets, men's and women's. The picture was a map of the state of Texas. Bart said it was a *graphic* picture of Texas, as you would see it if you were flying way up above it, just enough to see it all at once. The shape of Texas was like a fried egg with sharp corners, with different colors all over it and all kinds of lines, some squiggling and some straight, with numbers written on them. Down in the lower part of this map was a silver star and next to it said, "YOU ARE HERE," and Bart explained that this star was the spot where we were standing. He showed me with his finger how far it was from where we were earlier that day and said, "That was two hours driving, see? We go another two hours, another finger," and he showed me with his finger on the map how far that would be. Then he showed me, on the map, how the southern road we were taking ends on the *Gulf Coast.*

"This is where all the oil's being dug up. Here along the coast. And down here. You see all this blue?" His finger traced circles along an area on the map that was all blue, with no roads or rippling mountains.

"What's all that blue?" I asked.

"That's the Gulf of Mexico. It ain't an ocean, but nearly."

"What's the ocean look like?" I asked.

"You can't even believe it," he said. "You seen a river? Or a pond?"

"Yeah."

"Remember looking across the water, at the trees on the other side?"

"I do."

"The ocean is so much water, for so far, it just keeps going and going and going in all directions so that you can't see the other side. Just water and water and water," he said as I used my finger to *measure* how many two-hour drives it would take to cover that ocean. As Bart drove us away from that truck stop, I played a sort of game, of letting the wind flip the pages of the dictionary around, then stopping here or there to read a word, and then let it flip again, and that's how I found the word *gratitude.* It said *appreciative of benefit received.* That's when I realized that what I was feeling for Bart was gratitude.

I liked the way Bart looked when a cigarette stuck out the side of his mouth while he was driving. Bart had a bright, freckled face, with two thick eyebrows that stood out, dark, above his near-black eyes. He could move those eyebrows up and down separate from each other like they were dancing caterpillars. The way Bart's one brow would be straight up with his wide-open driving eye, and his other brow would be pushed down, shutting his eye down along with his mashed-down mouth, clamping on that cigarette, it was like his whole face would be in on the smoking of it. He'd smoke it down like that, letting the wind take away the ash, the way it had done with his tears. When it was my turn to drive, I let my cigarette dangle in the same way. I looked in the mirror to see if I looked like he did, but I saw a boy instead of the man he was.

"Trying to look cool?" Bart said. I thought he'd been asleep.

"What do you mean?" I said. "It ain't cool. It's warm."

"Not that kind of cool. Some words mean two things, right?"

"Yeah," I said, "the dictionary says *jerk* means pull on something hard and sudden but it also means a disagreeable person."

"Right," he said, sitting up and lighting himself a smoke. "It's also a hell of a way to cook a pig, soldier." He had started to call me soldier. "Cool can mean kinda cold. Just this side of warm. Or it can mean being cool, as a person, a way of being. Like keepin' it cool." He laid his hands across the air in front of him like there was a table there. "Goin' easy. Not getting ruffled. Cool, see? Cool." And he made his eyes narrow and his head bobbed up and down, with his hands still on the table that wasn't there. Then he looked at me and I couldn't help it but laugh. He laughed too. "I know, I know. It looks dumb. Because I'm trying to be cool. Can't try to be cool. The essence of it is that you just are cool. And that's why everyone admires a cool dude. You get me?"

"Yeah," I said. Bart lit up two and put one in my mouth as I kept driving.

Bart had three different shirts he wore. Kept them, along with his other stuff, in what he said was his brother's army bag. The bag had two letters on it, DG, which he said stood for his brother's name, Damian Grover. He was Bart Grover. When we washed up in the bathroom of the next truck stop, Bart took off his shirt and washed under his armpits, which were hairy, like my father's, and like mine had only started to be if I looked up close. Bart saw me looking at his shirt he'd taken off. "You like that shirt?" he asked. I did like it. The shirt was yellow, had black stripes and a big collar. The color was bright and there was something about it. "That's my coolest shirt, soldier," he said, smiling. Then he tossed it to me. "It's time you wore a man's shirt." I threw my Mexican shirt in the garbage can and put on Bart's yellow shirt. I felt the pits of the shirt wet against mine. I had to roll the sleeves way up, and tuck the shirt down into my coveralls. I liked the feeling of it. I liked the way I looked in the mirror.

One time, we were fueling up the car. Bart was squirting gas into the car at his side. I got out on the other side and leaned on the door, trying to stand in sort of the same way he did. I liked the way that Bart moved and carried his body. I wanted to do the same. Another car pulled up on the other side of the pump, and a lady started getting out of the driver side. When her door opened she swung her legs out to put her feet on the pavement. She was wearing a skirt, which slid up her waist, and suddenly I could see way up between her legs. Instead of undershorts there, she had something soft and almost shiny, almost the color of skin, and I looked right at it and felt my face get hot and I remembered the girl on the farm unbuttoning her shirt, and I remembered Sinema looking different in her sweater. But the shiny colored patch at the top of this woman's legs gave me a feeling of being stronger than I really was, but just for a moment. Like I got taller and my arms got thicker and my eyes could see further.

"That ain't polite," she said and I looked up at her face. She was smiling. Her lips were wet and very red but without paint on them and her face was so bright white I almost couldn't make it out as different from her hair, which was so yellow it hurt your eyes if you kept looking. I felt a hand on my shoulder and it was Bart, who'd finished pumping and put me in my seat, closing the door. Soon he was in his seat driving us away.

"You looked like you never seen a woman before." Bart looked at me and I looked away from him. "You never had that feeling before?"

"I don't know," I said.

"Well, you best be real careful with that feeling, soldier," said Bart. "It's a trap. Like a knife that goes in real slow, inch by inch, making its way to your liver. Anytime you look at a woman who makes you feel like that, your next thought needs to be, are you ready to feed her? To protect her? To pay for everything she needs? To do as she says? If you go looking between a woman's legs, you need to ask yourself, are you ready to care for the babies that are going to come out of there?"

"Babies?" I said.

"You know where babies come from?" he said. "You ever seen an animal give birth? You ever seen a cow calving? Anything like that?"

I remembered when my father's horse got fat around the middle and he said he'd had it sired by a neighbor's horse and it would have a foal.

My mother had asked if that foal could come to be my horse and my father said, "No way."

And then one day the horse wasn't fat anymore and my father said it had "dropped a dead one" behind the barn and he'd buried it.

My mother cried when he told her and she said, "Can't nothing grow in this place. This place is death."

And my father pointed at me with the neck of his whiskey bottle and said, "He sure grows. Look at him. That boy grows every goddamn day." And my mother ran up the stairs, crying, and I got this feeling like I'd done something wrong.

I had this memory so loud in my mind that I didn't realize that Bart had been talking all along. "Then you put it in her and you get this feeling, like good and bad at the same time, and you come out and go back in again because you can't help wanting to feel it and feel it and she'll tend to grab onto you tight, because she knows that if you find your right mind, you're likely to get out of her and take off running. I got scratches still on my back from women holding on and trying to trap you with that soft warm honeypot, trying to take all you got and swallow it up into her greedy self. Can't any man get out of that trap. Before you know it, you're spilling your seed right into her. She may not look like a chicken, but she got an egg in her inside nest, ready to hatch, and sooner than you know what happened she pushes that baby out the same place between her legs where you went in, and no sooner does she empty out than she wants to be filled back up again, and she'll take every drop you got until the next thing you know, there's a whole crowd of kids calling you daddy and grinding you down to dust." He kept on telling about men and women laying together and the man going inside of the woman with his spigot, and babies being born and how it all came from that feeling I got from looking at the soft shiny cloth between that woman's legs and I got where I was just feeling numb, like when you sleep on the ground on your arm and wake up to find your fingers won't move and your hand may as well be a rock, except I felt that way from my head to my feet.

THE AIR BLOWING IN THE windows got hotter, till it was like heat from a fire. I asked Bart what all that heat was and he said, "ME-XI-CO. We'll be just touching that border and then hanging a turn to the east. Then we'll be in Brownsville. It's still America. But you'll be wishing you talked some Spanish when it's time to order lunch." I told Bart I did speak some Spanish, at least enough to get some food. He laughed and said, "Well now there's something you know that I don't!"

Just then there was a popping sound from the engine. Bart's car began hesitating and then lurching forward and then hesitating, the engine roaring and popping and knocking. Bart reached over, grabbing the wheel, turning it off the road, and I hit the brake.

"Goddamn," said Bart. "Goddamn it all to hell." White and black steam started rising from all the corners of the hood. Bart popped open the front cover and pushed it up and open. That was the first time I ever saw an engine.

"Totaled." Bart looked up and down the road, deciding. "We might as well sleep in the car. Won't be no traffic till morning. But I'll tell you what. How'd you like to learn how an engine works on the inside?"

"Sure," I said. I tried to act *cool* like Bart had said to, but I was excited.

"As good a way as any to kill the last of the daylight," Bart said, as he got a metal box from the trunk. "I ain't got every kind of tool, but you need less to take one apart than you need to fix one." Bart got me hunkered down under the hood. "Good thing the sun's setting on this side. You'll be able to see for a while." Then he commenced to taking a wrench to every nut and bolt on that engine and taking it apart.

"Won't you break it?" I asked.

"Hell, it's broke already. You can tell cuz black smoke came out. White smoke is water steam. Black smoke means oil is where the water should be and water is where oil should be. Seals are cracked. Rod is thrown. She's dead." He took off the *crank case cover* and showed me the *cam shaft* going along all the *cylinders* with big springs that would snap the arm back after the firing cylinder would push it away, and how all that up and down turned to round and round by way of metal knuckles, and how the round and round turns the *belts* and the big fan in front and Bart showed and explained how the engine connects to the *drive shaft* through the *transmission*, which sends the round and round power to the wheels. I usually understood just a little of what people told me when it was about something new to me. But, somehow, I took to the workings of an engine, understanding it all quickly, like it was something I always knew but had forgot. It was more like remembering than learning.

Bart let me fix the wrench to a nut here and there and let me take them off and then put them back on. He showed me the workings on that car till the sun was gone and soon I couldn't see the car or his face, just his shadow. The sky above was splattered with stars, like shining paint spilled across a black floor.

Part Four

Chapter Twenty-One

Oil and Fire

The third day in Brownsville, we found jobs with a company called Matawaki Oil, which Bart said was a Chinese name. We were to be *pipe and drill men*, which Bart said was the lowest job in the system. "I qualify higher," he said as we read the paper posted on front of the building, "but I'd rather have you along than make a little more money. Anyway, the more they pay you, the faster you die."

The man who hired us asked a lot of questions. Bart had told me to say that I was seventeen, which he said I looked, which I did say to the man, who had a wide white hat, and he replied, "Means little matter to me 'slong as you don't show up criminal in the records. What's your first and last name?"

"My name's Ingram," I said.

"What's your last name?" the man asked.

"Don't know," I said.

"That some kind of joke?" he said. "I can't put you in the damn system with one name. You trying to hide something, you hide it someplace else." The man's anger was rising, and his loud voice was coming from such a big chest. "This ain't no place for aliases and outlaws. You better . . ." The man was pointing at the door with his pen.

"Mister," said Bart in a steady voice that stopped the man from talking, "this boy don't know his last name. He got thrown out of his house by his mama when a child."

"I don't care if his daddy done thrown him into a dumpster or if Santy Claus didn't bring him no Christmas. I can't hire a man who don't have two names because I can't put him in the system to be checked out, which is the only way I know you schemin', driftin', lyin' scurvy road rabbits ain't coming here hiding from the law and causing our company liability and me my goddamn job," said the man, with his face leaned way out into Bart's.

"Fair enough," Bart said, just staying *cool*, "put him down as Ingram Grover. He's my brother."

"You didn't say that before," said the man.

"Give him half wage. And don't worry about it," said Bart.

"What do I get out of it?" asked the man.

"Pro-duck-tivity," said Bart slowly. "That's what you fellows care about, right? You're getting a man for half a wage. Looks good on your record."

The man stared at Bart with one wide eye, his lips pulled back, and he said, mean, slow, and quiet, "And what do *you* get out of it?"

"That's my business," said Bart.

"Yeah. I'll just bet," said the man. He put his pen back to the paper and finished.

The next morning, before dawn, Bart and I and many other men climbed a ladder into the back of a great big truck, inside of which was two metal benches facing each other. The only window was in the center of the heavy back door that shut us in. It showed the road behind us, and not much else.

"We are officially out of government territory," said Bart. "The next thousand square miles belongs to the companies, just like we do now. Ain't no votes here. Ain't no rights, ain't no cops, courts, laws, no parks, no trains, or buses or doctors. You're a cog now, soldier." The other men in the truck just looked forward ahead of them, hearing Bart's voice but having no reaction.

The truck rumbled us down the company road, on and on, no one saying anything. I started to feel my eyes drifting shut, my body falling to the side, till Bart's hand clapped onto the back of my neck and pulled me up and over. I fell the other way, against his body. Bart put his arm around my chest and held me to him tight. I never quite fell asleep, but my mind and body rested as we rumbled along in that dark, hot truck.

The back door was opened from the outside and we all stepped out into darkness that was darker than just ordinary night. There were big iron trees, like the ones that held up the great road to Houston, but these trees held scorching bright electric lights pointed straight up into the night sky, which was like a big swallowing up of the light into its black darkness. All the men from the truck were standing around. I could see legs and arms, but a black fog, or mist, or something I'd never seen before, hung so low that I couldn't see anyone's head or face.

"How'd it get night so quick?" I asked Bart.

"It ain't night," he said.

Men walked around, talking to each other, but I couldn't hear anyone's voice and it took a while for me to realize that there was a sound all around us. A sorrowful but unnatural sound, like if a machine could scream in pain, like an angry hawk caught in one long screech, never stopping, never drawing a breath. The sound was all around, so that the men talking to each other had to put their hands on each other's shoulders and hold their heads close like kissing. I was so confused and not knowing where to be or what to do that I realized I'd lost sight of Bart. But then I felt his hand catch hold of my arm and he pulled me away from the crowd of arriving men.

We walked along this dark place till we got to what looked like the box on the back of a truck, but it was sitting on pavement instead of up on wheels, and cut into the side of it was a door, which Bart had a key for and he opened it up and we went inside, shutting out the dark and the screaming noise. Bart turned on a light to find two small beds and a table between, like in the motel room except nothing had any color or shape to it. The walls were gray. Each bed had a thin gray blanket. The table was black and the lamp was metal with a white shade. At the end of the room was a door where we found a bathroom. "This will do," said Bart. "Get used to it. It's home until you can't take it anymore." I looked at him when he said that and I felt a bad feeling. And I saw his face change when he saw mine. He said, "I never should have brought you to this place, Ingram."

"Why do you say that?" I asked.

"Because I guess you'll probably die here," he said. And he turned his whole body away from me so he was looking at a blank wall.

"Maybe I won't die here, Bart," I said, because I wanted him to turn and look at me again. Him not looking at me was like being left alone in this strange place. "You've been here before and you didn't die. Maybe we'll both make money here and then go live somewhere else."

He turned and looked at me, saying, "Man, are you dumb. Can't you see I'm no good?"

"What do you mean you're no good?"

"That ain't your business and it ain't your problem. Or least ways it shouldn't be," said Bart, sitting on the bed, facing me on my bed, our knees touching. "It's one thing I married that woman I never should have. She was grown. She took her shot. I was no good for her or the kids. So me coming here to sap whatever I can out of this place, and die doing it so I can send her a check that won't have a second of time on it. You know that, soldier? You can write a check for a billion dollars. But you can't write one for even one second of time. And here I am stealing time from you. Nothing but a kid." Then he laid his face on his hands, held up by his elbows on his knees, and I looked at the top of Bart's head.

"I wanted to come here," I said. "I would have come here if you didn't bring me. I'm glad you brought me." I wanted him to look up at me again. I was beginning to feel afraid.

Then Bart got all-at-once mad and swatted at the air in front of him like a fly was bothering him, but there wasn't a living thing in that room but me and him. "Man, your life ain't my fault," said Bart, getting up and whipping off his shirt. Then he took off his pants and got in bed and so did I. I felt unsettled and I guess so did he, but it was late and it had been a long day, so sleep came easy.

The next day we woke because someone pounded on our door and a voice shouted, "IT'S MORNING!" as a siren outside began to wail. Bart and I washed up and came out of the metal box we had slept in.

The outside was just the same as when we'd gone to bed. Dark black sky hanging down to the shoulders of grown men. Everything lit dimly by big bright lights. The constant scream of the hawk-like machine. Bart said, "There's no morning, noon, or night in this hell. Just a call to work, a call to eat, a call to quit. Only thing that breaks it up is a blow-out. Then they make you go under the blankets till the fire's out."

The big machines we worked at had nuts and bolts, same as the engine in a car. But the nuts and bolts on the drillers were as big as a boy's head. The wrenches that turned the nuts required three men to work them. One, a *nut hugger*, to hold the giant wrench to the nut, and two men to push the wrench, turning it left or right, with all their weight and might. The metal had to be thick and heavy to hold back the pushing strength, or *pressure* of the oil coming up from under the ground. "It's like the earth itself is trying to spit hot black blood up through the sky, clear out to outer space," said Bart. "Ain't one man, animal, or force of steel stronger than *pressure*, which is the will of earth itself."

I was a nut hugger. I had to hug my body against the up-to-down pipe and use the heels of my hands to hold up the open iron jaws of the wrench against the flat sides of the nut and keep it from slipping down or off as it jiggered around. The end man would grunt and push on the giant wrench while the middle man would huff and puff to hold up the center. As he pushed, I'd feel the head get tight against the nut, which would slowly begin to twist from the *leverage* of the wrench, either to the left or to the right, depending on if we were closing or opening the inside valve. "Lefty loosey, righty tighty," the supervising man reminded us every single time and as we turned it he would shout "SLOW, SLOW, SLOW!" It was difficult for all three of us to slow down while pushing and lifting so hard. But we knew that meant the pressure needed to be coaxed into the pipe and not blasted through it.

"It's like leading a nervous horse through a narrow canyon," said Bart. "Pressure is an almighty power. But it's dumb."

Bart explained that as we pushed, the nut turned and the valve inside swung open. When it did, the pipe started to shake and I could feel the oil under pressure being let in from the bottom section into the top section which would heave and buck, trying to take earth's spit all at once. That was in the case we were opening. When closing the valve, the bottom section bucked and shook as the top relaxed. With my arms and thighs wrapped around the iron I could feel the pressure of the earth pushing, wanting to burst out.

I knew the danger of that happening was real, because I'd been told that the iron gets weaker as you push it and that the company gets everything they can from every pipe but "burst they must and burst they does," said a man I ate across from at the long shiny steel tables where we had our lunch. He had only one arm, his shirt sewed up at the shoulder on the other side. I'd seen other men at the oil fields missing hands, fingers, arms, and feet. But I hadn't talked to one. This man's name was Jelly, and he was the only one at mealtime in constant motion, and that's because of his one arm. He had to take a heap of beans on his fork, shovel it in his mouth, and then put the fork down with a clang to take his cup and drink water, slam the cup down and pick up the fork. I looked at his sewed-up shirt, and he said, "You want to ask me where my arm went?" And I nodded my head yes, my mouth full of beans. "Well, I was born with two arms, just like you, boy," said Jelly. "And I was hugging on a pipe, which burst on one side into smithereens, my whole arm bursting out in a spray like red wet confetti. I was in a daze for a minute and when I come to my senses, the supervisor said, 'Jelly, where's your arm?' and I said, 'Well, chief, you can't see it cuz it's all over your face." Jelly laughed, showing his black teeth. Other men at the table laughed but only a bit, like they'd heard this before and it had stopped being so funny. "You feel bad for me, cuz I got one arm, boy?" Jelly asked me. "Well, every time you see a man here missing a limb, just know you're looking at one lucky bastard."

"Lucky?" I said.

"Lucky to be alive," said Jelly. "You a nut hugger, ain't you?"

"Yeah."

"Nut huggers all die unless they lose an arm, buddy. Losing an arm is better."

"Shut up, Jelly," said Bart who sat next to me. "He's just trying to scare you," he said to me.

"Am I lying?" said Jelly. Bart didn't say anything.

At night, which we only knew had come when the sirens sung, telling us to go back to our rooms, Bart and me would sit on our beds, quiet. When we weren't too tired, I'd read out loud from *Moby Dick* and Bart would explain the parts I didn't understand. Like how they'd lower a small boat from the big ship and fill it with men to go and kill a whale.

"See, a whale isn't like a fish. He needs to breathe the air. He must come up and blow out his hole that he has at the top of his head. When he does that, one man in the boat throws a harpoon, hard as he can, trying to stick it into the side of the whale."

"What's a harpoon?"

"Like a knife, with a blade as long as your arm. You haul it over your shoulder and heave it into the side of the whale, which is as thick as iron pipe but blubber and flesh. Whales were tough so it didn't kill them. They'd keep swimming. But the blade of the harpoon has a hook in it, so it sticks inside and the men in the boat got pulled and bucked up and down and all around the ocean in their little boat, till either they'd drown or the whale bled to death."

"And then what?"

"Then they'd drag it back to the ship and haul it on board, cut it up and render the blubber down to oil, and they'd climb down the blow hole into its head and get the oil straight out its skull. They put all that oil into big vats and sailed home where they'd sell it for piles of gold."

"You mean oil like what comes through the pipes here?"

"Just like that. Oil from the whales lit up the whole world. And that was the only way to get it. Until someone figured out it's down deep under the ground too." I laid there on the thin gray bed and imagined that the rock and soil we were drilling down into was like the skin of a great dirt whale and that the drills were harpoons and that every time we pierced the flesh and blubber of the earth it roared and bucked while we hung onto the pipes.

Sunday was the only day we didn't work. "The break ain't for us," Jelly told me. "It's to let the iron cool." There wasn't any preacher or church service on Sunday. But the screaming noise would stop and the dark sky lifted up a bit higher so you could see men's faces as they walked and stood around doing not much but talking. I asked Bart why no one sang songs or drank whiskey on Sundays like they did on the farm.

Bart said he didn't know. "I hate Sundays," he said. "Ain't nothing pleasant to do, no sky to look at. Can't smoke. All Sundays do is break up the misery so you know how long it is. Otherwise, these days would just slip one into the other and I'd sleep through it."

I don't know how many weeks and how many Sundays went by, between dark days of hard work in the black fog of the oil fields, before Bart just quit talking. At night after work, he'd go right to bed and sleep and at lunch if I asked him a question, he'd either say he didn't know or he wouldn't answer.

Then one night as I slept with my back turned to his side of the room, I felt my bed slump down behind me and I heard Bart's breathing from close and realized he was climbing onto my bed. I started to look back but he put his hand on the side of my head, keeping it looking at the wall, and he got himself under my blanket and sheets and soon I felt his body against the back of mine. I didn't say anything because, by the way his hand was firm on my head, I had an idea he didn't want me to. When he got close up behind me, he took his hand off my head and wrapped it around my chest. I could feel his breath on my neck and shoulder. It felt like when I used to sleep in Marion's bed, except her body was soft and warm and Bart's was muscles and bone like wood covered with leather. And his grip around me was strong. "Why are you in my bed?" I asked him.

"Just feels better than being alone," he said, sounding like he was in some kind of pain. And then he asked, "Does it feel better for you?"

I didn't know the answer right away. I didn't mind having him there. Something about it was uneasy though. "I'm not used to it," I said.

"Let's just try it tonight," said Bart. "Just sleeping. Just sleeping together is all. Okay?"

I didn't say anything. Bart started breathing hard and slow and finally he began to snore the way I was used to hearing him from his bed, but now it was right in my ear. There was something in his being closed in around me, like the way he held me up when we rode in the back of the truck, that was better than being in a bed by myself wondering if I'd get that feeling like there's nothing around me but gray till it would curl around into the shape of that creature and make me fall asleep in a state of fear. I also found it better to have him in my bed, saying the little he'd said, than how he'd been so quiet like he was hardly alive at all.

The next thing I remembered was the siren sounding for wake-up. I got up and Bart was gone. He wasn't in my bed, wasn't in his. I got up and went to work and found him having coffee with some other men. He saw me coming and put his cup down and walked away. All that day, as we worked, Bart kept looking away from me. At lunchtime he sat away from me. That night in our room he slept in his bed with his back to me. He had been quiet before. He was more than just quiet now. He seemed angry. "You mad with me, Bart?" I asked from my bed to his.

At first he didn't answer, but after some silence he said, "We shouldn't have done that last night. It was wrong."

"Done what?" I asked. "We just slept together is all."

"Don't ever be in a bed with a man again, Ingram," he said. "I got weak. It wasn't right. That ain't right."

"I didn't mind it, Bart."

"That's why it was wrong. If a man comes into your bed or otherwise puts himself against you, you fight him off."

"But you're my friend."

"I'm a man, Ingram. You need to be wary of me like anyone. I'm weak."

"Why do I need to be wary if you're weak?"

"On the inside, soldier," he said and I heard that he was sniffling from his nose. "I mean weak on the inside. Nothing more dangerous to you, young stupid boy as you are, than a man who is strong on the outside and weak on the inside."

I listened to Bart's struggling breaths until he started snoring. I wondered what it meant, being weak on the inside, being strong on the outside. I looked at my hand in the dark and squeezed it into a fist. That felt strong. I put my hand on my chest, pressing against my muscles. That felt strong. I closed my eyes and tried to feel if I could feel inside. There was something in there for sure. I tried to feel if it was weak or strong. I took a deep breath. My chest went up, lifting my pressing hand. I moved my hand down to my belly, which was soft and tender on the outside. From inside of my belly, the touch of my hand was warm. I pushed my fingers down and into my skin and I could feel the hard bones of my fingers. I'm weak in my belly, I thought. I moved my hand down lower. The rubbing on my skin caused a kind of twitch on the inside. I ran my hand lower till it was laying over my spigot. I knew if I pushed into it, I'd feel pain. My spigot being such a soft and tender thing, like a baby chick when I held it to pee. I held it in that tender way now, as I laid in my bed. The feeling on the inside, which had started in my chest, was in my hips now and partly in my spigot, which started having a tiny kind of shaking in it. My hips moved down into the bed and then up and I didn't know why. I didn't plan them to. They just did it. And then the strangest thing came along and happened. My spigot grew in my hand and filled up somehow, getting stiffer and longer until I could feel it buzzing like a tiny oil pipe, trying to push the earth's black blood out and my hand was like me being a nut hugger, except instead of iron it was skin, which could no way hold back what was coming and I started to fear I would pee in my bed and then came a roaring inside of my head and my whole body and mind went burning hot and I went someplace else where I'd never been born and the world wasn't the world and I saw two red eyes and a dead snake and I saw Anna Lee and I saw my father and I saw Sinema and I saw the world from up high. I saw water, for miles and miles, and I thought this must be the ocean and I saw Sinema and I felt my spigot jerk in my hand and something warm, like blood or oil, spilled out of it and I let out a sound like a hog when you kicked it off the porch and then I was back in that little room and Bart's snoring had stopped.

I froze myself still in my bed, laying there with my spigot in my wet hand, wondering how I would clean all that spigot grease off the bed and what Bart would say when he saw it. I fell asleep like that. And when I woke up there was no blood or oil, no mess at all. I would have thought I dreamed it all, but I was pretty sure by then I could tell dream from waking life.

Bart became even more like a stranger to me after that night. He got up and went to work without talking or looking at me, like he was alone in the room. Any time I tried to talk to him he walked away or stood there saying nothing. I still followed him to work. We still worked on drill gangs together. I sat next to him at lunch, and he let me. But no words passed between us.

One morning at lunch, a supervisor went around the eating tables asking men if they qualified for *small engine repair*. I looked at Bart, wanting to ask him what the man meant, but Bart was looking down into his soup and I knew if I asked, he wouldn't answer. So, when the man came up to our table, I just raised my hand and said, "I do, sir." Even though I didn't know if I did. The supervisor told me to follow him, which I did, to an area where a bunch of greasy engines like the one in Bart's car were held up by steel frames in various stages of being broke.

The man said that the engines had been hooked up to priming pumps, cable winches, and generators. Between the engines were black iron tables with metal shelves, stuffed with tools and various mechanical parts. "Find all you need there," said the man. "If you can get any of these running you got the job. If you can't manage it, I'll put you back where you were." He walked away quickly.

I'd been thinking about Bart's car engine since I'd had its heavy pieces in my hands. Here was a new, smaller engine in front of me. It was cold, quiet, and unmoving. I took a deep breath and wondered, why did it stop working? And what would make it go again? Without much of a plan or particular idea, I got a wrench in my hand and began pushing here, pulling there, finding that all the parts that ought to move were frozen. I took off a panel here and one there, not knowing what I was looking for, until I got to the front of the engine where I noticed a rubber belt that should have been threaded across three pulleys had snapped and was bunched up in the corner and melted stuck. I used a screwdriver to scrape out the dead belt and I looked on the shelves and found many belts in many sizes. The process of sizing a belt, fitting it to the pulleys, and adjusting them tight enough to hold the tension all came strangely easy to me. I didn't know why I could do it any more than I could remember learning to speak or to put my clothes on in the morning. In a few minutes I had the engine hooked up to a gas line I found that went to a tank that sat on the floor and to a battery with wires. "Fuel system, lubrication, coolant, electrical," Bart had shown me on the side of the road.

"It's just like a person," he had said. "Food is our fuel. Our brains are electrical. We need water to cool off."

"What's our lubrication?" I asked.

"Fun, I guess." Bart smiled and we laughed together. Made me sad to remember that as I hit the green button that said "go" and the engine coughed, growled, and sprang to life. It was about then the supervisor man walked by again, saw the engine running, and said, "Good enough, Hoss. What's your name?"

"Ingram Grover," I said.

"Good enough. You're small engine repair. Report here, every morning, now on. Be an increase in it. Don't know how much, but more is more." He walked away, leaving me standing there. I liked working on the engine. I liked finding I could fix it. And I surely liked that it got me a new job, with an *increase.* All that added up to liking the whole moment so strong, it almost made me dizzy in my head.

I kept working on other engines. One of them was easy—the distributor wire was gone. But the third engine, I took apart so much I got a little worried about keeping track of all the nuts and pieces. When I got deep enough into it, I found a crack in the cylinder, which was nothing I could fix. I was worried I would lose my job the same way I'd got it. Then Jelly came along, driving a forklift.

"Hi ho, Ingram," he said. "Looks like you got a safe job like mine and you didn't have to lose your arm to land it." I helped Jelly use a small hoist on the forklift to load up the engines in a pile. He was good with his one arm. When he got to the third engine, he said, "What's wrong with this one?"

"It's got a big crack inside," I said. "I can't figure how to fix it."

"Don't worry about it," Jelly said, smiling. "Take this red marker and write 'total' across the top whenever you can't fix it." He reached on the tool shelf and found a red marker, doing what he'd told me to do, and he hauled everything away, leaving me with no engines to fix.

"What do I do now?" I asked.

"You got a light load today. Knock off early," he said. "Enjoy it. Tomorrow you might work late."

Jelly went away on the forklift and I looked down at my hands, which were greasy like his face. I thought about wiping them off on one of the red rags on the table but I wanted to keep them like they were. I wanted Bart to see. Even though he'd been not talking to me and I didn't feel a friendship between us, I wanted to tell someone about what was happening, because it felt good. And I thought about how Bart had called me his brother, maybe only for convenience, but that was something. *Bart is my brother*, I thought. It shouldn't matter that he got upset about what happened in my bed. It shouldn't matter if he's not speaking to me. If something good happens to you, you should tell your brother. No one had ever told me that, and I didn't remember having a brother, even though my mother had told me I had one, when she gave me his hat.

I found Bart working on a drill crew, hugging a nut, which is what I would have been doing if I didn't go with the man to find my new job. Bart was having difficulty stabilizing the head of the wrench on the nut. I knew it was shaking bad because his voice quivered, even though he was sweat-hot, as he yelled, "Just open the goddamn thing and let it through!"

"SLOW, SLOW, SLOW," said the supervisor.

"Slow my ass!" said the end wrench man.

"It's gonna be MY ASS if you don't let her open!" shouted Bart's quivering voice.

"Bart!" I yelled his name, not knowing why. Bart looked over at me when he heard my voice and our eyes looked at each other's for shorter than a breath and then, with a sound like a giant dish breaking on a ten-acre-wide kitchen floor, the drill-pipe burst, spraying iron and oil out to the side. I saw a big chunk of iron smash right into Bart's chest, cutting him nearly in two bloody halves, held together by thread and bone, and I saw his face full of pain and fear as the oil sprayed all over him and in all directions. The oil spray touched a spark somewhere, which licked back in blue flame all the way back to the pipe and suddenly the parts of Bart that still stood up caught all on fire, his skin burning blue and his clothes burnt in orange fire. When he screamed he didn't sound like himself, didn't even sound human or like any animal. I watched Bart burn and scream and dance before I understood that there were four other men burning and I didn't see that Jelly had run up behind me and tackled me to the ground with an asbestos blanket and the rest of the commotion I only heard through the thick, fireproof cloth. I was glad I couldn't see it with my eyes anymore. I could feel myself putting what I saw, and what I could hear, into some place outside of my mind, not letting it get into my memory, so I'd never have to see it again.

Chapter Twenty-Two

Pa

In the oil fields, when a man dies, nothing happens. You might hear how it happened at the next lunch, but only by way of interest and wanting to have something to talk about. Past that, there was little to show the dead man was ever there.

Bart was only the first man I saw die in the oil fields. There were many others in the years I worked there, which were like years of mud, one dark misty day after another. It all ran together in the black fog. The only man I ever spoke to was Jelly, and never more than conversation about work. The only thing to mark time by was that I was learning to fix engines, more and better.

The company had moved me out of the room where Bart and I had stayed in favor of two men who newly arrived and wanted to room together. I came to know that most men roomed together, ate, and worked together—lived like a pair of shoes. Bart and I had been like that. I wondered how many of the men in the oil fields slept in the same bed.

My new room had only one bed and less than half the space. I didn't care. It was somewhere to sleep when I wasn't working. I never finished reading *Moby Dick*. I'd lost interest in it. The supervisor had scrounged up some manuals of the engines I'd been fixing and there was nothing I'd ever enjoyed reading more than books about engines, how they worked and how they were built.

I asked Jelly when he dropped off an air compressor engine that had blown a gasket and was covered in oil, "How come I'm the only one who wanted this job?"

"You're the only one who can do it," he said.

"But I'm only learning to do it myself," I said. "Why doesn't anyone else learn, to get the increase? And to be safer?"

Jelly rubbed his one hand on his chin, spreading grease on it, and said, "I guess most men don't want to learn themselves nothing. Easier to keep your mind where it is. Anyway, more money ain't so much more than less money around here." And he put his forklift in reverse, rolling away backwards, his grinning head fading into the black cloud, which was low and thick that day.

I had no idea how much money I was earning. Unlike on the farm, men didn't get paid until they left the job for good. There was no need for money while we were working there. Food was free and there was nothing else to spend on. The company men said that pay on-site would only be a "liability for theft."

"You get paid when you leave, if you leave, which you won't," Jelly would say.

I didn't think about leaving. I didn't think about staying either. I just did it. I liked finding the trouble with each engine I faced and being able to fix them brought me a kind of pleasure. But I began to feel something that surrounded all my other feelings like a blanket around my body. The oil fields were a bad place to be. If you looked at a man's face, you'd see the black fog go in and out of his mouth as he breathed, and that told me that I was breathing that fog into my body every day too, even though I couldn't see it. It was getting so every time I drew a breath, my chest felt tight and my head hurt all the time. I didn't dream about anything when I slept.

I had stopped thinking back on my past, the people and things I'd seen, like I had never been anywhere in my whole life except this black place. I'd stopped remembering my mother's face, my father's back, my time on the road. I'd quit thinking about Kyle, whose voice in my memory used to make me laugh. I never thought about the farm, or drinking whiskey. It was like I was never any place else except this black place. And I soon forgot Bart as well as everyone else had.

The only person that ever visited my thoughts as I'd wait to fall asleep was Sinema. I'd remember her face and lips and the shape of her sweater when I'd seen her in Austin. I'd think about the sound of her voice and the way she looked at me with interest. When I had these thoughts, I'd move my hand down my chest and belly and wrap it around my spigot. I'd close my eyes and wait for the rush to come over me and the visions to fill my mind and for my body to go stiff and for my spigot to spout whatever it was, which I never looked at, knowing it would be gone when I woke up. Touching my spigot never lasted much longer than a minute but it was the only minute I'd feel like I wasn't in that place, which I had begun to hate.

I sometimes thought about Sinema when I was working, wondering what she would think about me now. Wondering if she would be proud of the way I'd learned to do something useful. Wondering how she'd feel about the thoughts I had when I did what I did at night. So it was a great surprise to me, one day, to see a transport truck arrive with new workers, and to see Pa, Sinema's father, climb out of the back.

The last I'd seen Pa was when he sent me away from Black Town. Now he looked different. His belly was bigger and it hung down lower over his legs, which were skinnier. The crab apples in his arms had gotten soft. His hair was longer now, but thinner and gray. His face looked tight. I stood there, just a few feet away from where he was shaking out his ankles and stretching his back after the long ride in the truck. I reached in my pocket, putting my hand around my knife, which I had touched every day since he had given it to me.

A supervisor came to gather the men that had arrived in the trucks and bring them to sleeping quarters, which was behind where I was standing. As Pa turned himself toward me to follow along, there was a tingling on the parts of my skin that said I knew he'd see—my arms, hands, and face. He began to walk toward me and I waited for the moment when he'd see me. His walking gaze meant his eyes met directly with mine, but he walked past me, not having known for a moment that he'd seen someone he knew.

Pa might have looked softer, but he was as strong as any man in the oil fields, though his face carried the pain of the hard work more than some. I would sometimes see him on a drill crew if I walked by. We never spoke to each other.

"YOU'RE ALWAYS FIRST IN LINE," said a nasty voice behind me one day as I lined up for lunch. I turned to see a man I didn't know. "What makes you better than anyone else?" His whole face was pulled back tight with anger. His hands were balled up in fists at his sides and his back was hunched over like he was ready to do something. "How come you get to go always before everybody?"

"I'm just getting my food," I said.

"Well, I'm sick of waiting on you," he said. Other men were paying attention to us because we were holding up the lunch line. "Why don't you go fuck off some place?" said this angry man, who had a clean-shaven chin that ended in a point that curved up toward the tip of his long nose, which curved down to meet it. The man leaned his heavy body forward, close to mine. I could smell his sweat and his dark eyes were squinting into mine. I thought about what Bart had said about being cool. I took a breath in through my nose and let it out, and I said, "I don't have no interest in making you wait. If you want to go ahead of me . . ."

He hit me right across my face with his tin food tray. It didn't hurt much, but it sent me backward and made a loud metal sound, followed by all the men standing around all at once hollering and whistling. This fellow started swinging that tray at me again. He caught me on the jaw with the edge of it this time, which I could feel put a cut in me. I put my fists up in front of my face. He threw the tray down and started punching at me all over my face and belly. I was looking right at his angry face that seemed to stay still as his arms whirled around, his fists coming too fast for me to stop or even see them, putting hurt on me all over my body and face and all the men shouting made a wall of sound around us and then his fist came right down the middle of the world until it was all I saw as it landed between my eyes and blinded me. I fell on my back and tried to cover my face with my arms. My nose was filling up with blood. My ribs got a sudden shock of pain, which I knew was him jumping on top of me and sitting on my chest.

"Let me at ya!" he yelled as he tried to pry my arms off my face. "Quit coverin', ya coward bastard!" I didn't understand how he could be angry at me for covering myself as I'm sure he would have. He quit trying to pry my arms open and just started dropping punches down on them and all around my sides. I couldn't breathe or move and I wanted to die for so much pain and I hated the sounds of the men hollering until suddenly I felt the man fly off me and heard everyone around say, "Aw! No!" and make other noises of disappointment. I opened my eyes to see that Pa was holding the man around his middle and tearing him away.

"Get off me, black bastard!" yelled the man.

Pa drew his arms around the man's chest tighter, and I saw Pa's face grimace like he did when he was working and he squeezed the man until all at once the man went limp like a sack doll and Pa sat him down at a bench at one of the tables, saying to him, "You just calm down, mister. That there's just a boy." Pa then came over to me and took my elbow, pulling me up, leading me away from the situation.

Pa sat across from me, giving me some of his lunch, as I'd lost my place in line. I took a long drink from his water, tasting my own blood from my broken-up mouth. Pa handed me his napkin and pointed at his own face, showing me where to wipe the blood off of my own, which I did. One of my eyes was swelling up so I could see the skin in front of it. But the pain wasn't much to me. I was glad Pa was letting me sit with him.

"How'd you end up down here?" said Pa.

"Came here to work. Like everybody else."

"You're nothing but a boy," he said, spooning some beans into his mouth.

"I'm bigger now," I said. "I worked on a farm. Been on the road. I got a good job here. Small engine repair."

"Ain't no good jobs in hell," he said. "You want to die before you turn twenty?"

"It's safe doing the work I do," I said. "Plus I earn more money."

"Ain't safe," said Pa. "You get sick and die or get blown up."

"I thought you didn't know me," I said. "I saw you when you arrived. You walked right by me, the day you got here."

"Have you seen yourself lately?" said Pa. "You're almost as black as me. All the oil and smoke in the air is covering you inside and out. The boy I met back in Houston was a pink little boy. Now you're body's grown up, you're almost tall as me. And already you're worn out. You skipped straight from a child to a broken old man."

"A person has to work," I said.

"Work for what?"

"I want to earn enough money to buy a truck," I said.

Pa laughed. Some beans came out of his mouth. "You damn fool," he said. "I thought I told you to get smart. Only men that work in a hell like this, do so to provide for a family."

"I don't have no family," I said. I started to get angry back at him. "You ain't my family neither."

Pa stopped laughing. "I reckon I ain't," he said, and he got up and walked away, leaving me at a table of black men to finish his lunch, which he'd pushed the rest of in front of me.

A few days went by when I'd see Pa and he'd see me and we wouldn't say anything. Then one day I took my lunch tray to his table and sat across from him. He looked up from his food at me and then went on eating.

"I saw Sinema," I said, my words stopping his spoon right before it reached his mouth.

"You saw her when?" he asked. "Where?"

"Maybe a year ago. Maybe more. I lost track."

"How was she?" I saw his eyebrows, which were always pushed down to the center of his face, ease back toward his ears.

"She said she missed home. And that no one there will write to her. But she looked good. She was—" I got afraid to tell him the next word on my mind.

"What was she?"

"She was beautiful," I said.

Pa looked at me, his eyebrows now straight across his skull. "How long were you . . . with her?" he asked in a careful voice.

"She bought me a burger. I walked her home. She said she couldn't see me after that. She's working hard at school," I said. He nodded and went back to eating.

Pa and I started talking more often after that. We had our coffee together in the mornings and often lunch too. "I done had too many kids," he said one time. He started telling me things about himself and his thoughts. "Miss Maw loves a full house. Hell, she takes in every urchin off the street. But it's a hell of a load on a man's back."

Other times Pa told me about his life before he met Miss Maw. "I was a tom-cattin' young buck," he said, looking away, smiling, like he could see his young self in the black fog. "I wasn't nothing like you. You're a soft boy. Even now. Naw, I was full of spice and trouble. Fighting. Running away always. My pa used to beat me, trying to break me down. All he did was teach me to fight and not mind getting hit. He died. Left my mama alone to raise us. I was the only boy. So I had to go to work, feed and put clothes on my seven sisters. I was sixteen, surrounded by girls and women, all depending on me. No more fooling around. No more fighting and tomcatting. My friends, they all forgot me. I worked on yards, I worked on road gangs. Worked the steel into half the buildings they put up in Houston. Then my sister brought home a friend. Miss Maw. She was big and beautiful. Married her. And all I wanted was a son. I wanted a boy I could raise without beating him. Give him a full belly, a good body, the peace of mind to go get an education and have a better life than me. I end up having eight girls. One boy. But he was frail. A gust of wind would make him cower and cry. His knees couldn't hold him upright. And he never grew any courage. Maybe if it was just him, Maw and I could have pumped him up. He might have made it. But all them girls crushed him down to dust, poor little soul. So there I've been since, surrounded by girls and women all over again, all depending on me." And he laughed. "Listen, Ingram," Pa said, leaning on his elbows across our lunch trays. "You need to get out of here. You must have enough waiting for you on payroll. You got a skill now. You can take that anywhere and make a living. You got to get out of this place."

"Why don't you leave?" I asked.

"I'll never leave here again," he said.

"Ingram," said the supervisor one morning. "What the hell you doing?"

I told him I was cleaning the O-rings on a V8 engine.

"That engine weren't broke," he said. "How'd you get it?"

"I asked Jelly bring me engines that aren't busy, so I can maintain them."

"Maintain? You ain't supposed to maintain. You supposed to repair."

"I been reading the books on the engines, and they say if you keep the O-rings clean, if you replace the gaskets, in other ways keep it in good shape, it won't break so often. It's called preventative maintenance."

The man took his hat off, wiping the sweat from his brow, and looked at me for a long while. Then he put his hat back on, pushed it down on his head, pointed at me with his fat pink finger, and said, "You're fired," and walked away.

I picked up one of the O-rings and wiped the grease off it with a rag. The metal under the grease was shiny. I liked cleaning it off. I knew I liked that, turning greasy rings into shiny ones. I couldn't get the grease off my own skin anymore. But I could get this ring shiny like a new dime. I decided I would clean these O-rings and not think about what else to do for now.

As I stood there, cleaning that O-ring, I saw a white light all around me that made me shut my eyes. I felt the air in my lungs get pulled out. I heard men shout and scream. Without knowing why, I put my hands over my head and pulled myself into a ball under the metal table. I felt the blast. It was like being slapped by hot hard air from every direction on every part of my body. A bang noise pushed into my ears to the center of my head. Then came a roaring that went on and on along with orange and blue fire, scorching my back and sides and all of me that wasn't balled up together or protected by my own covering hands and arms. My mind shut off all at once, not like fainting when I was sick and not like falling down drunk and not like going to sleep. It was like I *was* and then I *wasn't.* My head was cold and wet and being sucked down into something colder and wetter and I couldn't breathe. I reached around with my hands, trying to touch my own head and instead I felt what I knew was the gray cold creature. He was eating me, head first. I tried with all my might to push him off and pull my head out of his mouth and I tried to yell out. I screamed, making the loudest sound of all my living days, and that scream brought the world back to me in shining warm light and I drew the longest deepest gasping breath, opening my eyes wide to see the white ceiling of a hospital, which is where I was, some weeks after it all had happened.

Chapter Twenty-Three

Burnt, Alive

The hospital in Austin was very different from the one in Houston. I was in a small room with three other men, and two of them were so burnt up in the blast that they had bandages all around their bodies and heads with only little holes for feeding with a straw. The man next to me had a plastic tent over his bed with air being pumped into it and anyone who reached inside his tent to feed him or give him medicine had to wear gloves and a white cloth over their mouth and nose.

They told me I had bad burns all down my back and legs. "You were a lot worse when you come in!" said a nurse who was tall, with very thin arms and a very small round head like an apple at the end of a long, thin neck. She had to yell very loud for me to hear her because my ears were *concussed*. The sound of her voice came to me muffled like she was shouting into a pillow. "You had all blood coming out of your ears, boy! And you hardly had any skin at all back there, boy! It was all charred and gooed! They had to scrape you down and rebuild you, boy! Good thing you slept through it!"

Her name was Abigail, and she was the one who told me, or yelled to me, that I was in Austin and that there had been a *phosphorous explosion* that killed ninety-seven men and destroyed all the machinery in that oil field. "No one could get near that flame to put it out for weeks! It burned all through Christmas and New Year's, boy! It was a miracle that any of you made it out of there! Some brave man in an asbestos suit went around grabbing folks and pulling them out with a forklift or something! It was a miracle! A Christmas miracle! He's a hero now, boy!"

"Jelly?" I asked.

"Yeah!" she shouted, excited. "That was his name! Jelly! Isn't that funny?!" And she grinned, showing that she had great long teeth and even longer gums. It was something a bit hard to look at.

Sometimes a doctor came in to see me with Abigail. They would take off my bandages, which were up to my neck. When the doctor talked to me, he didn't shout like Abigail did. He talked very slowly and clearly, which was enough for me to understand him.

"Does. That. Hurt?" he asked me as he peeled off a bandage.

"Yes, sir," I said.

"Does it hurt very much?"

"Yes, sir," I said.

"Well, son. I need you to report your pain. I need to know if it hurts. Or doesn't. Otherwise, I assume the nerves are dead, and then we have other problems. Okay?"

"Yes, okay, sir," I said. The doctor took his little silver scissors and peeled away a bandage, showing the red skin on my arm. He looked at my face.

I said, "That hurts very much, sir." And it did.

I didn't know why I didn't holler or twitch at the pain. The pain was worse than I'd ever felt. I just didn't care. I didn't care about anything at all. I didn't have any thoughts. I didn't remember anything. It's not that I'd forgotten. My memories were there. But I just let them lay, like an old shirt on the floor that I didn't care to pick up and put on. I'd listen to the quiet sound of Abigail screaming at me. I ate what she fed me. I told the doctor it hurt when he asked. And when no one was there, I looked at the ceiling and thought about nothing. I swear I didn't even think to myself, *I'm thinking nothing*, I just didn't think. For days and days. And I slept every night with no dreams.

My burns started to heal. The doctor cleaned out my ears. I could hear sounds in the room and even some from outside, coming in the window, like birds and cars. Then one morning, a man came in to our room wearing a red suit with a tiny white chip of collar at his neck. He walked by the first fellow's bed and touched his foot. He put his hand on the tent of the bed next to me and stood there looking sad for a minute. Then he came over and stood next to me, smiling.

"Hello, son," the man in the red suit said. "How are you feeling?" He put his hand on my shoulder. "Do you know that no matter how you suffer, someone is always there for you? Someone is always listening? Someone is watching over you and taking care of you? Someone who loves you and is with you every step of the way. Did you know that?"

He was the first person to speak to me since the blast who I could fully hear. And he was saying the most untrue thing I had ever heard in my whole life.

I began sleeping less in the day and remembering more. I remembered *Moby Dick* and I wondered what happened at the end of the book. Where I had stopped reading, the men on that ship saw the terrible white Moby Dick *breech*, which Bart had said is when a whale jumps clear out of the water, seems to fly up into the air and then comes crashing down, making a boat rock around, putting fear into the hearts of the men on board as they realize they are in the whale's home. While the whale can jump into their world and crash safely back down to his, if the men fall out of their ship, they'll just drop into the waves like little frogs, drown and disappear, to be eaten by Moby Dick, or just picked down into nothing by tiny creatures, smaller than a thumbnail.

In the book, the men have become afraid because Captain Ahab, being crazy and angry, wouldn't quit until he killed Moby Dick. Ahab was leading them all into great danger. The boy telling the story was called Ishmael.

Ishmael was weak and young but the other fellows on the ship were strong and there were lots of them. Yet, somehow, the one man, Ahab, had a power over them and they couldn't say no to the terrible things he made them do, and they all began to think he was leading them to their death.

I began to imagine my own ending to *Moby Dick*. In my ending, Ishmael talked to the great big fellow who he shared a cabin with, the one who threw the harpoon, and they agreed to take Ahab by the throat and hold him down, tying him to his own bed and stuffing rags in his mouth to shut him up, and then locked him in his cabin. Then, all the sailors worked together to sail the ship back to a safe and quiet country where they'd go off in all directions and live their lives peacefully on land where humans belong. I liked the feeling of this ending except I couldn't work out what would happen to Ahab. I didn't want him to starve to death, tied down to his bed in the abandoned ship. But if Ishmael stayed behind to free him, Ahab might have the power to force Ishmael back out onto the sea. So maybe Ahab had to die.

"Time for me to wash you!" shouted Abigail one morning. She didn't need to, because my ears had been cleaned and fixed. But I didn't say anything because it was tickling me inside to let her shout anyway. "I washed you lots of times when you were still under!" she said as she folded my blanket and sheets down to my waist, uncovering my chest and belly. Then she dipped a washcloth in a white tub of soapy water that had steam coming off of it. "It'll be easier you being awake! I won't have to move you around myself! You're a big strong one, boy!"

Abigail put her hand on my chest, and with her other hand, she ran the warm, soapy rag across my arms, across all the skin that wasn't covered by bandages. Then she dipped the rag again, wrung it out, and put it on my chest. The feeling of the rag on my chest was soothing at first, and then the water cooled as it dried. But the feeling that was the strangest to me was Abigail's bare hand on the skin of my chest. I felt her skin on my skin. She was quiet, looking where she was scrubbing, and looking up to my face, and then down to where she was scrubbing again. She moved down my chest and now she laid her bare hand on my belly, close to the chuck hole it had on its center, and she scrubbed the warm soapy water down lower. "Oh, he's breathing hard," she said in a quiet voice.

Abigail folded the sheet and blanket down to my feet. "Well, there it is," she said, looking down at the front of my underpants. Then she looked up at me and shouted, "You want me to take care of that?! I don't mind since you don't have your hands! A man has needs!"

I wondered how she knew that I had to sometimes touch my spigot. It never had occurred to me that another person could do that for me.

"It's okay!" she shouted. "I'll just get to it!" And she put her hand inside my underpants. When I felt her hand on my spigot I drew in a breath like I'd been punched in the stomach. Without thinking, I got my bandaged hand under her forearm and pushed her out from there, the way I might have suddenly lifted my hand to block my face if a rock was flying at it.

"Oh, I'm sorry!" she said. "If you don't want it, it's okay!" And she simply went back to washing my body with the cloth. I stayed excited the whole time but I had a certainty that I didn't want Abigail to make my spigot rush out its oil right there in the daylight. I didn't know why I didn't want it. But I strongly did not. If I wanted someone to do that for me, it would not be her.

One morning I was woken from a deep sleep by Abigail jiggling my shoulder. I opened my eyes to three people, a man and two women, all wearing fancy, clean-looking dark suits and ties.

"Mister Grover, we are here with the company to talk about restitution for you and your brother."

"My brother?" I asked.

"Your brother, Bart," said one of the women, who was black with short hair. "He was killed by an unstable drill pipe a few weeks before the catastrophic blast that left you critically injured. The company is committed to doing all we can for him and for you."

"Do what for me?"

"They owe you restitution for what you suffered and what you survived," said the other woman, whose face was white with red blotches. She didn't have any hair but I knew she was a woman by her lips and eyes and her womanly voice. "Ingram, I'm your lawyer."

"My what?"

"I represent you. I've been appointed by the state of Texas, which is asserting control of this case and making sure to hold Matawaki Oil accountable. I'm here to make sure you get paid for what they did to you. And to your brother."

"He wasn't my brother," I said. "He said that to the company man so he'd hire me." The black woman and the man, who looked Mexican except he was dressed in a suit and had his hair cut like an important white man, started whispering to each other.

Then the woman, who said she was my lawyer, broke them up by saying in a loud voice, "It doesn't make a difference what your last name is, Ingram. They owe you quite a bit of money."

"Well, I worked there for a long time," I said. "I was told I get higher wages because I was promoted to small engine repair."

"I'm going to make sure you get all of that and a lot more, for damages. For suffering."

"Suffering?"

"For the terrible trauma, and your suffering."

"Wasn't no suffering," I said. "I felt a blast and I woke up here."

"I'd like to talk to my client alone," said the lawyer.

"I'm sure you would," said the man. And then they all got in an argument talking about I don't know what.

After a few more days, I was able to walk around my room. My body was weak from being in a bed for so long. When I moved, my skin was tight and didn't want to stretch along with my bones so easy. But I walked around as much as I could, wanting to leave that hospital soon. I wanted to get my body better, get my money from the work I'd done, and get away.

The lawyer woman's name was Erica. She kept coming to see me as I got better in the hospital. She asked me a lot of questions about my time in the oil fields and I told her what I remembered, what I had noticed, which I didn't like doing because I didn't want to think about the oil fields. I was glad to be out of there. Erica met me at lunchtime in the cafeteria sometimes, which was on the end of a long hallway from my room. The walking there was like a long stretch of road for me but I would use being hungry to make me want to do it.

Erica paid me a kind of attention I'd never had from anyone. She asked me things about the oil fields, how Bart died, and the blast that burnt me up. When I told her, she put her fingers under her chin and looked at my eyes, her face changing with everything I said, making it seem important. She made me feel a little of what came along to my body when I thought about Sinema. I liked that Erica's face skin went clean up over her head without her hair. It made her staring eyes good to look at. When her eyebrows went up in surprise, the ripples would go all the way up to the top of her head. When she smiled, every part of the skin of her head twisted around, all the way to the back of her neck.

"When the blast hit, was it very painful?" she asked me.

"You mean did it hurt?"

"Yes. Did it hurt?"

Mostly what she asked me was about how much "pain and suffering" I had, because if I had a lot, I'd get more money.

"Tell me about the pain," she said, putting her pen on her paper.

"I don't know what to say about it. I could feel my skin was burning. It was like a sting."

"That's good, Ingram," she said. "Keep going. Really describe your pain."

"It was like a sting," I said. "Like a bee sting. But a little more."

"It must have hurt more than that," she said.

"Well," I said, "I guess it hurt like . . . Say you laid out on a meadow of grass. You know, when the grass is just a bit tall, so it hides the sides of your foot when you step in it. And say each piece of that grass, sticking up, was a little knife. A little green knife. And you laid down to rest in that grass, but your whole body is laying on tiny green knives. But somehow, the feel of it puts you right to sleep. Like you're just too tired from feeling so many little things at once." I looked at her, hoping that she heard what she wanted me to say. She smiled real big, her ears pushing to the back of her head.

"Ingram," she said, "you know what? You're a poet."

"What's a poet?" I said filling my mouth with mashed potatoes, which she said were made from powder. I didn't care. I liked how they tasted.

"A poet is writer who . . . writes poems," she said. "What you just told me was like a poem."

"I thought writers wrote books," I said.

"Some write poetry," she said. "That's called being a poet. I think you are one."

The next time Erica came to see me she brought me a fat book called *The Complete Poems of Emily Dickinson*. It was written in short sentences laid across each other in neat rows down the middle of the page, using words in a way that felt like singing when you read them. When I'd read one of her *poems*, I wouldn't rightly know what I read, but I'd feel it, the way there are things I feel instead of thinking them. Like feeling it's going to rain because the air around me is getting heavy.

I liked poetry. It was a way of describing how things are, how they look, how they feel. I felt this was a better kind of reading than fiction, where a writer is just making up a bunch of bullshit. I decided I didn't want to read things like that anymore. From now on, if I was to spend my time with a book, I would look for poems to read, to help me with what I needed, which was a way to look at the truth, at reality.

When Erica gave me the book, she had stuck a strip of paper in the pages and circled a poem. It was called *Awake ye muses nine, sing me a strain divine.* It was about how everything in the world, which Emily Dickinson called *this terrestrial ball,* comes in pairs. Men and women are supposed to be together. The sun and the moon go together and when bees come at the flowers, it's like they're getting married. But Emily Dickinson wrote it in kind of floating singing words like, *The wind doth woo the branches, the branches they are won.* It made me wish my dictionary hadn't been wrecked in the blast, but I could sort of feel I knew what *woo* meant without it.

One day at lunch, Erica came with a big envelope made of plastic with a zipper on the end. She opened it up and showed me it had a bunch of paper money in it and a few coins. "This is yours," she said.

"What is it?" I asked, looking at all the bills.

"It's your pay for the work you did. I got it in cash because you're not legally in the system. They're trying to use that against you, to not pay you, but it won't work. This was their first gesture to show they don't want any trouble. It's a good sign, Ingram."

I asked her, "Is it enough to buy myself a truck?"

Erica smiled and said, "It should be plenty. Yes. But there's a lot more coming."

"What do you mean?"

"Ingram, you're only one of seven men who survived that blast. The company owes you."

"For what?"

"For your pain and suffering. I've been trying to tell you. They have to pay for hurting you."

"I been hurt plenty of times. Nobody ever paid for it."

"I know," she said, "and that's not right. I want to get you justice."

Erica told me many times more that there was money I should get because my skin was burned. All I knew was I had enough, earned from my work, to get a truck. And I didn't want to stay in that hospital any longer than I had to. I went back to my bed and put the money under the mattress.

The next day I went to the cafeteria for lunch. Erica wasn't there. But on that day, in the cafeteria, I saw Sinema, sitting at a table, looking at a tray of food in front of her. She was crying. I came over and stood in front of where Sinema was sitting.

“Ingram,” Sinema said, her face shiny with tears. I sat in the chair beside her. She put her arms around my neck, her head against my chest. Her hands were right on my worst burns on the upper part of my back, but I didn’t care about the pain. The hurt helped me feel more that Sinema was touching me.

Chapter Twenty-Four

Sinema

Pa is in pieces," said Sinema. "His hands are gone. His face is burnt so bad. First time I came here I only knew him from the shape of his head. They said he might die. I've been sitting with him nights. He just sleeps. I felt like he was angry at me."

"Why would he be angry at you, Sinema?" I asked.

"Because I'm here. And Miss Maw's not here. Nor any of my sisters. And he's here because of me."

"He is here because of you," I said.

She looked up at me with her mouth open. I thought she might be mad at what I said, though I knew it was true. "You talked to him?" she asked.

I told her about when I first saw him come off the truck and about him pulling off the man who was beating me up. And I told her about talking to him about working to support a family. About being a man surrounded by women and girls, all depending on him. She wasn't crying anymore.

"Were you hurt bad, Ingram?" She put her hand lightly on my bandaged hand.

"I guess all hurt is bad," I said, "but I didn't mind it."

"You didn't mind it?"

"I don't mind hurt. It's just a way your body feels when it gets damage. Like an engine when it breaks. But they fix you up in a hospital and you can work again."

"I don't think they're going to be able to fix up Pa. They can't put back his hands." She started crying again. I wished there was something I could say to Sinema that would change her way of looking at things. But everything she said was true. A few days later, Pa died.

Erica the lawyer never came back to see me after she'd given me my earned money. Sinema came to the hospital to see me every day. I told her about Erica the lawyer, and about the money I had under my bed, telling her, "I think it's enough to buy me a truck."

"A truck?" she said.

"That's what I want."

"You want a truck," Sinema laughed.

"Well, what do you want?" I asked. I was laughing too.

"Want?" she said. "I don't know anything about that."

"Well, what are you going to do?"

"Well, I can't finish school on what they gave me left over for Pa," she said. "I might have enough education to get an okay job at the school. But I didn't get far enough to move on to stage three. So I'll be staying down here."

"What's stage three?"

"It's supposed to be the new place where folks live with new and better rules and where being black doesn't matter and no one is poor. But I don't get how that can be when things down here are worse than they were since way back."

"Down here?"

"Ingram, there's so much going on that you have no idea. I think the less you know the better. I tell you, the more I learn, I just get sick to my stomach."

I didn't feel concerned or interested in what was going on in the world. I just wanted to know what she was going to do. She went on. "The world is changing in two directions at the same time. Some folks are going forward and some are going back. The ones going forward don't care about the ones going back. I guess I'm looking to being caught in the middle. I think Pa was hoping I'd get up there and find a way to take care of the rest of the family. But I'm not sure how to take care of myself."

"Let me take care of you," I said. "I'll buy a truck and take you out of here. I'll fix engines. I got a skill now. I'll take you some place and I'll marry you. And we'll have a baby boy and then more children and I'll work hard and support our family."

"We can't have a baby together!" Sinema lightly slapped the back of my hand.

"Yes, we can. Listen, Sinema. I know how to do it." And I told her everything that I had learned from Bart and Bull. I told her how I could take my spigot and put it inside of her and how the walls of her mouth between her legs . . .

"My what?"

"I know you got a mouth down there. And fellows told me it's a trap. But I know they was wrong. I ain't afraid of the mouth between your legs. I want to put a seed inside of you to make a baby."

"My goodness, Ingram," Sinema said, shaking her head slowly.

I kept on talking.

"Sinema, when I touched my spigot, I thought of you. And now I know why." The words flowed hard and fast. "Something comes out of me that I thought was oil but I been thinking that maybe that's my seed and that's how we will make a baby. And I'll be your husband and I'm not afraid of you needing me and having kids that need me and being trapped. I can be like Pa and I can take care of everybody. Please, Sinema. Please."

Sinema looked at me for a long time. Then she put her arms around me and pulled me against her. Then she looked at me and said, "Ingram. I can't marry you."

"Why?" I asked.

"Because. For just one thing, you're a white boy. And I'm a black girl. Whites and blacks don't marry. Not in this world, boy. And they certainly don't have babies."

"I know. I got told that already by the mountain under the road," I said. She laughed at me again. "Quit laughing at me, please," I said. And she stopped.

"It doesn't matter," she said. "We're not meant for each other in fifty ways. We're not on the same path. I have to support my family. And you've got to go take care of your own."

"But I ain't got anyone," I said. "I don't have a family."

"Yes, you do."

"I don't. My father rode away and left us."

"What about your mama?"

"What?"

"Where is your mother?"

"I don't know where my mother is," I said.

"Don't you wonder where she is?" asked Sinema.

"No," I answered.

"Why don't you?" she asked.

"Because I'm a man now. I don't need her anymore."

"*You* don't need *her*? Ingram. Don't you think your mother needs *you*? Don't you think your mama is somewhere maybe suffering? Alone in the world? Don't you wonder if your mama is okay? Don't think you have responsibilities in this world? Outside of yourself and finding you a truck? Why would I want to have a baby with a man who doesn't take care of his own mama? You got to find somewhere else to put your spigot, Ingram. And you need to think about what you're supposed to do, not what you want to do. You need to live in reality. Not some dumb idea."

"I don't know what reality is, Sinema," I said, putting my face in my hands so I wouldn't have to see the angry look on hers.

"Ingram," she said, and she put her hand on my forehead and forced it upright, so I had to look at her. And she said, "Reality is what you make real. For yourself. For your family." Then she seemed to forget what she said and she looked at my face. She smiled without wanting to. "You look stupid," she said, and let a laugh crack out of her throat.

"What do I look like?" I asked, and Sinema took my hand and put it on her forehead and made me push it up. Her eyes stretched up like she was surprised. It looked stupid and it made me laugh. And she laughed more. We sat there laughing together at our two faces, stretched up by each other's hand.

Everything in my mind and in my feelings changed after talking to Sinema. Most especially when she had said, "Reality is what you make real." And what she had said about my mother. Once it got into my head that I needed to do something for my own mother, whose face I had completely forgotten, it meant everything I did next could come together by that idea. I needed to get well, get out of the hospital. I needed to get a truck, not so I could drive myself down the road, but so I could get home without walking all the way back, across everything I'd lived through to get to where I was. I needed to learn about money, about how to get a job and a home. The idea of finding my mother, whose face I couldn't see in my memory, gave me energy, almost excitement. Getting food for her and finding a home for her was a new idea that I thought of every night as I went to sleep in the hospital. Some nights I thought past my mother and I'd see my father's face real clear. I didn't want to find him, or take care of him. I didn't even want to think about my father. And when I couldn't help but think of him, it led to something else, that made me feel like a frightened baby. And I hated that feeling because I needed to be a man to take care of my mother. Somehow this feeling of being a scared baby was mixed up with something back home, something to do with the gray creature, who had stopped visiting me in my dreams and instead was in my waking thoughts. Every time I tried to work out in my mind what I would do to get home and find my mother, it would lead to thoughts of the gray creature. He was no longer just a haunting spirit. He was a real problem.

INGRAM

On my last day in the hospital, the doctor had me take off all my clothes in his exam room so he could see how all my skin had healed. I looked at myself in the mirror on the wall. My neck was long and thicker than I felt it to be. I had muscles around my shoulders and bulging along my arms. There was hair in the middle of my chest and above and around my spigot. My hands had gotten large. My skin was bright pink, almost yellow, except where it was burnt, which was red and bumpy.

"Well, you're healed, Ingram," said the doctor. I was discharged.

Chapter Twenty-Five

My Truck

The next day, Sinema and I sat at her kitchen table, counting my money. She said I had two thousand dollars.

"What can I do with that?" I said. "Can I get a truck?"

"Yes, you can get a truck. But you need to budget this money," said Sinema. She explained that *budget* means making your money last, by figuring out how much to put toward each thing you need in life. "Make a list of what you need," she said, giving me a pencil.

I wrote on the envelope:

Truck

Food

Clothes

Shoes

Home

Hat

Sinema looked at my list and laughed. "That's a good list, Ingram. You can just about get that done, except for a home. That's something you're going to need a job for. But if you're smart, this money will last until you get a job and a place to live permanent. The trick is not to spend all this money on one thing. Spread it even. Budget."

I found a store that sold clothes for men, women, and children, and other supplies. I bought myself a pair of thick, dark blue jeans that scratched at my legs. I bought three cotton T-shirts. One white, one black, one dark blue. Four pairs of white cotton socks. I bought three pairs of underpants, bright white, soft, brand new, clean, and never worn. I chose a red collared shirt with metal snap buttons down the front, and a dark blue hat with a bill in the front. "I need shoes," I told the salesman, who had glasses so thick his eyes looked giant.

"Let's fit you out with some cowboy boots," he said. "You'll never need anything else."

The man measured my feet and told me I was size nine and one-half. I looked at all the shoes on the wall and I knew right away that I wanted the black leather boots with a yellow toe and red stripes up the sides.

"Snakeskin!" the man said.

I bought those red, black, and yellow snakeskin boots. When I put them on, they hurt my feet, but not in a way that I couldn't take.

"Those boots will shape themselves to your feet," he said. "And your feet will shape to the boots. Then you'll be friends for life." He pointed at his own boots, which were dark yellow and looked like they were part of him.

"Anywhere around here I can buy a truck?" I asked the man.

"Looking to be a real cowboy?" He laughed. "Walk west on Essex Street, they got dealers there. Cars and trucks. Further west you walk, the cheaper the vehicles."

I walked west, in my new boots, to big wide buildings with tall windows and cars inside, new and shiny like they'd never been driven. Further west, big squares of pavement, full of cars and trucks with money amounts written on their windows in big white letters, along with some description like "Super Fast Runner" or "Clean and Easy."

"How much you want to spend?" said a man with a tall, stiff, brown hat, as he walked me along a row of cars. "They're not making these gas runners no more. That makes some of them cheaper, some of them more expensive. Depends on the appeal, on the need." Then he stopped walking and looked at me, saying again, "How much you want to spend?"

"I can't spend more than one thousand dollars," I said.

The man shook his head and said, "None of that here. You need to get off the auto-mile. Make a left there and go to Pete's Filling Station. Take your chance with him. He got vehicles, if you call them that. Mostly junk."

The rusted sign above the filling station said "Pete's Gas" in letters barely a different color than the rust. There was a row of dead-looking old cars under the sign, some without windows. In the very middle of them was a bright yellow truck, sort of like the one I rode in the back of when I was taken to the farm. It was leaning way over to the side because two of its tires had no air. There was a rash of brown rust across the top of the yellow hood. But all the glass was good and unbroken. I looked in through the window and saw that the seats were yellow and the steering wheel was black.

"What you want?" said a man who was standing behind me. He was tall and black, wide across the shoulders with big, angry eyes, shiny sweat all over his face and up over the middle of his head, which was bald between thick hair on each side.

"Are you Pete?" I asked him.

"What you want?" he said again.

"How much is this truck?"

"This truck? It's broke."

"I want it."

"I said it's broke," he said.

"How's it broke?" I asked. Just then a bell rang when a car pulled into the gas pump behind him. Pete went off to serve his customer. I opened the door to the truck and popped open the hood. The engine inside was red. I could see right away it needed two belts and two distributor cables were chewed through. There was a nest of mice by the shock absorber.

"What you doing?" Pete had come back.

"I could maybe fix this truck," I said. "How much you want for it?"

"Can't that truck be fixed," said Pete. But he let me poke at it as he wiped sweat off his neck with a red rag. Then he said, "If you can get it running you can give me a hundred."

"You got any tools I could use?" I asked. "And it needs some parts."

"You gonna use my tools, my parts, that'll cost you more."

"As long as it ain't more than a thousand," I said.

"It won't be near that," said Pete. "Come on with me." Pete led me into his garage and put some tools in a metal tray, saying I could use those. "But it's just a borrow. These tools stay with me when you're done." I said okay and began working on that truck.

First I took out the battery and put it to charge in the garage. I took off the valve covers. The cams looked good. It needed new gaskets all around. New distributor. New belts, everything rubber. But the parts, the steel, even the light springs and gears, were all solid. The more I dug into it with the wrenches, the more I put my hands inside it and all over it, the more I knew this yellow truck. This truck hadn't broke. It had just been left to die. There was a lot of working and figuring to be done if I was to get it running and rolling. But if I did, that would be my truck.

Pete had a busy filling station. The bell was always ringing and he'd run to the pumps. Inside his garage, he was trying to fix the brakes on a small car. "Damn it to hell," he'd say when the bell rang again.

"I can go pump," I said one time and started toward the car that had come in.

"NO, you can't," said Pete, stopping me, and he went to pump himself.

"Why don't you let me help?" I asked. "You don't have to pay me for it."

"Don't you know why not?" he said.

"No," I said. "Feels to me it makes sense that I help out."

"I can't have a white boy working that pump. Can't people be thinking that a white boy is working at a black man's business."

"Then let me help in the garage," I said.

"You know anything about brakes?"

"No. Only engines. But I need to learn brakes so I can fix my own."

"I got no time to teach you brakes or anything else," said Pete.

"I'll teach myself," I answered. "That's how I learned to fix engines."

"Can't teach yourself brakes on someone's car. They're gonna hit the pedal and go right over a damn cliff," said Pete. "Damn boy. Damn."

The next day, Pete and I put my yellow truck up on jack stands and pulled the wheels off. He showed me how the wheels were bolted to steel drums, which we pulled off to find the brake shoes, that push out against the insides of the drums to stop the wheels from moving. He helped me follow the hydraulic brake lines back from the *slave cylinder* that pushes the shoes out, to the *master cylinder* that sends fluid out to all four of them whenever the brake pedal gets pushed.

"You got to bleed the brakes," he said, which meant letting any air bubbles out of the line so that the fluid was like one solid thing. When you push on one side, the other side right away pushes on the brakes all the way down at the wheels. I never thought of water being something that could stop a car, but it wasn't so different from the pressure of the oil in the pipes.

Everything I'd learned about engines and mechanical objects had made something like a sponge in my head that could now soak up anything else about moving parts. Pete let me put new brake shoes on my truck and when he saw that I'd done it right for all four wheels, he said I could work on the brakes of the car in the garage while he pumped the gas. Which I did and I kept on helping with any car that came in for repairs, learning more and more along the way, giving him time to pump and tend to customers, which kept the line of cars moving faster through his station, which brought more and more cars. Pete would close up when the sun went down and I'd hang a light in the inside of my truck's hood and work on it. Sometimes he'd sit in his metal chair and read an old-looking book by another work light. The only sound would be my tools clickering and squeaking and Pete's chair creaking every time he adjusted himself and turned a page of his book. Sometimes we'd talk a bit.

"My daddy started this business," he told me one night as I put a new head gasket in my truck. "I'll be the one that finishes it."

"Your daddy left?" I asked.

"Left as in died, yes," said Pete. "I'm grateful to him. Every day. This is my business. My place. I don't have to work for nobody. Got just enough grease and steel moving through here to keep the gas truck coming, the cars coming, keep the lights on, the sign up, pay for my chicken and bread. Don't need no more than that."

"You think I could start a place like this of my own?"

"Well, this is a dying part of living. Cars, driving. Gas. Even the roads. They just passed a law to stop fixing them! Imagine that? They're gonna let the great highway system grow over and go to dirt. They say that's progress now! But I'll tell you what, young white, they never do what they say they're gonna do. And every day I see one after another drive in here for their gas, to take their vehicle where they want to go. These new-living folks that want to get in an electric car and be told which way to get where they're going? They may be smart and fancy, but they are few. Most folks are like you and me. We like the grease; we like the fire in the cylinder. We'll keep the cars going and the roads paved if they don't. At least you might. Young man, it's up to you. I won't live to see it."

I looked up from my work and saw that Pete was looking at me from his chair. I never could get my head around when he or Sinema or anyone else talked about the world. I asked him the only question that came up from what he said: "How do I go about making a place like this for myself?"

Pete laughed. "I suppose you'll figure it out. You could use some help. You got any fambly? Where's your daddy at?"

"He left us," I said. "Rode off on a horse."

"Couldn't have got too far, then." Pete laughed.

I worked every night while we talked and even after Pete went off home. When I got too tired, I climbed into my truck. I'd lie down across the seat with my head by the steering wheel and stare at the speedometer, the odometer, the radio, imagining the day that their needles would be jumping. I longed to be moving again.

Chapter Twenty-Six

Home

The yellow truck was humming like a happy drunk as it drove me out of Austin, with Sinema sitting beside me. We didn't talk much on the drive, having not much to say to each other. I was driving her home to Houston to see her family on my way back to where I'd come from. We stopped at the diner where I met Marion. She wasn't there. There were new waitresses and new cooks. I asked about her but no one remembered her.

Sinema and I got burgers at the diner. We'd bought a road map and we looked at it between us at the counter. I told Sinema the stories of where I'd been and she helped me trace along with my finger which roads I must have come along, but we did so backward, until we found the road I must have walked along to find Houston, and there was a tiny road, just before a small town called Liberty, Texas. The little road was just like a hair on the map, that stuck off the main road and just ended. It was called Draper Road, which must have been where my house was.

At the end of that day, I pulled up to Miss Maw's house and let Sinema out of the truck. We stood in front of the house together. Sinema reached into the dark red bag she had over her shoulder, and took from it a thick book, handing it to me. "Here," she said. "It's a dictionary. It has every word . . ."

"I know what a dictionary is," I said. I think I sounded mad. I was talking fast and tough because I was getting a feeling up in my stomach that I didn't want to have.

"Okay," said Sinema. "I'm glad you know. So keep learning new words, okay?"

I held the dictionary in my hands. I gripped it tight, like I needed it to keep me from falling to my death. I stared at it so hard that a tear fell onto it from my eye. Sinema was standing right in front of me and I wanted so much to look at her but I didn't want to stop looking at her so I didn't want to start. She had given me so much. She had helped me and listened to me and let me be with her so gently. And she had given me this book, just like Bart had. But she didn't want anything from me. I wanted to give Sinema something. To do something for her so that she wouldn't forget me like the people at the diner had forgotten Marion. I felt like my footsteps were disappearing behind me. Like everything I had done and seen had been nothing except for that she knew about it. I wanted to give her something so she would know she ever met me.

My hand reached in my pocket and found Pa's knife, which they'd given me back when I was discharged from the hospital, it being the only thing in my clothes that wasn't burnt.

"Your pa gave me this when I first left here," I said to Sinema as I handed her the knife. "He wanted it for his son. I guess since you're taking care of the family now, that's about the same." I saw her hand appear where I was looking and she gently took the knife from me.

"Gosh, Ingram," said Sinema. "Thank you." Her voice was passing through a part of her throat I hadn't heard before, like wind shivering by a new kind of tree. The knife was in her open hand, where it laid in the middle of her pink palm, like a bird that knew it could take off but didn't need to just yet. In her good hand, that knife was no longer a weapon to defend a boy, I thought. It looked more like a little finger bone, like she was holding a place for what was left of her gone, frail brother, Martin. I had given that to her. And she had said, "Thank you."

I began knowing, as I looked at the knife in her hand, that doing something for another person, and feeling them being thankful, will fill you right up and keep on flowing. I looked down at my own hands. I was clutching that dictionary so hard my fingers were white to keep me from falling into the gray, gray, gray that was clouding my mind with fear as quick as I was filling with gratitude. I thought I might black out like I used to when I was a tired, hungry child.

"Hey, boy," Sinema said and she put her other hand on my forehead and pushed my face up to look at her. We both laughed just a little. I saw in her face that she was a bit sad like me, and that felt good to see.

"It's okay, Ingram," she said. "I'm your friend. You understand that? I am your friend. I'm not going to stop being your friend. You got your truck now. Go home. Get your life together. Start your car business. We'll see each other again."

"You mean it?" I said. "No bullshit?"

"No bullshit, Ingram." She slapped my cheek and laughed. I heard Miss Maw's voice coming from inside of the house in a way I knew she'd be out on the lawn with us soon. I didn't want to see her. So I hugged Sinema real quick and I got in my truck and took off.

I drove through the busy parts of Houston. I drove past the hospital where I'd been sick, the construction site at the edge of town, the factories with tall smokestacks, and though I couldn't see it, I knew the concrete river ran behind them, where I swam naked and gotten sick from green sewage. I drove on the first great road that went up over where I'd met the mountain. I didn't know if the mountain was still down there but I didn't figure he had any reason to be happy to see me or anyone else. I kept on driving till the road glided me down to level ground, where it went from three lanes to two lanes with yellow lines down the middle. I drove past the diner where I'd stolen meat from the man, which made me laugh a little at remembering it, so I pulled over and went into that diner, sat at the counter, and bought myself a cheeseburger and a Coke. The sun was going down and I wanted to see my home by daylight, so I slept that night in my yellow truck.

The next morning, I simply woke up, sat up, and started the truck. It only took me a few minutes to drive what must have taken a day to walk when I was small, before I saw the straight, short dirt road that ended at our house. I drove down that road to its end. I turned off the engine, got out of the truck, and walked to the spot where my mother, tired and covered in rashes, had told me to leave. I looked at that spot, thinking how I must have been about as tall as my belly button was now. Because my mother had to squat down to be looking in my eyes.

I looked past where my mother and I said goodbye, and instead of seeing the house there, I saw only its roof, sitting on a short pile of collapsed, rotted wood that had been our house. Looking down at the top of my roof had me feeling even bigger and less belonging to this place. Next to the house was the shed I had slept in since I could remember. It was still there. The door was open. I had to bend my head down a little to look inside. I never had seen my father do that when he went in there to drink. I wondered if I'd grown even taller than him. I looked down at the floor, where I used to sleep. There had been a blanket there, which my mother had given me to sleep with. It was gone. I wondered why this little shed had been left standing, just like it was, but my blanket was gone. Had my mother taken it to remember me? Or to wrap me in if she ever saw me again? Or to give to another boy? To my brother? She gave me a hat that day, which she said was my brother's. Where was he now? I thought this blanket was some kind of clue. I thought remembering it might help me remember what else was hiding in my mind. But I couldn't even remember what color that blanket was. I only remembered that it never kept me warm much.

I walked around the place for a little bit. I didn't see anything else that could be any help to me in finding my mother. Hanging around there, I figured, was about as good to me as it would have been to stay when I was told to leave.

I got back in my truck. It felt good to start it up and hear the engine turn and burn, because I had put it together with my own hands and made it work. I had taken money that I had earned with my hands and my mind and bought gas with it, which was now running through the cylinders, pushing them out with each firing.

I drove back up the road, this time turning toward town, onto what I used to think was a hissing monster but now saw as a small country highway. I quickly found myself in Liberty, Texas, the town where my father had taken me to find out that I couldn't go to school. I parked my truck on Main Street and walked until I found the Liberty town hall, where I was told to go to the records room. I found a woman who smiled from her desk and said, "Can I help you?" She was the shortest person I'd ever seen, almost as small as a child. By her face and hair she was probably Mexican.

"I need to find my mother," I said to the small woman.

"Well now, what is the last time that you saw her?" she asked.

"A long time ago," I said. "I was a child. She sent me away from home. We lived out on Draper Road."

"What's your last name?" she asked.

"I don't know," I answered. Unlike the many people to whom I had explained the facts of my life, this tiny woman was not surprised by any of it.

"What is your first name?"

"Ingram."

She wrote down the things I told her on a small piece of paper and she got up from her desk, not growing even an inch in standing up from sitting down, and went into another room, saying, "I'll be back in a few minutes."

"Mister Kessler?" she said when she came back. She saw the confusion on my face and smiled. "I'm so sorry. Your last name is Kessler. You're Ingram Kessler. Here are your family records." And she handed me a brown folder with all kinds of papers in them. I asked her if I could stay sitting at her desk to read them and she kindly said, "Sure," and got me a glass of water. The small woman sat at her desk writing and looking over records while I read everything that was known about my family. What I learned was this: My father's name was Phillip Kessler. My mother's name was Sarah Kessler, but her name was Burroughs before she married my father. She was from Beaumont, Texas. They were married in Liberty. I learned, as I sat there reading about it, that I was seventeen years old, and that I must have been nine when I left, because that's when the house we lived in was foreclosed on by the bank. And I learned that I had an older brother named Albert, who died of pneumonia when I was six. The records only said of my mother's whereabouts "unknown" and that my father was living in Liberty, on First Avenue.

"I'm looking for Phillip Kessler," I said to the man who answered the door that was supposed to be my father's home.

"He ain't here," said the man, looking angry. "He ain't *ever* here. Good riddance." I saw that the man, whose skin was pale from never leaving the house, which inside I could see had all the shades drawn on the windows, had tears starting up in his eyes. "Excuse me," he said and he started to close the door, but I stopped it with my hand.

"Where can I find him?" I asked.

"Same place anyone can find anyone," he said. "In the fucking bar." And he pushed the door harder. I let it close.

There was only one bar in Liberty. It was called Wally's Bar and Pool. I pulled up in front of it and got out of my truck, looking up at the sign. There was music and drunk voices coming through the door, which had a diamond-shaped window, through which I couldn't see much. It wasn't much different than the canteen where I'd learned to drink. The ragged sound of drunk men's voices. The darkness trapped inside while outside the sky was bright blue. I didn't want to go in. I didn't want to find my father drinking in there. I only wanted to know what he knew about where my mother might be. I got a bad feeling in my stomach, imagining seeing him, looking down at me with his anger and violence. I wondered if I'd be scared. His name was Phillip. I had only known that for part of a day.

"Phillip," I said out loud, looking at the door of the bar. "Phillip," I said again.

"What?" said a voice. I looked over and saw a man crumpled on the sidewalk with his back to the outside wall of Wally's Bar and Pool. I hadn't even noticed that man when I drove up and got out. His clothes were so gray and he was in such a collapsed heap that I'd taken him for a pile of trash set against the building. I came over and stood above him. He was looking down at the sidewalk between his spread knees. He saw my shadow there and looked up at my face.

"You a cop?" he asked me, sounding weak and angry.

I got down on one knee in front of my father. I had never in my life looked straight into his eyes. His eyes contained no anger. With a dark misery, a kind of death, he stared at my nose. I could plainly see that he was part of me.

"Phillip," I said. It didn't make a difference in his face so I said, "You're my father." He looked back down at the pavement.

I'd gotten a room in a motel on Main Street. My father didn't protest when I took him there because I stopped at the liquor store and bought him a bottle of whiskey. I told him he couldn't have it till we got up to the room. "I know what you're trying to do with me," he said, his words all garbled together. "You should be shamed of yourself. Who are you anyway?" He'd known me right away but he seemed to keep forgetting it. I got him back to the room and made him shower. Then I opened the whiskey bottle and brought the glass from the bathroom to my father, where he sat on the bed, knowing that a drunk can't talk unless he's drunk.

"Where is my mother?" I said as I poured him a glass.

"I don't know where the hell she is," he said, emptying the glass into his throat. "That was the idea of walking out."

"Well, where do you think she went?"

"Listen, boy. You may think you have a right to be angry."

"I'm not angry," I said, which was true. But he kept on going, as drunks do, like I hadn't said anything.

"Goddamn country went to hell. No work nowhere. No money. Can't raise the money to feed the pigs. Can't feed you. House foreclosed on. That woman looking at me like I'm nothing. What the hell was I supposed to do?" He held out his empty glass for me to fill it. I put the top back on the bottle and screwed it on tight. That made him look me in my eyes for the first time.

"Gimme a drink, boy," he said, sounding like he used to sound when he was getting ready to hit. My father reached for the bottle. My hand reached out and swatted his away. It made a slapping sound on the back of his wrist. He looked up at me.

"Goddamn devil," he said, his head dropping down till his chin was on his chest. I looked at the top of his head. His hair was thin there.

"I could beat you to death," I said out loud before I was done thinking it. "I could beat you to death right here." I was breathing in and out real deep and loud. My hand was a fist. I didn't know what I was doing anymore. He just sat there, limp, on the bed, holding the empty glass in his hand.

"Gimme a drink," he said, "or go ahead and kill me." I stood above him and I hated him. He was weak. Like Bart said, he was weak on the inside. But he was also weak on the outside. And I started to see that he had always been weak. I wanted to know why. Why was he different than Pa? Other than being black and white. They both had life bearing down on them. They both had it hard. But why did Pa stay and work, raise and protect his girls, give Miss Maw a stove to cook at? Why did he keep on going till the earth exploded through the pipes and broke him in pieces? And why did my father get up and quit, walking away, trading his family for whiskey? When his only son was just nine years old?

"Why'd you quit?" I said. "Why didn't you try harder?"

"You don't know how hard the world is," he said. "You're still a boy."

"I ain't a boy no more," I said. "I know how hard the world is. It's a whole lot harder for a boy on his own than a grown-up man." I was shouting at him. "I was out there all alone. I got sick, I got beat up, had my arm broke. I walked and I starved and I worked and I worried. I even drank whiskey, but I learned to put it down. I learned to read and write and fix engines. I got blown up and burnt and saw everyone I know walk away from me or die. Now I got myself a truck and some money. I'm wearing clothes I picked out and bought. I can get a job fixing things. Why couldn't you do it? What makes you so damn weak and special?"

My father was sitting on the bed, his spine crooked over, his face pointed to the floor. He picked up his big head and looked at my eyes. I saw hate in his.

"You're a devil," he said. "A devil can do anything." I didn't know what that meant. But it hit me hard.

"Why you calling me a devil?" I said. "What did I ever do to you?"

"You took my firstborn child. Albert." I took in a big long breath and held it. His eyes got narrow.

"My brother?" I said.

"You laid beside him in his deathbed and sucked his last breath out into yourself. That boy was the onliest thing I ever loved, and you laid there and watched him die. Could have helped him. Could have told someone. But you took his place. Took his breath. Watched him die. Like a devil. You just let him rot before your eyes, because you have no heart, boy. That's why I never loved you. You can't love a piece of stone."

Looking tired from what he said, my father slowly keeled over, laying on the bed on his side. I sat down on the other small bed. I closed my eyes and tried not to hear what he had said but it was too late. The knowing of what had happened started in the center of my chest and began to swell out to my shoulders and up my neck. I set my teeth shut so hard I thought they'd shatter. Then I felt something bumping on my knee. I opened my eyes and saw my father's glass. He was gently poking at me, wanting more whiskey. I looked at his eyes. He looked like he was dying. I opened that bottle and I poured his glass full. My father drank his and I filled it again. I let him have as many drinks as his hand asked for. Then my father rolled over onto his back and began to snore. I had a feeling that somehow didn't belong in the moment, but there it was. I was happy that he was sleeping.

That he was safe. I was relieved, just like I would be whenever I could get Kyle to sleep after he'd been in a state of agitation.

I watched my father sleep. The satisfaction of having put him to rest was mixed with the still-rising feeling, like a hot stone, coming up in my throat. I looked at the bottle in my hand. I tipped it up to my lips and took a long drink. As I knew it would, the hot burning whiskey shrank down that lump in my throat and dimmed the light in my mind. I took another drink. I drank until there was no more in the bottle. Then I laid back on the bed and started to see things in my mind that I hadn't seen before. They were frightening and dangerous, but I was drunk enough to see them without wanting to die.

I saw a face that I'd never seen before, though I knew it was living in my memory. It was a boy's face. A narrow face with red hair on top, freckles all over his cheeks and the bridge of his nose, and a smile that looked easy to keep. My big brother, Albert. Albert, walking next to me, holding my hand, telling me things, helping me learn how to play.

"You're a fox and I'm a rabbit," he said. "We're pals, Ingram. And we are both running from a coyote. Ready? Go!" Albert and I ran across the grass behind our house, stripping off our clothes along the way, and finally we jumped into the pond. There was always a game of being animals and having to run when we jumped in the pond.

Albert, talking to my mother and making her laugh. "Mama, what if I stole Daddy's pants while he's sleeping?" My mother laughing while she cut a carrot. Covering her mouth because her smile was so big. "He'll come down here hollering and huffing!" Albert imitating my angry father: "Who took my damn pants?! Who took my damn pants!" My mother laughing so hard she had to put down her knife and do nothing but laugh, her body swinging forward and back.

Albert making my father laugh. "That horse took a dump so big I might name it."

My father laughing, trying not to. "Now quit, boy," he said in a laughing, shivering voice.

Albert pointing down at a heap of horseshit. "I think I'll name it Mickey. Mickey! Wash up for supper! Say, Daddy, how does a heap of shit wash up? Just keep scrubbing till it disappears?" My father walking away, laughing, rustling Albert's hair.

Albert and I in bed together in the room above the porch. I was afraid of the dark and couldn't sleep. "Count the frogs croaking, Ingram," said Albert. "It'll help you sleep." Under the singing of the insects, only now and then there was a low croak of a frog.

"One!" I said.

"Two," said Albert. And he helped me count till I forgot and woke up the next morning, hearing him talking to my parents downstairs.

Albert coughing. Albert getting so sick his smile faded and his skin turned green. And I slept in the bed beside him and heard his breaths getting smaller and smaller and I begged my big brother Albert not to die. And he put his cold hand on my head and said, "Shh. Go to sleep, Ingram. I'll be all better in the morning. I promise. Go to sleep."

And I believed him because he never once lied to me. I closed my eyes, but I never was really asleep. I was in some fearful place where I couldn't move. And that night, the gray creature of death came into our bed and climbed inside of Albert and killed him till he was still and cold with open eyes. And I stared at my dead brother, his face getting grayer and grayer with the sun coming in the window, and I whispered his name again and again and I begged the gray creature inside of him to crawl out and kill me too and when my mother came in and screamed my father came in and found me next to his dead firstborn son and in one instant he hated me forever, dragging me out to the shed saying, "You not in this family no more. You are an animal."

I WOKE UP THE NEXT morning on the motel bed. My father was still sleeping. I remembered what had come flooding into my mind the night before. Albert. My brother.

"Albert," I said out loud. I was glad to have him back. It was peaceful now. My memory of him was sitting in my mind now. It was just there, like anyone and anything else I could remember. I thought about Bull and how him and Albert were alike in some ways. In how they were both lively and looking for a good time. They had both been kindly to me. I thought about how Bull's family probably never knew what happened to him. But he was in my memory now, next to Albert. In a funny way, they could keep each other company. I thought about Bart. Somehow I knew that Albert would have liked Bart okay. But he might have told me to stay clear of him. He would have liked Sinema, I thought. That was sad to me, that they never met. I closed my eyes and I saw Albert. And I saw my mother's smiling face, clear as day. And I saw my father smiling, looking strong. Remembering that my family had been happy, even when times were as hard as ever, because Albert brought us all together, made me miss him so bad. And a feeling of tender sadness started in my chest, the way the hard rock had grown the night before. But I didn't mind it. I wanted it. I laid there thinking of my brother and what had died with him and I cried for the first time since I'd grown hair under my arms. I cried willingly and easily. I felt the sadness. The gray creature was gone.

"Get up, Pa," I said, pulling his arms to make him sit up. "Let's go."

"Where we going?" he groaned, opening up his eyes and looking at me from his world of a hurtin' head.

"We're going to find my mother," I said, and took him out to the truck. We drove out of town and onto the east-going road, toward Beaumont. I reached across my father and opened his window to get some air in his lungs. Out of my own window, the moon was rising.

THE END

About the Author

Louis C.K. was born in Washington, DC, in 1967. He was raised in Mexico and Massachusetts. He then became a comedian, writer, and filmmaker. Ingram is his first novel. He lives in New York City.

Photo by Blanche Gardin